The
Trouble
with
Rent Boys

LIAM LIVINGS

Beaten Track
www.beatentrackpublishing.com

The Trouble with Rent Boys

First published 2021 by Beaten Track Publishing
Copyright © 2021 Liam Livings

Paperback ISBN: 978 1 78645 495 9
eBook ISBN: 978 1 78645 496 6

Cover: Debbie McGowan

Beaten Track Publishing,
Burscough, Lancashire.
www.beatentrackpublishing.com

Dedication & Thanks

Thanks to Deb, Ames and Jor, the Beaten Track Publishing team for making this book better than I could have done alone. Your editing, cover-creating and proofreading skills are splendid.

Thanks are also due to two authors who inspired me to write this story, a bit of a departure from what I've written before: Jackie Collins and Penny Vincenzi. They're both sadly no longer with us, but their stories continue to give readers, including myself, such joy.

Penny Vincenzi wrote wonderful, escapist doorstopper novels with elaborately woven lies and conflicts containing characters so lifelike that I missed them after finishing her stories. Her books have kept me eagerly turning the pages while on holiday, long after my separation from my fellow holidaymakers had verged towards the antisocial. I regret nothing.

Thanks to Jackie Collins, whose romantic suspense novels have entertained and captivated me since I was a teenager. Writing strong heroines, compelling, conflicted heroes that have kept me reading way past bedtime, and weaving plots that zip along like a red Lamborghini.

Thanks to you, readers, I hope you enjoy this escapist, gossipy, romantic suspense with plenty of *gay* sprinkled throughout!

Love and light,
Liam Livings xx

Character List

Danny Traviati – a high-class male escort; lives in London Docklands.

Paul – Danny's boyfriend and manager who runs their escorting business with Danny; friends with Sharon Smith through the dog circuit.

Charlie Frost – an ex-city banker, mid-thirties; runs a veg box and baking business from his home in Chelsea.

Neil Bingham – Charlie's boyfriend; same age; a management consultant who lives with Charlie.

Camilla Constantine – Sloaney woman, mid-fifties; Fred Smith's ex-wife; lives in Chelsea next door to Charlie and Neil; can't cook a thing, buys it all in from Harrods.

Tamara Smith – eighteen-year-old daughter of Fred and Camilla; studying business at college.

Aaron Smith – nineteen-year-old son of Fred and Camilla; not sure what to do with his life; strawberry-blond hair.

Hugo Jones – runs Reece Jones Instruments, family business; lives in Chigwell, Essex.

Isabella Jones – Hugo's wife; late-twenties; runs and owns Lux Sunglasses with her brother, Fred Smith; lives with Hugo.

Lord Reece Jones – Hugo's father and Isabella's father-in-law.

Lady Reece Jones – Hugo's mother and Isabella's mother-in-law. Both live in Reece Jones Park, a large, crunchy-gravelled estate in Hertfordshire.

Fred Smith – mid-fifties; ex-city banker, now runs Lux Sunglasses with his sister, Isabella; ex-husband of Camilla; father to Tamara and Aaron; now husband of Sharon Smith; lives in Wanstead *village* with Sharon.

Sharon Smith – mid-thirties, bottle-blonde, surgically and non-surgically enhanced; loves her dogs, Jacuzzi, new Range Rover and her husband, Fred Smith; friends with Paul through the dog circuit.

Part 1
Summer 2013

Chapter 1

IN A KITCHEN just off the King's Road in Chelsea, Charlie Frost, a well-preserved thirty-something—wearing only socks, bright blue designer underwear and a short, red, silk kimono his boyfriend Neil had brought him from China on his last business trip—danced. Sliding across the floor, twirling and throwing shapes with his arms, he closed his eyes and lost himself as the chorus of his favourite song by his favourite singer, 'All The Lovers' by Kylie, reached a crescendo.

The vegetables lay on the work surface, half of them arranged into boxes, ready to dispatch later that day. *They can wait. This is necessary*, he thought, briefly allowing himself a moment to reflect on what grey-suited corporate Neil would make of this little performance, smiling as he remembered how they used to dance together in nightclubs.

He gracefully continued across the rustic-tiled floor of his cottage kitchen, throwing his arms either side of his body and singing at the top of his voice that no other lovers compared to you, when, out of the corner of his eye, he noticed a face at the window. He stopped the music and tugged his kimono around him to cover the little bit of middle-aged spread that seemed to be extending a bit farther than he wanted of late due to all the cake testing he needed to do, of course—all part of the job.

Composing himself, he opened the door. "Aaron, how lovely to see you! You should've knocked."

Aaron stuck his hands in his pockets, arms ramrod straight. He glanced up at Charlie, flashing his blue eyes. "Rang the doorbell, but you didn't answer. Music." He pushed his strawberry-blond hair off his face. It immediately fell back into his eyes.

"Sorry. Working hard, you see." Charlie gestured to the vegetables and boxes.

Aaron shrugged. "Mum sent me round to ask if you and Neil wanted to come for dinner at the weekend."

"What's she cooking?" Camilla's meals were legendary among her neighbours in the row of cottages where she lived. Legendarily awful. She'd boiled a kettle dry once when Charlie had popped round for tea.

"Beef in pastry, she said. Sounds nice." Aaron rubbed his dark-ginger-stubble-covered jaw.

"She's not making beef Wellington, is she?" Charlie was already planning his 'suddenly very busy weekend'.

"Harrods." Aaron folded his arms, his sleeves taut over his triceps.

Charlie glanced at the front of the T-shirt—a large Z and A in silver across the middle—and then the arms and thought how Aaron had changed since they'd moved next door to Aaron's mum four years ago. Nineteen and fifteen years old might as well be thirty and ten for the differences Charlie had noticed in Aaron. Charlie shook that thought away, reminding himself he was happily with Neil, and besides, he was friends with Camilla and Aaron, which made things even more complicated. Still, he did have nice arms.

Aaron yawned, rubbing his eyes. "And?"

"Keeping you up, am I?" Charlie walked to the wall calendar, confirmed they were free the whole weekend and offered Aaron a drink. "Bit of caffeine to wake you up."

4

"Mum woke me up, told me to get out of my pit and make myself useful. It's the summer holidays. And I'm definitely not going back to uni. Hated it. Sleeping is what they're meant for. Yeah, strong tea, please." He stood by the table now.

"Don't stand on ceremony! Sit. Any closer to working out what you want to do now you've left uni?" Charlie worried for Aaron and felt responsible, since Aaron had told him the whole story of hating uni, pretending to his parents he'd return in September when he'd already made up his mind never to go back. Aaron had explained it all on another quiet afternoon like this, over lots of coffee and a few tears, and he'd made Charlie promise never to tell his parents.

Now, Aaron let out a long, loud, teenage sigh. He rested his head on the table, using his arms as a pillow, closed his eyes and waited for Charlie to bring him his tea.

Charlie sat next to him, tapped Aaron's arm and slid the mug along the table. "It's hot. Don't knock it over when you sit up." He shook his head, both admiring and bored with Aaron's dramatic display.

"What if I don't know what I want to do, but I do know what I don't want to do?" Aaron said.

"That, I think we can work with."

"I don't wanna work for bloody Lux Sunglasses. The more Dad wants me to work with him the more I want to run away and join the circus."

Charlie smiled over his mug at the return of the drama.

"And it's like cos he's not with Mummy, he gets extra Dad points for getting me to work with him." He shook his head. "Doesn't make sense. I think they talk about me like they talk about maintenance payments—rotas of who gets us which weekend and all that stuff. They wouldn't do that if they were still together. Anyway, whatever, I wanna do something with my hands. I dunno—cooking, fixing things, making things. Something."

"Can you cook or fix or make things?" Charlie thought it best not to go down the road marked 'Camilla and Fred's childcare post-divorce'.

"Mum can't boil an egg, and her definition of DIY is GSI. She's straight on the phone to Malic the Polish guy whenever anything needs fixing or changing."

"GSI?" Charlie was lost already in teenage speak, but not so deep down he loved it; it made him feel young again.

"Get someone in."

"I see." Charlie paused, pondering how he could be helpful but not patronising, and settled in for what he knew would be another morning wonderfully whiled away in Aaron's company.

***

Isabella Jones sat by the pool in southern Italy, surrounded by her parents-in-law, watching her husband, Hugo, swimming. She noticed he hadn't allowed his hair to become wet and was doing a fastidious breaststroke—was it possible to swim in a fastidious way? Hugo certainly appeared to be giving a bloody good go.

Hugo waved to his mother, shouting, "Oh, Mummy, you *must* come in the water! It's simply blissful!"

Isabella shuddered at her husband's turn of phrase, regretting that she'd agreed for yet another year to come on holiday with her parents-in-law.

Lady Reece Jones pulled back her enormous sun hat and cooed, addressing both her son and daughter-in-law, "Oh, darling, I do so love you both coming on holiday with us. It really is such marvellous family fun."

Lord Richard Reece Jones turned to Isabella. "Isn't it, dear?"

Keeping her eyes on her *Vogue* magazine, Isabella smiled sweetly and sipped her double gin and tonic, wondering when it would be polite and unlikely to be noticed if she made herself another.

Lady Reece Jones shrugged off her towel and walked, wobbling slightly from side to side, to the steps at the shallow end of the pool, holding onto her hat as a gust of wind threatened to remove it. She lowered herself into the water and began to splash playfully with her son. "Hugo, darling, you were right. It *is* simply blissful." She turned to Isabella. "Would you like to join us?"

With pursed lips, Isabella looked up from her article about the perfect luxury beach holiday and said, "Not quite yet. I'm trying to get an even bronze."

Hugo swam backwards from his mother. "Oh, Mummy, not the hair, please. It's taken me such a long time to style it correctly. I shall have to borrow your hairdryer if it's wetted."

Isabella stared at the pair playing childishly in the water and allowed her mind to return to the dark-haired man at the car hire desk in the airport. He'd definitely winked at her as she'd signed the form. His cheeky grin. The crisp, white shirt straining to contain the arms within, three buttons open at the neck, dark hairs sprouting out. And those hands! Such enormous hands, she'd noticed, as he'd handed her the pen. She was well aware of what that meant. His light-brown trousers had been a bit tighter than a British man would wear but—based on the others at the car hire desk—perfect for an Italian man. Tight enough to show her his large hands were matched by the contents of his trousers. He'd shouted at his colleague to hurry up as the beautiful English lady was waiting, and she'd felt a flutter in her stomach and her chest flush red.

"Mummy, when are we eating? I'm absolutely famished!" Hugo shouted.

Isabella returned her focus to the magazine article and counted in her head the number of days until they would be home, away from her parents-in-law and able to resume their normal *ships that passed in the night* marriage.

Chapter 2

A FEW DAYS LATER, well-tanned and at least partly rejuvenated, Hugo and Isabella sat at opposite sides of the ten-feet-long, dark-oak table in Lord and Lady Reece Jones's oak-panelled dining room at Reece Jones Park, a hotel-sized estate in Hertfordshire. The housemaid had just served the second course: a duck breast in a rich cherry sauce with a bed of golden sautéed potatoes and asparagus spears.

Lord Reece Jones said, "Hugo, old boy, when do you think you'll get around to giving us some grandchildren? You've been married...how long is it?" He looked at Isabella, who'd been staring out the window.

"Four years." She counted on her fingers. Or was it five? It felt like fifty. Just like the rest of that bloody Italian holiday. Interminable discussions stretching well into the night about the family heir and who would inherit the silly business and estate. Every night, she'd gone to bed, her back to Hugo, over three feet away in bed. Not even so much as a kiss goodnight or a peck on the cheek. Women had needs. She was a woman, and she certainly had needs. Two years and he'd not touched her in that way. Could anyone blame her for... She looked up. "Yes, four years."

Lady Reece Jones put her cutlery on the plate, wiped her mouth with the white cotton napkin bearing the family initials and crest and took a deep breath.

Isabella knew what was coming. It was what always came at this stage. She put down her cutlery too.

9

"Have you been to your GP? I have the number of the most marvellous Harley Street doctor you can see. He'd fit you in tomorrow if needs be. One call is all it would take." She raised her head and pursed her lips, staring at Isabella. "Hmmm? Anything?"

"We've not been trying very long, so I don't think that's necessary, not yet anyway. But thank you so much, all the same." *And he's not been anywhere near to having sex with me in years. Maybe that's why I'm not pregnant, possibly?*

Richard Reece Jones said, "How's Reece Jones Instruments, old chap? Making me lots of lovely money? The money mill— that's what your mother and I call it!"

"It certainly rumbles along, Father," Hugo replied.

"But does it rumble along *well*? What new ideas have you to keep up with the incessant march of technology? We can't bank on everyone using violins and cellos forever. There may be some electronic competitor lurking around the corner. What are you doing to prevent that happening?"

"I'm sure it'll be fine. We make the things, and the musical instrument shops buy them, and from there, people buy them, I suppose." He shrugged.

"What about new products? Is there something—some little widget we can make to do something whizzy for guitars? I mean, a guitar is only a violin on its side without the bow, isn't it? What?"

"I didn't say anything, Father. Maybe." He paused and, checking his reflection on the back of a spoon, smoothed his eyebrows with a wetted finger and adjusted his hair.

Isabella shuddered. How on earth had she ended up with this man?

"Father, Mother, have you heard the most marvellous news about Isabella's job? She's frightfully busy. I hardly see her. She's out the house at first light and doesn't come home until well into the evening. They are such workaholics at her place!" He looked at his wife. "Aren't they, darling?"

"Yes, *darling*, but I wouldn't describe them as that. It *is* my own company. Fred worked bloody hard to buy Lux Sunglasses, and I'm beggared if I'm going to let it fall apart."

"See, isn't she marvellous, Father and Mother?" Hugo looked at his parents, eyebrows raised. "She was at a fashion show in Milan last week, trying to sell the products to some of their fashion houses. She's started business-expensing her dresses, haven't you, darling?"

"Yes, darling. My accountant said it's a legitimate business expense, and part of that is my looking smart and professional. So I treated myself—well, Lux Sunglasses treated me—to a few cocktail dresses from the new Alexander McQueen collection. Clean, simple lines, exquisite fabrics, perfection in every way. I can hardly turn up to these fashion shows in a sorry little affair from the high street. What's the point of having an accountant if he can't save you money like that? That's what I've always thought."

"It is, isn't it, darling? That's what you've always said." Hugo beamed at his wife, then at his parents, who were picking at the last bits of food on their plates. "Tell them about the company car, darling."

"My accountant told me I needed to upgrade and explained some beastly business about benefit-in-kind tax or some such. Anyway, long story short, I've a new Mercedes. It has a tiny little petrol engine and a most marvellous electric one too. Air conditioning, built in satnav, leather throughout, of course. It's like the bridge of one of those spaceships in the films I don't like. And all for less—in this kind tax, or whatever it's called—than for my last one."

The housemaid cleared the plates then returned with the dessert—a four-layer strawberry pavlova with mountains of thick, peaked cream and a dusting of white chocolate.

Lady Reece Jones shouted, "Dessert wine, please. Don't forget the dessert wine."

The housemaid nodded and quickly disappeared.

Lady Reece Jones plucked a toothpick from a silver dish in the middle of the table and began to root around her mouth. "Marvellous, Bel. Any other news from our favourite daughter-in-law?"

Isabella, the woman's only daughter-in-law, shook her mane of dark-brown hair. "It's a soft top too. One little button on the dashboard and it's all open to the elements. Of course, in winter, there's a neck heater to keep things bearable. And I bought myself a beautiful Hermes scarf to wrap my hair when the roof's down."

Hugo leant back in his chair and examined his nails, spreading his hands out in front of his face, moving from one to the other slowly in turn.

Isabella, noticing him doing this, rolled her eyes and continued with her story about how the Italian fashion houses had lapped up her presentation and ordered 'simply shedloads' of the most expensive sunglasses in their range. She told them about a party in London to launch a new diffusion range of sunglasses, at which Hugo had joined her. "We're such a marvellous team, Hugo, Fred and myself. My brother and I, we work like Irish navvies for the company. But we love it. Fred was pleased we'd filled our order books. The retailers—premium high street, some of them I'd not heard of before—they were eating out of my hand when I told them the mark-up they'd get for the products. I almost added that it's all made in a factory in China and just boxed and finished in Italy, so we can have the assembled by hand on the boxes. I checked with our lawyers. It's all perfectly above board and legal."

Lady Reece Jones pushed the toothpick silver bowl across the table. "So no news on the grandchild front?"

Hugo jumped in. "Oh, Mummy, do please give it a rest. It's such an exhausting conversational topic. Can't you see how busy we've both been, running our little empires for the families? When do you suppose we'd fit in the…err…baby-making?"

"I'm simply thinking of your poor father. He worries about this place and the business. We don't want Reece Jones Park and Reece Jones Instruments going to the state if you've no male heir to pass it to." She paused, wiped her brow with the napkin. "It would be such a terrible shame." She rang a small silver bell next to her fork, and the housemaid immediately reappeared, leaning forward slightly as she cleared the plates. "Now, do we have a date for us to come to you?" She reached into her handbag and pulled out a thick, bright-pink Filofax stuffed with business cards, sheaves of paper bursting from the edges. She flicked through and shouted a few dates across the table.

Hugo shrugged. "No good asking me, Mummy. It's Bel who handles the diary arrangements." He smiled at his wife.

Isabella smiled back, noting that his eyes remained dull and joyless—the usual continuation of the ridiculous charade they put on for his bloody parents. "I'm exhausted. Must we do this now, this very instant?"

Lady Reece Jones put her pen on the table slowly and rested her hand on the Filofax, keeping it open. "It isn't absolutely essential, my dear, but I have found it makes it so much simpler in the long run. My poor, dear son has never been blessed in the organisational department, and since we have to run everything through you, and you are—as you've ably described—so *awfully* busy, I do feel it would be most beneficial for all parties if we were able to close this off here and now." She smiled at Isabella, having picked up her pen once again.

Date agreed, kisses and handshakes exchanged, Isabella and Hugo made their way to her brand-new, bright-red, soft-top Mercedes, across the expanse of crunchy yellow gravel of the drive.

Isabella turned and waved at her parents-in-law as she got in the car.

"Aren't you going to open her up, darling?" Hugo tapped the roof.

"Not while we're in earshot, I'm not, *darling*."

In a cloud of petrol fumes and spray of gravel, Isabella left the redbrick, fifteen-bedroomed with ballroom and servants' quarters, Victorian-faux-Tudor Reece Jones Park, its double iron gates and its box hedges behind.

She turned to Hugo and said, "Must you always be so *completely and utterly* fucking useless?"

"Darling, I thought we made a good team tonight." He tapped the roof, and his hand hovered over the roof button.

"Don't you fucking dare, *darling*. I swear to God, if your interfering old mother asks us one more time when we're having kids, I will tell her the real reason. See what she has to say about that." She stared straight ahead, concentrating on the road and willing this closeness with her husband to be soon over.

He lifted his hand from the button and folded them both in his lap. "I'll do my best for her not to ask again. Maybe you could say there's something wrong with your plumbing, just keep things simple."

"My plumbing—*my plumbing*? What would you know about my fucking plumbing? Thank God it's Monday tomorrow and there's not much of the weekend left." She pushed the roof button, and it lowered as they sat at a T-junction before leaving the countryside behind and returning to their suburban world of Chigwell.

Hugo started to say something, but he was drowned out by the loud music she'd turned on.

Chapter 3

FRED SMITH WAS in the middle of telling his twenty-five years his junior wife Sharon how surprised he'd been at Hugo's performance at the party in London.

"Turned out my funny brother-in-law actually pulled it together, and the clients loved it. He managed not to do any of the things that make me cringe and want to run from the room screaming. He was…" He tried to think of the right word. "Like a normal bloke, I suppose. Isabella was on good form too. It all ran like clockwork. For once."

"Sounds lovely, babes." Sharon flicked her waist-length, very out-of-a-bottle, very blonde hair and combed it with her long pink and white nails, leaving it to rest on her right hip. "When you seein' the kids next? I'm trying to work out when to get the dogs groomed."

"Dunno. I've gotta talk to that old cow Camilla. She's bleeding me dry. I told this bloke at work how much maintenance I'm paying, and he thought I was having a laugh. He said cos the kids are over eighteen, there's no need. I don't need to pay her a penny."

Sharon clapped her hands and picked a stray eyelash extension off her cheek. "Didn't I always say dogs are so much better than kids? I dunno why you said you'd pay her so much. I mean, what does that Camilla need all the money for, eh? She looks like she's just come from a jumble sale in them clothes. And her skin—

it's so pale I thought she had a deficiency or somethink when I last seen 'er."

"That's why the party was so important. The business don't run itself, sweets. Me and Isabella—she'll always be just plain Kylie to me, before she got all these fake airs and graces and forgot she was brought up in Mile End with me—we're both working our fingers to the bone for that business, and half my money's going to Camilla. I'm so proud of my sister, running it with me. We make a good team, we do."

"I thought you paid it to the kids, so Alvin and Terry can do what they want with it."

He rolled his eyes. "How many times, sweetheart? It's Aaron and Tamara. It's not like you don't see 'em. They're here one weekend a month. You are their step-mum." And he'd hoped her being only ten years older than his children would have helped them bond, but unfortunately not.

"I know, babes. I do try. I'm all right with other people's dogs and cats, but kids—you've no chance, sorry." She shook her head, allowing her hair to shake all around herself. She examined one of her nails. "You seen this? One of 'em's split. I only had 'em done down that new nail bar in Chigwell last week. What am I s'posed to do now, eh?"

"Go back and have them done again." He paused as she made kissing noises back to him. "Actually, second thoughts, scrub that. We ain't got the money. Can't you make do and mend until the next appointment?"

"Do I look like a make-do-and-mend sort of girl? This—" She gestured to her whole body encapsulated in a pink Juicy Couture towelling tracksuit and silver high heeled shoes. "—this don't come from make do and mend. This takes time. It takes effort—"

"Yeah, and money, don't forget money!" Fred said.

"Oh well, I suppose that means the party you mentioned is off, if we're—" She lowered her voice and looked out the window theatrically. "—*cutting back.*"

"Oh, no, babes, you can get on with that. I mean to say, there are limits."

She filed her nails with a small emery board she'd taken from her white, fluffy handbag.

"Did Aaron call? Or Tamara? Either of 'em?"

"Not that I remember. I did check the messages earlier, and nothing. Do you want me to see if the little red light's flashing? That means it's got a message, doesn't it?"

"Only if you're getting up anyway, babe."

"Why? You expecting a call from them?"

"No. Well, I wanted to talk to Aaron about coming to the office a bit—a little introduction, rather than throwing him in the deep end. Tamara's all right, doing her couple of days a week. She's a real boon, typing and filing her little heart out. I told Aaron I want to pass it on to him." He put his hand on his chest and looked up to the ceiling. "You know, when the time comes..."

"Oh, babe, don't say that! I don't know what I'd do without you. I'd just be lost. I'd have no reason to put all this on if you went."

"Babe, I will go. I am going to go, one day." Fred stared at his wife.

"I know, but can we not talk about it now, please? I want to watch my programme. The one with the man who opens the shop in London in the old days. Mr. Marks and Spencer's, or Harrods, or John Lewis..." She turned up the TV volume and settled in to her programme.

Fred checked his mobile phone: still nothing from Aaron in reply to the text he'd sent a few days ago.

Chapter 4

Danny Traviati lay on the large, black, leather sofa with chrome edging as his boyfriend—manager—Paul handed him another glass of champagne. They chinked their glasses, and Paul walked to the floor-to-ceiling window of their Canary Wharf apartment that looked out to the perfectly manicured square beneath, where private security guards patrolled for anyone breaking any of the management agency's strict bylaws.

Danny put the champagne on the glass coffee table and smiled at himself when he noticed the well-endowed marble men whose hands held up the table's top. "Who paid for this, then?"

"It was the last one, with the awful wig and the flabby belly."

"Who used to tell me how much he loved me every time he handed over the money?"

"The very one."

"In that case, I've earned this. I've earned this in spades. On my knees, on my back, my front..."

"Don't you ever think it's a bit sad?" Paul asked.

"That they pay, or that they think it's love?"

Paul shrugged and took another sip of champagne. "Both, I suppose. It's all fairly vile when you think about it."

"Don't knock it. That 'vile' pays for all this." He gestured around the four-bedroom apartment. "And don't forget the car in the basement, in our own parking space. It doesn't grow on trees, you know."

"No, but sometimes I think it grows from the end of your cock!"

"So do I, my darling, so do I." Danny stared out the window, thinking about the last sugar daddy he'd lured in gently and then milked for tens of thousands of pounds' worth of gifts and other gratuities, on top of the hourly or nightly rate he already charged. He'd come a long way since those early days of a little advert in the back of a free gay paper and a pay-as-you-go mobile phone. How he'd moved up in the world, from wanking off old men in their cars or Soho doorways and giving blow jobs to office workers on their way home to their families in the home counties, to the exclusive escorting in hotels with busy, rich businessmen he did now.

He caught the twinkle of his blue eyes in the table's reflection and adjusted the dark, wavy quiff of his hair. He was pleased with the fake Italian persona he'd created over the years. Growing up in Dagenham, there were pieces of furniture in the apartment that were more Italian than him, but a quick name change and a bit of a fake Italian accent, and presto! Danny Traviati had been born from the ashes of Danny Taylor.

"Why did he stop booking again?"

"His wife found out," Paul said. "She asked about the money. He rang me, begging me if he could count the gifts against future bookings."

"Bloody cheek!"

"That's what I told him. I said, if he wanted to give you those presents, they were completely separate from the normal fees. And if he wanted to book you again, I would be happy to oblige if he gave me his credit card number or wired a money transfer."

Danny shuddered. "I'd had enough of his saggy arsehole and tiny, flaccid cock, I can tell you. What was the last count when you closed it?"

"All in? The gifts and all the bookings?"

"Yep, the whole kit and caboodle. Tot it up in your little spreadsheet thingy. You know how it makes me stiffen." He licked his lips at Paul.

Paul sat with his micro-thin laptop, adding up figures and checking the bookings record. After a while, he looked up from the screen. "Have a guess."

"Oh, come on. I'm getting bored here. Get on with it, man. If you're my manager, manage, do it, add it. Earn your keep. You don't do fuck all else around here."

Paul said to himself under his breath, "I don't need to."

"What was that, sweetness?"

"Nothing. So, drumroll, please."

Danny made a winding-up sign with his hand.

"Come on, give it a bit of theatricality! It's worth it, when you hear it." He smiled and glanced back to the screen.

"Let's see. He was seeing me for…five months, was it?"

"Six, actually."

"Once a week for six months at two fifty an hour. That's…" Danny counted on his fingers and then gave up. "Plus the stuff. What did he give me? I can't remember. It all blurs into one after a bit. Poor me, eh?" He looked at the half-inch thick TV that filled the longest wall in the living room.

Paul shook his head. "That wasn't him. That was the other guy—the one who worked for the electrical goods company. Said it fell off the back of a lorry, and if he gave it to you, would you do a whole Sunday like a proper boyfriend, cos he was alone?"

"I remember. What did the old guy give me, then?" Danny looked around the apartment, tapping his dazzling-white capped teeth with his perfectly manicured nails.

"How about starting with what you're sitting on?"

"Oh, yes, I remember. That holiday he paid for on his card—two weeks in the Maldives in winter. Did he pay for that gay cruise that we went on with him?"

"How else do you think I'd have let him come along? And we charged him double time every time you went to his cabin, not mine," Paul said.

"Ahh, yes, of course. I needed a holiday after that holiday. I was sore in places I didn't know you could get sore. Chafed. I couldn't work for a bit after we came back."

"You didn't need to, not after what we'd made that fortnight. And don't pretend you don't love it. You love fucking your way to exhaustion. Always have, always will. It's one of the reasons I fell for you. That and your magnificent—"

"Stamina?" Danny fluttered his eyelashes—the only gesture of campness he ever allowed himself. "Fucking well come on, now. How much was it? All in?"

"Ready. Drumroll."

"Come the fuck on, will you? Can't you just get on with it? Why does it always have to be such a bloody performance? Just tell me how much fucking money!"

Paul's eyes opened wide, and he began to back away

"I'm sorry." Danny moved closer to Paul, who shrugged out of his reach. "Please, I'm overworked. I'm tired. Sorry. I love you. Come on."

Paul returned to his seat and kissed Danny, who reached down to Paul's groin and felt a pleasant swelling.

"Come along, drumroll, *please*." Paul smiled and lifted Danny's hand from his groin.

Danny rolled his eyes. "If I must, I must." He drummed with his hands on the table.

"That's better." After a few seconds, Paul said, "Forty-five thousand pounds."

"And how much do we need to tell the taxman about?"

"Just under half was for services rendered, so we'll have to declare that, or we'll be audited. I'm not going through that fucking rigmarole again with the fucking HMRC goons. I know it's nothing to do with them what exactly the business is we're doing, and that, strictly speaking, prostitution is illegal…"

"I'm not a prostitute, I'm an escort. A high-class, male escort, actually. Haven't you read the business card?" Danny shook his head, tutting loudly.

"Honey, who do you think wrote it, while you were drilling away behind some saggy old man's arse, kneeling on a hotel bed? Fucking taxman, looking at the bookings, going through the books to see if they matched up with what I'd declared. Did I tell you he went through the diary for the whole of that year? Checking the booked time against what I'd said I'd received for every entry. Little man. Tiny little man, taking pleasure in stuff like that. Tiny little cock too, I bet. He was so fucking patronising about what we did. Even though I told him you escorted men on evenings out, he knew what you really did. Patronising cunt. I nearly told him if he had a good fuck from Danny Traviati, he wouldn't give a shit about the profit-and-loss columns or checking our accounts. But I didn't, I bit my tongue."

"Thank fuck for that." Danny paused, thinking about what Paul had just said about the money. "So about twenty thou in six months. That's one client, yeah?"

"Yep."

"How many clients you got on the books at the moment?"

"Active or lapsed? By which I mean those who haven't repeat-booked in the last six months."

"Yeah, just the active ones." He laughed to himself. "Although, chance'd be a fine thing. I don't think there's one guy in the whole of London who books me who really is active. Bottoms, the lot of them. Needy, desperate bottoms. Fuck knows how the bi or straight ones satisfy their wives and girlfriends. If you can call them straight after they've been fucked by a man for a whole afternoon."

"Here we are again—that endless debate about what makes someone bi, gay or straight. It's like 'does a falling tree make a sound in an empty forest?'"

"It's nothing like that. Nothing like that at all. I just don't understand..." Danny continued with his ongoing theory about men's sexuality and what defined them, their relationship or their bedroom activities.

Paul let him talk while poring over the bookings for the next few weeks. There were only a few odd days without any bookings at all.

"Hey, you listening?" Danny straddled Paul's legs, getting between him and the laptop.

Paul looked up at Danny's groin close to his face. Danny pulled Paul's face upwards and squinted, licking his lips.

"Aren't you tired?" Paul asked. "You had two half-day bookings yesterday, and you've another one—he checked the time on the laptop—in a couple of hours. Better save yourself for them who's paying."

Danny moved the laptop from Paul's lap to the glass table then pushed Paul down on the sofa, unbuttoning his fly with one deft movement of one hand. Paul turned his head towards the black sheepskin rug by the window, and Danny knew what to do. He scooped Paul up and placed him on his back on the rug. Always a man prepared from every eventuality, he pulled the equipment from his back pocket, and they arched their bodies together, enjoying the gaze of neighbours through their apartment windows.

23

Danny didn't need to rest for the next client; he could handle another session, especially if it was with Paul. He didn't need to close his eyes and think of David Beckham. Paul was just as dirty and depraved in the bedroom as Danny, and that was exactly why they'd stuck together for so long after that quick wank in the stationery cupboard at the office where they'd met years ago.

Afterwards, they lay on the floor, entwined together, sharing a cigarette and laughing about the neighbours' view and whether they'd get another of the 'Cease and Desist' letters citing lewd behaviour reports from fellows of the management company.

Paul offered Danny a bit of cocaine. "You look tired."

Danny waved it away. "Better not or I won't be able to get it up later. When am I due?"

Paul checked the bookings diary on the laptop. "An hour or so."

After a while of lying entwined together, Paul returned to a computer game, naked with the laptop on his lap.

"Going for a shower," Danny said, kissing Paul on the way past and looking down at himself and laughing at how his sizeable cock swung from side to side as he ran across the floor to the bathroom.

Chapter 5

IN CHELSEA, CHARLIE Frost and Neil Bingham knocked on their neighbour's door for the weekend lunch. Despite Neil wanting to make an excuse not to attend, Charlie had convinced him it would be another pleasant afternoon, even if Camilla's food was pretty dismal, and so here they were.

Camilla Constantine accepted their homegrown, home-cooked rhubarb crumble, which immediately made her feel inadequate.

"Oh, boys, you really didn't have to. I did say *I* was cooking. I did say, just yourselves and a bottle." She smiled and kissed them in turn, showing them through to the low-ceilinged living room of her cottage, where she'd lived for the past thirty years, for the first twelve with husband Fred Smith and the rest happily without him. She'd always despised her married name so had, as soon as was practical after the divorce, changed back to her maiden name.

"It rather suits me, I feel, like the Alice band I found at the back of the wardrobe," she'd told her baby daughter, Tamara, in 1996 when the divorce finally loomed large on the horizon, after years of ploughing on through Fred's silliness and indiscretions.

Tamara had reached from her highchair, grabbed her mummy's hair and put it in her mouth. Aaron, her toddler son, had been walking around the house, grabbing books and toys and asking Mummy to play with him, completely oblivious to his parents' dissolving marriage. Camilla wasn't bothered her children didn't have the same surname as her. She'd made it clear they were to

25

stay with her after the divorce; bringing them up made them closer to her than any silly shared surname with their father.

Charlie and Neil took a seat on the squashy, seen-better-days sofa as Camilla ran to the kitchen, calling to ask if they wanted a drink. "Some fizz, maybe?"

Charlie looked at his boyfriend and shrugged. "Fizz would be lovely," he called back. "Do you want any help?"

"No. You've done more than enough. Just you sit there and relax. What do I have to do with this crumble? Did you tell me?" *Why is food so complicated?*

Charlie started to stand, but Neil stopped him and frowned. "Sit. She can manage."

Charlie sat again but shouted, "There's a note with the instructions on top of the Bacofoil. One-eighty for forty minutes, and it'll be done. I can show you."

Neil pushed him back in his seat. "It's rude. I've told you before. It's rude to cook for someone else in their home. It basically says to them, 'Poor you. You're incapable of cooking, you useless idiot. Let me help.' You might as well pat her on the head."

"I don't think it quite says all that." Charlie paused. "All right, who shat in your handbag?"

"Tired. Long week. Busy week next week too. I'm all over the place."

Charlie squeezed Neil's shoulder. "We won't stay long. Get home for that thing we watch on a Sunday night. I've ironed all your shirts and restocked your travel wash bag with things."

"You are perfect. I don't know what I'd do without you." Neil leant forward and kissed Charlie's lips. His eyes closed, inhaling slowly as if to take in the smell of Charlie. "Love you."

"Love you," Charlie replied.

Camilla bustled in with two old-fashioned champagne glasses with expensive dark cherries at the bottom. "Sorry. I would have made a cocktail, only I can't. So it's champers. I've put the cherry in, bit of colour. Bit of fun. Did you say what I had to do with the dessert? I've a mind like a sieve, especially when it comes to food!" *And everything else!* She patted her forehead while closing her eyes.

A female voice shouted from the kitchen, "Mum, come in here. We need you, please."

"Sorry." *What now?* She touched both Neil's and Charlie's hands and left the room.

Charlie whispered, "She's like this every time. You'd think she was catering for a wedding. It's only us and her kids."

"I don't think they normally cook if they don't have guests. So for us, this is rolling out the red carpet."

"It's all bought in. She gets it catered from Harrods. Doesn't cook a bit of it. Even the starters are bought in. I saw the packets last time we came round."

"Why the drama, then? What's she got to do? Put it in the oven and serve it?"

"Not even that. It's delivered hot, I think. I rang once to check."

Neil rolled his eyes.

"Quiet day," Charlie justified. "Between projects. I'd done the dinner, and the next day's dinner, delivered the veg boxes for the day, and met my knitting quota."

"I believe you. Thousands wouldn't." Neil shot him a smile.

"I do work hard, running the house, you know. And with the craft fairs and the veg boxes all over London, it's a full-time job. It just happens I'm at home all day."

"And here's to that." Neil chinked his glass against Charlie's. "What did Harrods say?"

27

"Well, they can do cook-chill so it's delivered frozen, or for a bit more—quite a lot more, actually—they'll deliver at the time of the dinner party, hot, and all you have to do is plate it up."

"Honestly, some people." Neil shook his head.

"I know, and every time I tell her, 'I don't mind us always hosting,' but she won't have it."

"She can't be short of money, then. Was it expensive, this Harrods service?"

"I asked them for a quote for a normal-typed dinner I'd do." He leant forward and whispered so quietly Neil could barely hear. "Let me put it to you this way. It cost a bit less than the first car we bought together."

"What, that old Fiesta?"

"The nice one. Thirteen years old. MOT and tax."

"How much did they quote? Just tell me."

"For a three-course meal for five, like tonight, they wanted just under six hundred quid."

Neil whistled, then fished the cherry from his glass and ate it.

Camilla shouted in the kitchen, and Neil and Charlie pretended not to notice. She appeared in the living room, red-faced, hair escaping from her Alice band and a tea towel over her shoulder, and banged a gong above the fireplace. "Dinner is served, gentlemen. Please follow me to take your seats." She sighed loudly, wondering why she put herself through this every time.

They sat at the scrubbed wooden table on pine wooden seats with chintzy cushions in the farmhouse-style kitchen, complete with powder-blue Aga, wooden laundry rail above, copper saucepans suspended, shining perfectly in the light, floor of aged terracotta tiles and sprigs of lavender dotted all over the place. Camilla had based the whole look on a feature she'd seen in *World of Interiors* magazine, and it all looked so perfect until she started to actually make anything to eat.

Tamara handed out the prawn cocktail in small glasses. She caught Charlie's eye. "I said I could do this, but she wouldn't listen. She got it all in—again."

Charlie smiled and took his prawn cocktail.

Camilla offered wine and poured some into the glasses. "I added the paprika, darling. I did do something." She looked around the table hopefully. "Has everyone got what they require? Then I suggest we begin before the next course burns or cools or something. I swear to God, I've lived here thirty years and I still can't get the hang of that bloody Aga. I said to Fred when we moved in, 'Either it goes or I do.' Turns out he went and we're still both here, stuck with one another." She raised her glass and proposed a toast to friends, tagging onto the end of it, "Aaron, darling, did you call your father back?"

"No," her son answered flatly and dug into his prawn cocktail. He was such a worry. Children always were at that age.

"He rang the house phone, darling. Said he'd texted you as well. He wants to talk to you about the business. You ought to take an interest. Just pretend to be interested, will you, darling?"

Aaron pushed his mane of strawberry-blond hair out of his eyes. It immediately fell back, covering half his face. "How am I meant to fake it? I can't. I hate it, Mum. It's just so awfully boring. I want to do something more creative—something with my hands." He flicked his hair back again. "Hairdressing. That's a trade. No one's exploited in hairdressing. Not bloody boring sunglasses. I mean, sunglasses—luxury ones—they're all made in the same factory in Japan or China. He told me, like it was something to be proud of. All those people being exploited, earning a pittance to make them, and then Dad goes and sells the bloody things for thousands of pounds. It's disgusting. It's immoral. It ought to be illegal."

"It's capitalism, and that, my dear, is what makes the world go round. What do you think paid for you and your sister to go to school? What pays for Mummy to keep this darling little house and stay at home to look after you?" She paused, glass of wine in hand, looking at the others in the room. "Right, darling, clear the plates and see if the lamb is OK. I don't want it getting cold or hot or whatever it is…" She trailed off as Aaron and Tamara cleared the table of the starter.

Aaron opened one of the Aga's doors, and a powerful blast of meat and burning filled the room. "Mum, I think you'd better have a look at this."

"Excuse me, please." *What on earth now?* She jumped up from the table then peered at the dish with the braised lamb casserole in a tomato sauce. It looked lamby and tomatoey and not at all burned. "What's that awful smell?" She began dishing up the lamb while Tamara checked the other doors of the Aga until she removed a black, round disc, an inch tall and a hand's span across.

"Mum, what's this?" She held it above her head.

Camilla dropped the spoon, splattering a bit of sauce on Charlie's and Neil's shirts as well as her own flowery blue-and-white blouse. She ran to the scene of the crime by the Aga. "Shitting fucking fuck. You know what that is, don't you, darling?"

Tamara shrugged on her way to the bin.

"That's what happened to that fucking Victoria sponge I made and forgot about." *How absolutely mortifying, and Charlie a professional baker too. What an idiot they must think I am.* She returned to the table and resumed dishing up the lamb, taking deep breaths to compose herself in front of her guests. "Still, we can't all be Delia Smith, can we, eh, boys? Neil, you're not so into cooking, are you? So you must understand what it's like for me."

Everyone tucked into the main course, while Charlie explained that he was the lead chef in their house, since he was at home more. "Neil's travelling means he's often back so late. It wouldn't make sense for me to wait for him to get home and cook. Overall, it's a fairly even split, isn't it?"

Neil nodded, smiling at Charlie and taking another bite of the food.

Tamara said, throwing her napkin on the table, "Never mind *Aaron* calling Dad back. What about me? I'm at that bloody sunglasses place two days a week, and it's like I don't even exist. All he gets me to do is the bloody filing and typing up things he's written by hand. I mean, who does that nowadays? Everyone types their own letters. He asked me if I'd learned shorthand in college." She rolled her eyes. "Shorthand!"

"Darling, he's from a different era. He's not a modern man, not like these two." She gestured to her *gaybours*, as they jokingly referred to them in her house, and to their faces.

Tamara's hands hung by her sides, and she stuck her bottom lip out. "But, Mum, I'm doing business studies, not typing school. I don't want to be a *secretary*." She spat the last word like it was a piece of burned lamb.

Camilla put down her cutlery. "Now, now, there's nothing wrong with being a secretary. That's how I started at the magazine when I met your father, in that bar with my girlfriends while he was out celebrating his bonus." Her eyes lost focus as she thought back to how much simpler life had been then, when they'd first moved into this house, all so full of hope and promise, setting up a family together. Building a home together. Until it had all gone to hell in a handbasket, as her mother used to say, God rest her soul. She felt a hand on hers.

"Mum, are you all right?"

She looked at her daughter and smiled. Something good *had* come of it. Two 'somethings good' to be precise. "That's enough complaining about your father. He's a very good man. He's always

31

been so generous to me—when we were married and afterwards. If it weren't for him, we wouldn't be able to live here. Imagine that—moving out of Chelsea. Where would you be then, Tamara, without the King's Road five minutes away? So look sharp and think on. We'll have no more complaints about Daddy."

***

Over the dessert of Charlie's rhubarb crumble, which he served since Camilla had insisted, Charlie asked Aaron where his interest in hairdressing had come from. It hadn't been discussed when Aaron had popped round to chat earlier that week. It was good to see the young man working it out, but it struck Charlie as a bit...well, a bit random.

"Dunno really." Aaron pushed his hair back from his eye. "Wanna do something creative. Something that's not just sitting in an office all day with a computer, filing cabinets and that."

"Yes. That's why I stopped my job in the city," Charlie said. "I'd always wanted to do something creative but just didn't think I would be able to make a living out of it. Turns out we manage just fine." That made sense, he supposed.

Neil nudged him to eat his dessert; he'd been talking so long he hadn't had a mouthful yet.

"Of course, having another wage does help," Charlie added, scooping up a spoonful of crumble. "And Neil's very good at bringing in the consultancy bacon, aren't you, sweetheart?"

"You do the cooking too, don't you?" Aaron asked, pointing to the rest of the crumble in the white earthenware dish in the middle of the table.

Charlie nodded.

"And didn't you make these for Mum last Christmas?" He held up his napkin holder—a carved wooden ring decorated with painted flowers in the style of old-fashioned gypsy caravans.

Camilla interjected, pushing a stray hair back from her eye and tucking it under her Alice band. "So, Neil, how *is* your work? Busy, varied, or are you going through a quiet patch, hang over from the last recession, which apparently, we're meant to have come out of. But it simply doesn't feel like that to me." She laughed quietly to herself and twisted the napkin in her lap.

"Busy enough. I increased my day rate, so some of the older clients who'd had me at the cheaper rate fell away. I went to an industry thing for freelance management consultants, and that was the day rate to aim for. No point in filling my diary with work at a rate lower than I'm worth when I could be spending time at home instead." He smiled at Charlie.

"Yes. Quite." Camilla continued to play with her napkin and its holder. "So what exactly is it you do again? I've heard of management consultants, but it's a bit like wi-fi, isn't it? It's something you've heard of, but when you really think about it, you're not quite sure how it all works, how it all functions." She looked at her children. "Or is that just me?" She raised her eyebrows.

Aaron and Tamara shrugged, so Neil explained exactly what it was a management consultant did all day and went through a typical week in the life of his job.

Camilla said, "Well, that sounds marvellous, doesn't it, Aaron? Isn't that the sort of work you'd like to do with Daddy? At his business? Helping them sort out problems, maximising the flows of..." She made circling motions in the air.

Neil rescued with, "Profit flows? And customer satisfaction?"

"Yes, quite. Customer satisfaction. Isn't Daddy always talking about the customer satisfaction and building their customer bases or something?"

Since Aaron showed no inclination for replying, Tamara said, "We did the different types of business—limited companies, public limited companies, sole traders, all those—at college. And we're about to do profit, turnover and cost and what the difference is. It sounds so interesting. I can't wait to explain to Daddy about it all."

Neil and Charlie raised their eyebrows at Tamara, waiting for Camilla to reply. Instead, she clapped her hands and said, "Hadn't we mooted the idea of walking your darling dog? Bit of fresh air, walk off some of these calories?" She rubbed her stomach. "I'm fit to bursting—your dessert has just about pushed me over the edge. Lovely as it was." She smiled at Charlie, who just nodded back in agreement.

"I'll go get Judy," Neil said and left to fetch their black-and-white Papillion.

Charlie started to stack the plates and take them to the dishwasher; he found it hard to sit and watch while others worked around him.

Camilla waved her hands about frantically. "No, no, no! *You* are the guest. I will not have it. Put those back at once! We will deal with all this mess later. Now it's time for the guests. It'll all wait. Besides, what's the point of having two teenage children if you can't make them earn their keep?" She smiled and put on her green Barbour jacket and matching Hunter 'gum boots' as she called them, which were by the door. "Come along, children, put on your walking boots."

Aaron reluctantly put on his and reminded his mum, in a slightly whiny tone, that neither of them were really children any longer. "I'm nineteen and Tamara's eighteen. We can vote, drive—get married even," he added with a quick shake of his head and a quiet tut to himself.

"Yes, but you'll always be children to me. Because you are. It's something you'll understand when you have children of your own."

Chapter 6

A SHORT DRIVE AND they were in a fairly natural-looking park to enjoy the autumn sun, and Charlie let Judy off the lead. They had divided into groups: Charlie and Aaron; Camilla and Neil; Tamara floated between the groups, trying to interject in conversations.

Aaron and Charlie had been discussing what Camilla had said about him being always a child, and Aaron was in the middle of explaining how he didn't feel like a child any longer. "Nineteen is nothing like fifteen. I've left school, I'm shaving, I could get a job if I wanted. I told her, I could get married if I wanted to. Fuck's sake, I can vote, drive. I'm not a bloody child anymore. You understand, don't you?"

Charlie nodded. He'd already noticed how Aaron wasn't a boy any longer. "'Course I do. Nineteen's not that long ago for me, you know."

"How long have you and Neil been together?"

"Six years. But we were friends first. We've known each other for over ten years, but as a couple, yep, six years. Why?"

"Just wondered. Wondered if you've had other boyfriends before him."

"'Course I did. And so did he."

"Right. And how many did you have?" Aaron asked.

"What, boyfriends before Neil?"

"Yes, proper boyfriends."

"Depends on what you define as a proper boyfriend. When I was younger, that was quite a loose definition." He coughed,

35

thinking he needed to rescue this situation quickly, sensing he could be venturing into dangerous ground. "Anyway, when I first came out, I went out with a load of guys, only a couple of weeks for each of them. Is that a proper boyfriend?"

Aaron shrugged, despite it being a rhetorical question.

"Thinking back, not really. Some of them, we just held hands and did a bit of kissing. Then, that was enough."

Camilla appeared in between the two of them. "What was enough?"

Charlie explained what they were talking about, underplaying the sex part.

Camilla clipped Aaron around the head gently. "Have you no manners? Have I brought you up to respect no one's privacy? Why on earth have I spent all that money—Daddy's money, actually—on schooling, for you to ask a friend how many sexual partners they've had?"

Charlie said, "To be fair, he didn't ask me that. He actually asked how many proper boyfriends I'd had before Neil. That's a much less intrusive question and one I don't mind answering."

"Yes, well. That's as may be, but I'm not convinced it's a conversation a teenage boy should have with you."

Charlie and Aaron caught one another's eyes behind Camilla's head as she ploughed on with the walk, well wrapped up in her Barbour jacket and gum boots.

"OK, that's interesting, so why's that?" Charlie spoke first.

Camilla said, "What about the girls at uni? Aren't you interested in any of them?"

"I thought he wasn't sure about uni anymore. He said he finished at the school, went to uni and didn't think it was for him, so he's taking some time out."

"Did you?" Camilla asked, turning to Aaron with a furrowed brow.

Aaron nodded and put his hands in his pockets.

Charlie bit his tongue. Aaron had said he'd finally told his parents, he was sure.

"Why didn't I know about this? It's like you're not my children sometimes. I wonder if one day you're going to run away and join the circus or something." She shook her head.

"I *did* tell you. I *have* told you. And Dad." He looked away for a moment, watching the dog run in a long arc back to them. "But neither of you would listen. You kept saying I should stick with the course and I'd come round to it. Well, I didn't. I hated it. It was fucking terrible, so I'm taking a break from it all to work out what I want to do. Why do you think I didn't go back at the start of term? I've been here since then."

"Language, please."

"You swear all the bloody time."

"I do a lot of things you don't do. Besides, guests, company."

Charlie said, "Don't mind me, honestly."

***

They walked on in silence for a while. Camilla nodded slowly as she thought about the news she theoretically already knew but now was having to absorb for the first time. "I did think it was an awfully long Christmas break, or half term or whatever it's called these days."

"Reading week."

"Yes, exactly." Not that he'd done much reading, she thought. "So is Daddy still paying for the accommodation and tuition fees even though you're not there?"

"Like I said, I *have* told him. If he listened or not, I don't know." Aaron thrust his hands in his pockets.

She was positive he'd not told her or Fred, but she did have a mind like a sieve, so there was no way she could prove it. Important thing was to work out how to move forward from here. "Anyway, we can sort that out with Daddy later. Why didn't you stick with it? What was wrong? I mean, it's University College London. It's *the* place to go. It's where they all went doing PPE. It's a must-attend university! You have the grades, and so you simply must go."

"You bloody go, then. Cos I'm not going back at the moment. I need a rest from it all." He folded his arms and stuck out his bottom lip.

Charlie said quietly, "If I may? I think what he's saying is he didn't know if it was for him, the academia of university—and it *is* academic. He wants to think about what else he can do, maybe not going to uni, doing something more with his hands, something more creative, like a trade. Is that right?"

Aaron nodded. "Yep. That's exactly it." He smiled at Charlie. "At last! Someone who gets me."

Camilla tried to grasp the concept that had been thrust into her lap to deal with. "So where would you do that? Which uni is good for those things?"

"Depends. I may go back, or I'd go to a college, like Tamara."

"But you were *always* going to uni. That was always the plan. You can't go to college. You've already done sixth form or whatever it's called now. It's just not right—"

"Was I *always* going to uni? Who asked me, Mum? Did anyone check if I wanted to do politics, philosophy and bloody economics at that place, or did you just fill in the forms, sign the cheques and ship me off on my own?"

"But, but...why didn't you say?" She'd always done it all with his best interests at heart.

"I did! I have. I'm doing it now, but you're *still* not listening. The only person I've told about this, who's actually got what I'm on about, is Charlie. No one in my own family gives a shit about what I do." He stopped walking, but Charlie and Camilla continued so quickly passed him.

Charlie put out an arm to stop Camilla when she turned to walk back to her son. "Leave him. He needs to be on his own. Give him some time."

Aaron stood alone a few steps behind them, fists balled and arms held straight by his sides.

***

After a while, Aaron walked with Tamara. "It's like she listens but doesn't hear. I mentioned to them I was thinking about stopping uni for the moment, and now it's like it's some big fucking surprise. Some big thing to be dealt with. Whatever."

"Dad's not much better. I explained about the NVQ in business I'm doing, and what does he ask me to do last week?"

"Go on, make me laugh. I could do with a laugh."

"He showed me a filing cabinet and asked me to sort out from A to M. And the next day N to Z."

"Sort out?"

"Any files older than five years had to be moved to the archives in another part of the office. It was, like, so boring. I tried to ask him about what new product ideas he'd had, and could I talk to some customers, and do you know what he said?"

"'Why would you want to talk to customers?' Something like that?"

"Exactly!" Tamara paused. "What you gonna do? You can't just hang about the house all day, now Mum knows you're having a break from uni. Mind you, you've got away with it for a few months. Not bad, I suppose."

"Dad'll want me to help with Lux Sunglasses. Like, to do all the stuff you want to do. But I couldn't give less of a shit about the sunglasses. It's all sweatshop exploitation, you know that, don't you? Disgusting, capitalism."

Tamara shrugged. "Someone's gotta make them. And someone's gotta sell them."

"Typical. Just the thought of sitting at a computer in an office, with a filing cabinet and one of those office chairs, it makes me want to scratch off my skin with boredom." He flicked his hair from his eyes and stared at the expanse of the park, a few trees around the edge, his mum and their friends a few hundred yards ahead, throwing a stick for the little dog. He breathed deeply.

"Dramatic, much?"

"Whatever. Charlie and Neil got it right. They both do stuff that fits with their skills, what they want. They're a good team together, I reckon. Shame Mum and Dad weren't so good."

"You don't know what goes on at theirs. Who knows what Charlie and Neil are really up to when the door's closed. So what do you want to do, like, for work? All you've said is what you don't want."

"Knitting, pottery, woodwork, cookery, engineering, hairdressing. Stuff like that. That's what I want."

She put her arm around Aaron's shoulder. "I think you might need to narrow it down a bit before you tell Mum and Dad."

***

An hour or so later, as they reached Charlie and Neil's front door, the Smith family stroked the little dog, and Charlie reminded them it was his and Neil's turn to host next time.

Camilla leant to Charlie and said, "I'm awfully sorry about what he said. Those questions, really inexcusable. I honestly don't know what I'm to do with him sometimes. I've simply no idea."

"Don't worry. I've been asked far worse by colleagues at work." Some people were malicious or tactless, but Aaron's questions had been innocent. He had a good heart.

Camilla frowned. "Really?"

"Someone once asked me, over coffee before a meeting started, who was the woman in my relationship."

"What, with Neil?"

"Of course." ·

"And what did you say?"

"I said, no one, that's the point. Now *that's* rude, so don't worry about Aaron. Honestly, any time he wants to talk about my businesses, or any of the crafting, baking, knitting whatever, creative things to do with his hands, just send him round. I'm at home alone, just me and Judy most of the time. I'd be glad of the company. You're welcome for a tea and a digestive biscuit any time too, if you're at a loose end."

Whiling afternoons away chatting to Aaron would break the monotony of being alone all day long. He found somehow, despite the age gap, their conversations flowed easily from one topic to the next, punctuated by more tea and coffee being made. Charlie also felt responsible for mentioning the uni thing to Camilla. Despite Aaron saying he'd told his parents, it really hadn't been Charlie's place to bring it up. He wondered if Aaron really had told his parents or whether it was an elaborate ruse.

***

Camilla so often found herself at a loose end, rattling about the house alone, with Tamara at college and Aaron doing…well, she wasn't sure now what he had been doing all day. She relished a good old chinwag with Charlie. She'd tried to learn from him about how to become more domesticated but had failed every time and ended up dialling Harrods caterer instead. But there was something about Aaron's questions and his friendship with Charlie that worried her. She couldn't quite put her finger on it. If she said it out loud, it would be as bad as saying one of those old-fashioned phrases her mother had used to say that were terribly offensive these days, so she wouldn't say it.

Even so, the idea of Charlie and her son learning about *knitting* and *cooking* did something to her stomach, and she wasn't quite ready to share with anyone because she wasn't quite sure if she *should* feel that, not now, in the politically correct twenty-first century world. Charlie was always so helpful, such a great friend to her, and Aaron got on with him well. She didn't want to spoil that with her old-fashioned worries, about…well, nothing really.

Charlie and Neil were such a lovely couple. Such a marvellous addition to the neighbourhood, despite what the elderly lady at the end of the row of cottages had said when they'd moved in. It was so modern to have a couple like them nearby, and they were friends too. Just not too friendly or inappropriate. That was the word she could verbalise, now she'd turned over the thoughts in her head a while—*inappropriate*. Was it *appropriate* for a nineteen-year-old and a man in his early thirties—a *gay man* in his early thirties—to have a friendship like that? Like what, she couldn't still put her finger on, but she knew Fred would not be happy in the slightest. Once he'd got over the Aaron-maybe-not-going-to-uni news, a conversation about Aaron talking knitting and baking with their gay neighbours wouldn't be well received. Not one bit.

But that wasn't for now. That was for another conversation with Fred. And how much she relished and enjoyed those conversations with Fred, knowing his wife would be filing her nails and getting her roots done in the background on their call. They were the highlight of her day, week and often her season. What on earth had Fred been thinking, marrying that terrible plastic woman? Still, not her problem now.

But onwards, always onwards. She brought her thoughts back to the matter in hand. Tea and biscuits with Charlie would be such fun.

"I'll give you a tinkle to work out a date next week to pop round."

Charlie nodded. "And Aaron, any time."

"Of course!" she said a bit too brightly.

Aaron waved and followed Camilla back to their house, where all three of them tidied the kitchen in complete silence.

Chapter 7

O N SUNDAY NIGHT, Charlie handed Neil the four shirts he'd ironed and two pairs of shoes he'd cleaned and shined.

Neil added them to the packing for his working week.

"Where is it this week?" Charlie picked a bit of dog hair from one of the shirts.

"Manchester, Birmingham, Leeds, Cambridge. I'm properly on tour. Going to all the glamorous places."

"I'm alone four nights next week?" *Again!*

Neil nodded. "But I'll call you every night still."

"I think I'll pop round Camilla's. See how they're doing with Aaron taking a break from uni. I wonder how the ex-husband took it."

"I'd have loved to be a fly on the wall when she told him. Poor lad, though. Doesn't know what he wants to do."

"Who does at that age? I barely knew I wanted men, never mind what career I wanted to have for the rest of my life. How are they meant to make that choice at that age? It's all the wrong way round."

"It is," Neil agreed. "What's with the probing questions he asked you?"

"Nothing. Perfectly innocent. And it wasn't that probing. I said not to take any notice of what his mother told him. He's just confused, looking for someone who'll listen. Maybe he's not seen a couple like us before. I don't think there's any gay uncles lurking in their family. He's certainly never mentioned any to me."

43

"But everyone comes out so early now. He'll have some friends at school, I bet—posh school like theirs, they'll all be playing soggy biscuit, having daisy chains and buggering each other in the dormitories."

"He didn't board. In fact, I don't think they do boarding."

"Public school, though. You know." Neil smirked.

"I think someone's been watching a bit too much gay porn. Let me explain, sweetheart, there's real life, and there's porn." He made two fists, one to represent each different concept. "And the two are different. OK? One is here—" he shook one fist "—and the other is here." He held the other fist in the air.

"He fancies you."

"No, he does not. Don't be so ridiculous. He's not gay. And anyway, even if he was, I'm far too old for him. I could be his dad." How had Neil picked up exactly what Charlie had thought himself more than once? The looks Aaron gave him, a bit too much arm and hand touching—it was a dead giveaway.

"If you were his dad, you'd have been fourteen when you had him."

"Really?"

"Think about it, he's nineteen, you're thirty-three."

Charlie waved it away with a shake of his head. Best move off this conversation quick. "He doesn't fancy me. I'm friends with his mum—I'm like an uncle. You remember your mum's friends when you were a kid. They were aunties, and your dad's friends were uncles. Not real uncles and aunties, but it was different from people your age. We're Uncle Charlie and Uncle Neil. That's all."

"And there's a whole swathe of porn about that too." Neil sighed as he shuffled through some papers he'd taken from a pile on the bed.

"What's up?"

"Just looking at who I'm seeing this week. It's full on. Two days of training, then a diagnostic session with another client and a review on the Thursday. And I've still got all the prep to do."

"Can't you do it on the trains?"

"Some, but I need to get a bit done now or I'll be behind all week. If you leave me, I can do a good hour or so without interruption and clear more than I could on the train in two hours, with emails and phone calls pinging in. Then we can watch that programme you like together. Is that all right?"

"If you must." Sadness filled Charlie's heart.

"I must. Take Judy for a walk. Get a bit of fresh air. Or just loll about, watch some TV I don't like. The whole place to yourself until I come down."

Charlie lingered in the doorway of their bedroom.

Neil looked up from his papers. "Yes?"

"I'll miss you."

"I'll miss you too." Neil gave Charlie a broad smile. "But when I come home, you and Judy greet me. I'm so happy to be back, and I remember that's why I'm doing this schlepping all over the place."

They kissed, and Charlie brushed his palm around Neil's jaw. "I'll really miss you. It's been such a busy weekend, and we've not had chance to...yet. Do you want?"

Neil nodded, instantly ditching his paperwork. "Get 'em off, then." He undressed quickly, and Charlie copied then lay on his side, in their favourite position, ready for Neil to lie behind him.

Neil slicked himself and gently lifted Charlie's legs, kissing his neck, pushing and kissing and pushing and kissing until slowly, slicked bit by slicked bit, with a gasp from Charlie, they were one.

Charlie turned his head to kiss Neil, who moved behind him. He loved how close he felt to Neil, how now their flesh was together. Since the clinic and the test results, they had left behind the little silver packets they'd been using until then. "I fucking love you," Charlie said, smiling as he felt Neil filling him, his warm body against Charlie's back and his hand grabbing Charlie's cock, pumping in time with his deep thrusts.

"I love fucking you," Neil replied with a smile and a wink, then leant forward and kissed Charlie.

***

Afterwards, leaving Neil with his laptop and papers spread out on the bed, Charlie showered and went downstairs, where he cuddled up with Judy. The TV and sofa all to himself—what a treat. But now he thought about it, it wasn't such a treat. Although it was *their* home—office, kitchen, craft room—he was the one who spent most of his time there. Maybe once or twice a month he was out and about, taking care of delivering the veg boxes or going to a craft fair or a farmers' market to sell his cakes and veg, but the rest of the time, it was just him, Judy and the house. All to himself. Just like now, on the sofa, with the TV. He shook that from his mind and focused on being thankful. He wasn't the one working on a Sunday evening or doing hundreds of miles a week, criss-crossing the country on trains and in taxis and sleeping in hotels.

Part 2
Winter 2013

Chapter 8

Hugo Jones sat at the bar in a Soho club known for being somewhere a man in need of a man's touch could procure such services. If that was what he wanted, of course.

He'd shown his face at Reece Jones Instruments, made a few calls, checked in with his secretary at eleven-ish and left just after midday for "...a long client lunch—I'll be gone all afternoon." Well, there had to be some perks to being the company owner's son, didn't there? And quite honestly, how much was he really required to do? The products hadn't changed in decades, and people didn't tend to update musical instruments for the sake of it. The shops they sold to were happy with their service; he'd certainly not heard any rumblings to the contrary. The customers continued to buy the things just as always—when they expired and needed replacing. As CEO, he really should know more about their products, but what a terrible crushing bore that was. A few signed papers here, the odd cheque there, and it all ticked along nicely, allowing him plenty of time for afternoons such as this one.

Am I gay?

Of course not. He was a married man. He wouldn't go as far as to say happily because that would be a lie. But he *was* married to a woman and had only ever dated women before that.

But what about the men I sleep with?

Well, of course, *that* was just sex. That was completely different. There were no emotions there. It was mechanical, animalistic, brutal, biting, sweaty, painful—and how he loved that deep, stabbing, aching pain inside him every time—but it was sex. Nothing more, nothing less.

Hugo sipped his second cocktail—a properly made Manhattan—that was starting to have the desired effect. He almost asked for a cigarette from the dark-haired, Mediterranean-looking man next to him at the bar. He didn't normally smoke, but now he was loosened up a bit, he quite fancied one. Yes, a nice, smoky cigarette. That was one of the things he wanted.

Grabbing a box of matches from the black marble bar counter, he passed them from one hand to the other.

The dark-haired man leant forward and put his hands over Hugo's. "What do you want?"

"Oh, thanks awfully, but I'm fine. I was just wishing I'd brought my own blasted cigarettes out with me." He patted his jacket pockets. "Nope, left them at home. It's been such a stressful day, with work and not knowing if I'd get away. I must have forgotten them."

The man handed Hugo a cigarette.

"Thanks ever so much." Hugo accepted, noticing the man's blue eyes and inviting smile. He felt a shift in his underwear as that familiar itch returned. Only one thing would scratch it sufficiently.

The man shook Hugo's hand. "Danny. And you are?"

"Hugo. Shall we...?" He gestured to the patio doors to the smokers' balcony.

"Yes, let's, and you can tell me all about it."

They stood on the balcony, smoking, and Hugo told Danny about his stressful day at the office and how he hadn't been sure he'd make it to the bar. He was gabbling and nervous, spoiling it all somewhat, he felt.

Danny listened intently to every word and when Hugo paused said, "If we could get the paperwork sorted, we could both relax. You do want to relax, don't you, Hugo?" He put his hand on the small of Hugo's back.

Hugo reached into his inside jacket pocket and pulled out an envelope filled with bank notes, handing them to Danny. "It should all be there. I counted it twice." He shot Danny a half smile, the butterflies dancing in his stomach and the itch in his underwear radiating out, towards his thighs, backwards over his bottom, resting down low, below his stomach, staying there, in anticipation of being scratched in just the right way.

"Marvellous." Danny smiled, quickly opened the envelope, leafed through the notes and put it in his pocket. "Now, you were saying, you had such a stressful day at the office. I want you to relax, completely and utterly." He leant forward, one arm resting on the balcony rail, his head on his hand, looking into Hugo's eyes.

Hugo stared back into those deep-blue eyes, the face of the handsome man before him, listening to his troubles, and he disappeared into the space between them, the hot atmosphere that hung there, willing this moment of anticipation to continue forever.

Over the next hour or so, Hugo bought a few more rounds of drinks and shared how unhappy he was with his wife, how they never had any intimate relations, how they hadn't for years. "I'm a man. I need to feel flesh against mine. I'm not sustained otherwise. I want to feel so I know I'm alive, not some automaton who only works and sleeps like she does."

Danny subtly checked his watch and then gently took Hugo by the hand and led him out the bar.

Hugo swayed slightly as the air hit him. Soon after, they were in a taxi, and Hugo found himself leaning forward to touch

Danny's face, and then a bit more until their lips met. The feeling of Danny's slightly stubbly jaw against his sent a jolt of electricity to the bottom half of his body, which had been radiating warmth and anticipation since he'd arrived at the club.

Danny kissed him back and felt up Hugo's hard-on as it strained beneath his suit trousers. "Easy, there's plenty of time yet. No rush."

And then they were in a hotel room. Danny had swept them in from the taxi, past reception and up to this room. No delays, no credit cards, one smooth movement.

Hugo lay on the bed and watched Danny undress, one garment at a time. His body was naturally tanned, not that awful orange fake tan so popular where his brother-in-law Fred and his wife lived. He immediately shook the image from his mind. Danny's was an outdoor, gardening, builder's kind of tan. His thick chest hair formed a narrow triangle between his nipples. A dark trail led from his belly button under the waistband of his crisp, white, fitted trunks—designer, of course, although Hugo didn't recognise the name. Danny looked like the sort of man who'd fuck you and it would hurt, but he'd make sure you enjoyed it too. The thought left Hugo's cock stiff and straining.

Danny pretended to pick up things from the floor, lingering as he bent forward, his bottom to Hugo, moving around the room, repeating this little dance.

Hugo, still dressed, allowed his hand to creep to his groin.

"No touching," Danny commanded. "Not until I touch you."

Hugo's hand returned to the bed, his body quivering in anticipation. He worried if he didn't get a release soon, he would burst.

Danny slowly removed his underpants and stood side-on in front of Hugo, casting a crane-like shadow on the wall behind him.

Hugo's hand moved down again, and again Danny told him no and repeated his little dance, bending down, touching the plush, white carpet, taking a few steps, always with his bare bum towards Hugo.

Hugo whimpered, his splayed fingers clutching the bedspread in desperation.

"Yes. That's right." Finally, Danny turned to face him and walked towards the bed. "Is this what you want?"

Hugo nodded. At that moment, he hadn't wanted anything more in his whole life. With his whole body, he wanted, *he needed* to have Danny's magnificent cock deep inside him.

Over the next couple of hours, Danny fucked Hugo in various positions, with breaks for champagne.

By the third time, Hugo could hardly see straight. He felt bruised, battered, abused and used. It was exactly what he'd asked for in his email to Paul.

Danny left his business card on the bed after showering and dressing. "Take your time. The room's paid for, so leave whenever." And he was gone.

Hugo lay on the bed, the blinds closed, the lights dimmed, his body covered in sweat and other bodily fluids. He was spent, totally spent. Feeling Danny's hard body against him, in various parts of him, had been exactly what he'd needed. The afternoon had gone precisely as requested. Paul, who had handled the booking, had done a good job. He and Danny were a professional team. A classy escort business. Hugo smiled to himself as it had all gone to plan, to pain. Pulling the duvet around him, he rolled over and closed his eyes.

***

Out the front of the hotel, Danny blinked, getting used to the sunlight after an afternoon in the darkness of the hotel room. He rang Paul to confirm when and where his next client was.

Paul confirmed details and asked how the new client had gone.

"I love this job. The straight or bi ones are always so grateful. Grateful for the hardness of the sex, and the cuddles and pillow talk afterwards."

"Do you think he'll be back for more?"

"How much did he pay for?"

"A couple of hours."

"For what he got in that couple of hours, he'll be back. He won't be able to get that anywhere else."

"I don't know how you do it. I need a cold shower just hearing about it."

"I like sex, what can I say? Lucky this is my job, I suppose." He hung up, put on his designer sunglasses, hooked his suit jacket over his shoulder and set off for his next client meeting, a smile across his face, wondering how he got to have all this fun and be paid for it too.

***

Neil looked around the budget hotel room, courtesy of his client, off a main road to the west of Birmingham city centre. The day's training had left him exhausted and only just able to call Charlie to see how things were back home. Content all was well, he'd slept for a while. Now awake he wanted two things: some food and a man.

He scrolled through his phone and ordered dinner with a few swipes of his finger. He moved on to the next app, entering his location and time before clicking send. As his food arrived, his phone rang. "Hello, sir, this is Tiredman Escorts calling. I wanted to go through a few details of your request, then we'll be able to send one of our escorts round very shortly. Are you OK to talk now?"

Neil nodded, a mouth full of pizza. "Yep."

"We have some preferences listed, based on your previous requests. Are they all still valid?"

"Yep." He chewed loudly and swallowed. "How long will it be? I've got to be up early. I don't want moonlight and roses, if you know what I mean."

"Yes, sir, I know exactly what you mean. We just have the payment details and then we can proceed. Cash or card?"

"Cash." Always cash, because Charlie paid the credit cards, and this—what would happen in this room tonight—was nothing to do with what happened in their cottage in Chelsea.

"If I could just confirm the total, you will be required to pay the escort at the start of the session. Otherwise, the credit card we have on file will be debited."

"No need for that. I've got the cash." Neil reached across the bed and counted a pile of money that had been next to his laptop and work papers.

Chapter 9

FRED SMITH ARRIVED at the Chelsea house of his ex-wife and children to find a small Harrods van delivering and Camilla out the front, directing the delivery man into the kitchen.

"Hello, Fred. She's all ready for you."

"What's this?"

"Just a few bits and pieces. It's all going straight to the kitchen. It's all food. No luxuries." She tapped the delivery man on the shoulder and said, in a mumble just loud enough that Fred could still hear, "Put the oysters straight in the fridge, would you? But you can leave the caviar on the side. I'll have that now—a late lunch."

"Caviar, oysters. What are you playing at? The money's meant to be for the kids, not for you to eat like the fucking queen."

"I am not! How dare you! I resent that insinuation. It's a rarity. Just a few little treats for me every now and again."

"Tamara said you get it all catered in when you have guests round."

"Ah, well, yes, *that* was in extremis. They're both very foody, our gaybours, and I didn't want to disappoint."

"I wanted to talk to you about these two—" he looked over his shoulder "—friends of yours. I'm hearing all sorts of crap about hairdressing, college and cooking, girly stuff like that, for Aaron. And I'm not happy. That's why I want him coming to work with me too. If he's deciding whether to go back to uni,

56

then he's not sitting around here all day in his underwear playing computer games."

"Ahhh, talk of the devil." Camilla hugged Tamara as she passed. "What did you say, you want to take Aaron too?"

"What else has he got planned today? Finding a cure for cancer? Repainting the Forth Bridge? They're *practical* things, *things he can do with his hands*. That's what he wants, isn't it?" Fred rolled his eyes at each emphasised word.

"I'll get him. I think he's up." Camilla left Fred and Tamara at the front door and shouted to Aaron that his father wanted to see him.

After a protracted process of getting Aaron off the sofa, then into the kitchen, Fred left Tamara and joined his son.

Fred stared at Aaron across the table, his hands resting either side of the place mat. "I'll overlook the fact you let me pay for another whole term of tuition and rent when you weren't even there, while you were deciding whether to stay or go. I'll even overlook that you say you told us, but we didn't listen. I know I can be busy and sometimes miss things, and your mother's a bit all over the place at the best of times. But I will not let you sit around all day, moping about the house, not knowing what to do, watching daytime TV and eating cereal. You're coming to do an honest day's work with me and your sister." He banged the table. The place mat jumped in the air then quickly fell, and one of the tall brass candle holders tipped over. "Don't suppose you've got a tie, have you?"

"My old school tie's all cut up after leavers' day."

"A shirt maybe? Something a bit more formal than this." Fred waved at his son's attire—a faded grey pair of very skinny jeans and a black T-shirt with the logo of some band or another

Fred hadn't ever heard of. "Proper trousers, not jeans, and a shirt. Come on. We're late as it is."

Aaron didn't move. He slumped further down into the chair, examined his nails, then flicked his fringe from his face.

Very quietly, Fred said, leaning across the table, not breaking the gaze the whole time, "I won't say it again. If you don't get a fucking shift on, I'll tell your mum about the little incident with your laptop when I came into your room unannounced. Or we could just keep it between us two, man to man."

Aaron ran upstairs and shortly reappeared in an un-ironed white school shirt and black school trousers, outside the front of the house.

Fred passed him, noticing the shirt's state. "Ain't you got an iron in this place?" He looked at Camilla. Honestly, he didn't remember her being this messy when they'd been married. Letting herself go, definitely.

"Me? Is that directed at me? Of course we have an iron. It's just that I happen to not take an awful lot of time using it on shirts for a school he left some months ago, since I have many other priorities, like looking after our children and running this house. Not that you'd know, of course, having never even put a wash load on, stacked the dishwasher or paid a utility bill. I expect *she* does all that for you now, doesn't she?"

Fred ignored the jibe at his wife, standard Camilla behaviour really, and ushered his children into the car, shouting he'd be back with them at sixish.

*

One of Camilla's neighbours had been lingering on the pavement during the interaction, and once Fred had left, she finally walked past. Camilla waved and smiled. "Oh, yes. All's fine. Marvellous here." She slammed the door and sat at the kitchen table, crying. "Fucking marvellous."

***

At the office, Fred sat at his desk, opposite Tamara and Aaron. "You can't just sit about all your life. You've got to pick something and do it. What do you want to do? I'm not paying you to sit about."

Aaron stared at the ground and tapped his dirty trainers against each other.

"Can I please do something that doesn't involve filing today?" Tamara asked. "We're studying using customer feedback at college at the moment. Can I, like, do something that's, like, linked to that, please?"

Fred stared at his son. "What about you? Anything from you, under all that hair?"

Aaron sat up and stared at his dad. "This is a new haircut, and I like it. I bet you did stuff with your hair when you were my age that your parents didn't like. Do you, like, even know what manscaping is?"

Fred shrugged. "It's when men shave in places that's not their face." He shuddered. Load of old cobblers. "Though, why any man'd wanna, I do not know. Not a bloody Scooby! Why'd you ask?"

"Right, so, I was reading a magazine, when I went to the hairdresser's, about this new beard style, and clippers you can get to cut it into the style. And I was talking to the senior hair stylist— she did my hair, I was well lucky to get her—about colouring and how the different colours bond to the hair. How you can't perm hair if it's been coloured too, cos it damages it and it can break off in clumps, stuff like that. We talked about this competition she does every year for the young hairdresser of the year. It's in Birmingham or Manchester or something. Anyway, it's like this big show, and they all do their best new styles. It's like New York Fashion Week—for hair, in Birmingham." He paused.

Nothing from Fred as he tried to absorb what Aaron had said, most of which he'd not quite understood. He felt the words slipping off him and landing on the ground. "And what's that got to do with the price of—" He looked up at the pictures of their bestsellers, hung on the office walls. "—designer sunglasses, eh?"

"Fucking hell, Dad. Can't you see it? I'm not interested in all this crap." Aaron waved his hands around the room. "It's got as much creativity as one of the *bip-bip* people at the supermarket checkout. I want to do something creative, something with my hands, and I *think* hairdressing is what I want."

Tamara said, "He won't be out of work. People always need their hair cutting."

"Quiet. Enough," Fred snapped. "Where's this come from? How do I know you won't start this and drop out quietly? Turn up one day, bags packed and it's all over? And muggins here's got to fork out for another NQT or whatever it's called."

Aaron replied, quietly, "You don't. It's NVQ, Dad. But if I don't try it, I won't know. All I know is I'm not coming here to work with you. Why don't you ask *her* to help? She's, like, much better qualified than me. I don't know my L-T-D from my P-L-C and wouldn't know turnover from profit and loss if they bit me on the bum an' stuff. But she—" He pointed at his sister, who stuck out her tongue.

"Who's she, the cat's mother? As Mum always says." Tamara grinned at her brother.

Fred looked at Tamara. "I was going to ask you to type some letters for me, but bang goes that idea." He turned to Aaron.

"And what's this I hear about these two gaybours? Is this where all this crap's coming from?" He was determined to get to the bottom of it.

"It's not catching!" Aaron spat.

"That's not what I meant. I don't have a problem with *those* people. Nothing wrong with *it*. As long as I don't think about what they do to each other in bed." The thought made him queasy. Two men together in bed. Disgusting.

"Thinking about you and Mum in bed makes *me* puke. Never mind you and Sharon." Aaron put his fingers in his mouth and mimed being sick.

Fred put up his hands. "OK, fair point. What does this pair do? Why am I hearing so much about them all of a sudden?"

Aaron explained what Neil and Charlie did, paying particular attention to Charlie's homebased crafts.

Fred asked what Neil did for a living. He seemed to be making progress here with Aaron.

"He's a management consultant, whatever that is." Aaron rolled his eyes.

"I know what one of them is—someone who charges you five hundred quid to tell you something you already knew, then asks for more money to fix a problem you could have fixed yourself. Bloody waste of time. That's a bloody management bloody consultant." He had calls from those people every day of the week. Fucking con merchants, the lot of 'em.

Tamara interrupted, "Actually, there's more to it than that." She started to explain what she'd learned about that particular career.

Aaron stood. "If it's all right with you, I'm gonna get off." He looked at his dad. "Unless you want to hear more about why

61

I don't want to work here and need more explanation of what I do want to do?"

Fred realised he'd done enough with this issue for today and waved Aaron away. Meanwhile Tamara was still going on about management consultants. Fred shushed her.

"I just need a bit of time to get my head around it."

***

Later that day, Tamara was given some letters to type by her dad and protested about how Aaron always got away with it. He'd not even stayed for an hour. "I've like, got some ideas about customer feedback if you want. I could, like, call some of the shops we supply to, ask them if there's any issues with the supply chain."

"The who chain? Look, don't worry about that, love, we've got someone in Marketing who does all that for us. Just type up those letters, and then you can go home. I'll give you money for a cab. I'm gonna be here late tonight, sweetheart." He left the room.

Tamara stared at her college notebook on the desk, full of her ideas, and then looked at the pile of handwritten letters her dad had given her to type. *What do I have to do to make him see I can do this? How much longer can I put up with being overlooked like this? Will I ever get to make use of my college course?*

She stared at one of the pictures on the wall—a pair of red, square sunglasses. She remembered seeing it months ago when she'd started coming to the office. It had all seemed so positive and hopeful, and she'd been optimistic she'd learn so much. Yet here she was, months later, having learned nothing, with a dad who didn't see what potential she had.

She picked one of the hand-scrawled letters from the pile, opened a new Word document and began typing it, her vision blurring from tears. Why couldn't something happen? Why was her life so monotonous and boring? Why couldn't her mum make her dad see her properly? Why had her mother said she must keep Daddy happy and not upset him?

***

Another town, another train, another night in a hotel for Neil. This time, in Cambridge, he lay on his bed, just out of the shower, wrapped in a large, fluffy, white towel. There was a knock on his door. The pizza, he thought. He opened the door to be greeted by a man with dark, wavy hair and blue eyes, holding a twelve-inch pizza.

"Come in," said Neil, dropping his towel as he closed the door. The man was exactly as his picture and profile had described, unlike some of the others he'd had the displeasure to try on other occasions. He'd often wondered if there was any sort of money-back, satisfaction, Sale of Goods Act clause applicable to this sort of service. Some of the booking companies he'd used had been woefully inadequate, and he'd been itching to do them a time-and-motion study to improve their service. But no, that was work, and this was pleasure. He was well able to separate the two, as well as the other parts of his life: his life and what he did with Charlie and his life and what he did in these hotel rooms.

Some of the escorts—rent boys was such a dirty word and not one applicable to the men he *procured*; that was a nice, business-appropriate word. Some of the *men he'd procured* through the websites were just ordinary guys, often models or actors in the adult film industry making a bit extra on the side. These escorts weren't anything like the rent boys he saw with business-card-sized ads in the back of free gay magazines. They were a whole different class entirely, and the one standing in front of Neil now was certainly a cut above the others he'd seen.

Danny—*I wonder if that's his real name or just his escort name*—put the pizza on the desk then asked where Neil wanted him.

Neil pointed to the bed and ordered him to strip as quick as he could.

Danny removed his clothes then lay on the bed, playing with himself as Neil watched from the chair doing the same. With the nod, Danny approached Neil and, on his knees, gave him what he'd been craving since the last time they'd been together. With his eyes closed, Neil's mind darted to Charlie and the last time he had done this with him. With a bite, Neil returned to the sensation of now, pleasure tingling and coursing through his body.

Following the detailed instructions Neil had sent to the person he'd booked the escort through—Paul or Pete, he thought it was—they fucked twice, animalistic, bitey, sweaty, dirty fucking. Exactly what Neil didn't get at home. Danny had even thrown in a bit of cocaine for fun, no extra charge, so Neil had agreed, remembering how much he used to enjoy doing it in his twenties, working in the city of London.

After the last fuck, Danny offered another go—"No extra, fancy it?"—with a twinkle in his eyes.

But Neil was all passion spent and waved from the bed, which Danny took as his cue to shower and leave.

Once Danny was gone, Neil rolled around in the bed for a few moments, enjoying the dirty smell and feeling over his skin, before turning to his work papers to prepare for the next day.

***

Hugo had tried to sleep for a couple of hours that night, but no matter how much he scrunched his eyes shut, sleep hadn't come. Isabella lay with her back to him, three generous feet from his back. 'The marital bed' it had been called when they bought it. What a joke. He crept downstairs to the kitchen and called the number on Danny's business card.

Straight to voicemail. *Actual complete bloody buggeration.* He laughed to himself.

He knew a local spot in the forest known for cruising, where he could get someone to scratch that itch. But what he wanted, what he really wanted was Danny. He wanted to stare into his piercing blue eyes. He wanted to feel the beam of his smile as he looked down on him. He wanted to revel in his laugh and attention as he listened, with total and utter concentration, to Hugo's every word. But most of all, what Hugo really, really wanted was another few hours in bed with Danny and his acrobatic sexual exploits.

Chapter 10

A FEW NIGHTS LATER, Isabella Jones sat in a bar in London meeting a 'simply charming and delightful man' she had happened to bump into at one of the London afterparties she'd recently attended for work. It had all been such a frightful mix-up; he had sworn he was meant to be on the guest list, but patently he wasn't because she'd checked, and she'd asked her assistant to check twice. But as he stood at the front of the guest list queue, a wide smile across his face showing perfect white teeth, bright, bright blue eyes, and just enough of a tan to look swarthy and Mediterranean—such a complete contrast to Hugo's white, saggy body—she hadn't been able to resist his offer of a special cocktail at the bar. So she'd waved him through into the party and joined him at the bar.

There they'd talked about the sunglasses business, about which he was surprisingly knowledgeable. He had worked for other similar luxury-goods brands before—watches, the diamond people, De Beers—and he knew her world intimately. He talked of many of the same contacts she knew from the business world. She had been so grateful Hugo had had a headache that night. Unhindered by her dead-weight husband, she was able to sparkle and flirt—perfectly harmlessly, of course—with this charming man all evening. The three or four mysterious cocktails he'd shared with her had oiled the wheels somewhat, but she wasn't doing anything wrong, not in public. She wasn't that stupid.

At first, she'd been unwilling to share his business card, saying that night had been perfect on its own, why did they need any more? And besides, she was married, so nothing could come of it. The Mediterranean man had been so considerate and selfless. Eventually, she'd agreed and given her mobile number, never expecting to hear from him again. A few days after their first meeting, he'd sent a text asking if she wanted to meet again, and over the next few days, their texts became more flirty, and they managed to arrange a little tête à tête in a small club in London he'd suggested.

Now he greeted her by the bar and led her to a private booth, signalling to the barman for two of his special cocktails.

Isabella excused herself with a smile, went to the ladies' loo to be very slightly sick. Her stomach tensing at seeing the man again, she calmed herself, retouched her make-up and returned to him, and soon they were deep in conversation, her stomach settled and the memory of the incident in the ladies' pushed from her memory.

"Where does your husband think you are now?" he asked matter-of-factly.

"No idea. He's not asked. We both come and go as we please. It's not even like ships that pass in the night. It's just two ships."

"You are so deep, I think. That is like poetry, I think."

"Go away. Don't be ridiculous. I'm just a bit drunk, thanks to you. This is what you do. You get me drunk, and heaven only knows what happens then."

"We will have sparkling water from now on." He snapped his fingers, and a bottle arrived at the table. "And I will not make you do anything. I will be the perfect gentleman for you, the perfect lady. Was there anything that happened last time you didn't want?"

She poured herself a glass of sparking water and pondered for a moment. "Actually, you were the perfect gentleman." *Sadly.* She sipped her water.

"Did you tell your husband about me?" He smiled and topped up her glass then his own.

"What do you think?"

"I think we should finish these drinks. It would be such a shame to waste two perfectly good cocktails that the wonderfully talented barman made for us. Once we have finished our water, of course. No need to rush. I'm not trying to get you tipsy. Then I'd love to take you to a quiet little members' club just around the corner. No one will know you there. It is the ultimate in discretion, you can be assured of that, beautiful lady." He smiled. "What do you think? And any time you want to go home, just say the word and—" he snapped his fingers "—you will be on your way home, promised of safe carriage."

***

After three more cocktails, and the rest of the sparkling water left untouched, in the back of the large black limousine that had appeared outside the club, Isabella told the man that her husband didn't understand her or didn't fulfil her, and it had been too long since she'd felt the weight of a man pressing down on top of her.

"And what do you want me to do, beautiful lady? What sort of man do you think I am? I am, as I hope I've proved, a perfect gentleman."

She leant forward and kissed him. "But I don't want you to be one of those. I want you to be an imperfect gentleman."

"Well, in that case..." He pushed the privacy glass button, and the back of the limo was isolated from the driver's hearing and sight.

The limo circled around central London long enough for the imperfect gentleman to have sex with Isabella twice in quick succession. He pulled a condom from his pocket, and she waved it away, explained she was on the pill and couldn't have children anyway—she and Hugo had been trying for years.

"Even so, I should." His eyes glinted as he opened the silver packet with his teeth.

She took it from him, half-heartedly attempting to do as he'd suggested, but slippery fingers, and a part of her brain needing this now more than it required her to be sensible, and she pulled him closer, welcoming his stiffness into her, giving up on the condom as it slipped from her fingers and fell onto the floor.

She lay on her back, her dress pushed up around her stomach and her knickers on the floor of the limo, panting, her make-up smeared across her face, her hair looking like she'd been dragged through a hedge, her body covered in bite and scratch marks and beads of sweat on her brow and between her breasts. At every moment, she had wanted it, with her whole body, and willed him to go on, to go in, to drive deeper, harder, more, and again. "Yes, now," was all she'd said when they'd started, making her wishes perfectly clear to the imperfect gentleman.

"I take it you don't want the limo to take you home?"

She gathered up her things, put her knickers in her handbag, pulled her dress back into place, brushed her hair and reapplied her make-up. "Of course not. A taxi will be fine." She suddenly felt a bit used and dirty, a wave of regret starting to build inside her.

The limo stopped by a taxi rank.

"When can I see you again?" she asked hopefully. If she could make it more than this, it would make her feel less dirty, more worthwhile at any rate. More fun? She wasn't sure which, but she knew she wanted to see him again for whatever reason.

"You're seeing me now." He smiled and put on sunglasses.

"I'm not going to beg. I'm not some lovesick teenager. Well, it was nice knowing you." She got out of the limousine, slammed the door and jumped into the first taxi. She shouted her address, and once it had been established it would be extra for leaving London, going over the River Lea for the wilds of Essex, she threw a note into the driver's compartment, told him to do whatever he had to, and while she was in her purse, she found the unopened silver packet of a condom.

She brushed away the worry, knowing she'd taken her pill that morning as usual, yet she felt a twinge, a memory of a feeling from earlier, pressed up against each other, locked as one, in the back of the limo. He'd brought alive parts of her she hadn't known existed until that night. Did she really want to forfeit that for a bit of arrogance? He *had* been pretty arrogant, but given that and the alternative of Hugo's simpering to 'Mummy's' every wish, she knew which she preferred. *Let's keep his number*, she thought. She could always delete it later. Better to keep it for now and see how she felt in the morning.

She put the unused condom back into the silver packet, wrapped it in a tissue and stuffed it into her handbag.

Chapter 11

A FAMILIAR CONVERSATION—LADY REECE Jones and Lord Reece Jones at either end of their twelve-foot-long dining room table, talking about when they could expect a grandson from their dear darling son Hugo.

"How long have they been married?" Lord Reece Jones said, peering to one side trying to obtain eye contact with his wife, past the candlesticks and flowers.

"Five years. It's simply unacceptable." She paused to wave the housemaid in to serve the main course. "It's not darling Hugo. It can't be. It's got to be the bitch."

"Steady on. That's a bit harsh, calling our daughter-in-law a bitch."

"No, darling. I mean like with animals. If there's a problem with the puppy, there's a problem with the bitch. No puppy, something wrong with the bitch. Stands to reason."

"Maybe, maybe. But what are we to do? He's not that far behind us. If it all goes to him and he goes before her, she gets it all. Every last acre, brick, table, ballroom, bedroom, box hedge. To her."

"I know this. Do you not think I know this? Why do you think I've been so keen for them to get a bloody move on and breed?"

"We'll just have to put our thinking caps on and come up with something, old fruit."

Lady Reece Jones smiled, staring into the distance, playing with the silver napkin holder absent-mindedly. Yes, a plan.

That's what she needed, a plan. She already had part of a plan, which would, in part, resolve at least some of the problem—poor dear Hugo stuck in a marriage to a barren wife. But that would take a while to bear fruit. In the meantime, what on earth was to be done for her poor son?

***

Paul hunched over his laptop in their flat, trying to work out with Danny ways to make more money from their business.

"Is that strictly legal?" Danny asked, parading about the apartment in amply filled underwear and nothing else.

"Blackmail?"

"Yes."

"Oh, no. That's completely illegal. We can't call it that. I'll have to put it down as some other business income or something. I wonder if I could call it professional services. Maybe, but that's more what we do anyway. Do professional services need the services of other professional services? I'm not sure."

Danny looked at Paul. "Come on, you're getting us tied up in knots."

"Chance'd be a fine thing!" Paul looked down at Danny's underwear and lifted the laptop from his lap. "I tell you what, we both need a break from all this brain power. We need some good old visceral action. Where to this time?"

Danny nodded to the table. "I'll get a video camera. We can film it from below, put it on the website for repeat booking clients, some extra added value."

"That's enough. No more business talk. Get those off." He reached for Danny's underwear as he walked away, making a snapping sound as they pinged back onto his bum.

"So that's a 'no' to the camera?"

"Oh, no, get it. Might as well make use of it all." Paul shrugged his clothes off, then lay on the table on his back, his legs high in the air, poised for the return of Danny and the camera.

***

After two long sessions, Paul said his arse couldn't cope with any more and they had to get back to work. They resumed a different position, on the sofa this time.

Danny had tried his little-boy-lost look and said he could easily go again, just a quick one, but Paul stuck fast, rubbing his bum and shrugging on a bathrobe. They continued brainstorming ideas for making more money from the business.

"So are we saying no to blackmail?" Danny put on a pair of tracksuit bottoms, deliberately leaving his chest uncovered, knowing it would tease Paul.

"I don't think we should cross it off the list. We just need to be careful how we do it."

"What else?"

Paul scrolled through his bookings system. "There seems to be more requests for lover/boyfriend typed bookings."

"The ones who ask if I can spend the afternoon with them, then go back to a hotel for a romantic evening. Not just your wham, bam, thank you, mam types. More..." He thought for a moment how to describe it. "Love."

"On the meter, though."

Danny nodded. "Of course, but the illusion of love. Anything we could do with those, do you think?"

"They do have a tendency to give you gifts, and that holiday was rather special, wasn't it?"

"Even if we don't put it through the business, it's still more money for us, so not a bad thing." Danny stared out the window, tapping his chin.

"But what is it you do to make them shower you with gifts?"

Danny turned to face Paul. "That, my dear, is why they pay me the big bucks!"

"Seriously, what?"

"Let me see…well, it's a gradual thing. A little word here, a word there. A discounted booking or an extra fuck thrown in once the meter's stopped running. But they always pay for it in the end. And then some."

"Genius. That *is* why they pay you the big bucks. I'd say, let's do that then."

"Yes, *I* will do that." Danny knew it was all down to him. It was his business, after all. Paul was just there to do the admin, which anyone could do. Without Danny, there would be no business. And of course, there were the little jobs he squeezed in without telling Paul. They could be quite lucrative. And interesting. Yes, an interesting diversion from the usual merry-go-round of bars, hotels and men.

"Right, no need to get touchy. We're a team, remember?"

"'Course we are," Danny said and leant forward to kiss Paul on the lips, allowing his bare chest to press against the open neck of Paul's bathrobe.

Chapter 12

HUGO ARRIVED SLIGHTLY late to meet Danny for brunch at the Oxo Tower in London. "I'm most awfully sorry. I seem to have lost track of the time." He glanced at his watch, then pushed his floppy hair out of his eyes.

Danny stood and kissed both of Hugo's cheeks before resuming his seat by the floor-to-ceiling window overlooking the Thames. "I've taken the liberty of ordering a Bloody Mary. It goes so well with brunch of eggs, I find." He smiled. "I'm having the eggs Benedict. It's what I always have when I'm here. What about you?"

Hugo scanned through the menu. "I'm not awfully familiar with brunch. I'm more of a lunch or dinner man. A bit traditional, I suppose." He shrugged.

Not in all senses, Danny thought. In some senses, Hugo was very untraditional, especially compared with what his wife thought about him. Danny smiled to himself and allowed Hugo to talk about the different types of egg he may choose. Who knew someone could say so much about so little? Danny's spiel to Hugo when he'd called him a few days after their last meeting had worked perfectly. Danny had laid it on thick, lots of talk about how it didn't feel like work when he was with Hugo, but of course, he unfortunately would still need payment to balance the time in his diary with the money coming in. Paul was such a hard task master. To avoid the awkward handover of money, or 'the paperwork' as Danny liked to refer to it, they had set up a direct bank transfer twice a month. For that, Hugo would have two blocks of two hours with Danny every month to do with as he wished—lunches, afternoons in bed, brunches—anything he wanted. Hugo had been so pleased when they'd arrived at that suggestion, he didn't have any ideas for the first 'date', so Danny had suggested brunch, and Hugo, being so frightfully polite and English, had gone along with it.

Hugo was still talking, and Danny focused on his mouth moving, then slowly brought his mind around to the words coming out of it.

Hugo's hands flapped in front of his face, fanning the menu in his right hand. "So I'm not sure about the eggs. There are, as I've said, benefits and disadvantages to all sorts. And it does seem eggs *are* certainly *the* thing to have for brunch. So on balance, overall, what I'm trying to say is, I'm not sure which type to have. What do you think?" Hugo put the menu on the table and took a sip of the coffee.

"Eggs Benedict, same as me. Can't go wrong." Danny snapped his fingers and gave their order as well as another round of Bloody Marys before nodding for the waiter to leave.

They talked about plans for the rest of their time together. Danny suggested the Millennium Wheel; Hugo instantly agreed.

When the food arrived, Hugo was in paroxysms of ecstasy about the eggs Benedict, saying he couldn't believe he'd never tried them before, and they must come here again sometime soon. He babbled about his family business and the pressure he felt to keep it going, the pressure from his parents to give them a grandson, and how he felt sometimes the pressure was all on him.

Danny squeezed his hand across the table. "You like to be not in charge sometimes, I think?"

Hugo nodded, talking through a mouthful of food. "Exactly, yes. That's it!" He sprayed a bit of egg on the table and quickly reached to clear it up.

Danny looked out the window, not wanting to stare at the egg Hugo had spilt down his shirt. OK, so this didn't really feel like work, not as much as some other clients. But fucking hell, what a fucking terrible bore this man was! He could bore for England. He could bore for the fucking Olympics, taking *droning on about nothing* to levels Danny hadn't previously thought possible. And how sad that Hugo thought they were like partners, when actually he was paying for it.

As they finished, Danny settled the bill quickly. It would all be billed back to Hugo in time, but him paying on the day helped add to the relationship illusion Hugo and similar clients craved, as specified with Paul beforehand.

"So where is this wheel? I feel awfully silly, living in London all this time and never going on the wheel. I suppose that shows I'm not a tourist or something." Hugo pushed his hair from his eyes and stared at Danny.

"Did we say definitely the wheel? Or we could have a walk along the South Bank, get a coffee there, or..." Danny paused. He knew what the answer to this would be, and at least it would stop Hugo bloody talking, give his mouth something else to do, or fuck him so hard he wouldn't be able to prattle about nothing. "I have a reservation in a quiet little hotel near here. We can go there and do exactly what you wish. It's totally up to you." He held out his hands, palms upwards, and closed his eyes in fake prayer.

***

That afternoon, as expected, they went straight from the restaurant to the hotel without passing the Millennium Wheel. But they didn't have sex, which was *not* as expected. Hugo wanted to lie in bed with Danny, watching TV and talking. He cuddled up to Danny and kissed his chest, telling him how much he loved him.

"I can show you how I feel," Danny replied, his eyes indicating a growing lump under the duvet.

"I don't want that. I want this." Hugo stroked Danny's chest hair.

They lay like that for most of the afternoon until Danny had to leave for his next client. He was so frustrated from not doing what they'd planned—although he still collected his £500—that he was a bit too keen to get down to it with the next client, a rather timid first-time customer.

"You drive me crazy. I need to be with you, to be inside you," Danny panted to the young client as he pressed him against the hotel room wall.

***

Later, Paul called Danny to tell him he'd received a complaint from the young, timid client, saying Danny hadn't stuck to what he'd requested and he hadn't enjoyed it.

"He *sounded* like he bloody well enjoyed it! Shouting and gasping for more," Danny protested.

"Yes, well, customer feedback is king, and if he gives you a bad review on the website, it'll cost us money."

"OK, what do you want me to do?"

"I said he could have half an hour free and that you'd stick to exactly his requests. He's very new to this whole thing. He told me to remind you he doesn't want to be pinned against a wall and bitten before being flipped over and fucked into the floor."

Danny allowed himself a deep breath and pinched his nose. "As I said, he seemed to like it at the time. Couldn't get enough, actually. But if you think it'll make him come back, I'll do it."

"Bloody right, you'll do it. Next time, tender, gentle, the full boyfriend, like you do with that Hugo man."

"It was his fucking fault in the first place."

"How so?"

Danny explained what Hugo had wanted to do instead of sex. "I was like one of those men holding up our glass table when I left his hotel room. I could hardly walk."

"If that's what he wants, that's what he gets. He's called to up the regular payments—says twice a month isn't enough. He wants to see you every week."

"What for? A proper session or more of that lovey-dovey crap?"

"That *lovey-dovey crap* pays five hundred an hour plus expenses. Besides, it means you're not all passion-spent when you come home to me. I get a bit more of you."

"When have I ever come home from work and not been able to give you what *you* wanted?" Paul didn't answer, but there had never been a single occasion. Even when Danny had been drunk or after a session with cocaine and alcohol, he'd always come home and given Paul a good seeing-to. It had been one of the reasons Paul had agreed to it in the first place. Danny's libido was indefatigable.

"So you're seeing him for a country drive later this week," Paul said. "You're booked out the whole afternoon. I'm arranging the hotel, the restaurant, and he said he wanted to go to a spa place with you. Sit about with cucumbers on your eyes in white towelling gowns, that sort of thing."

"And no sex?"

"I don't know. If he wants it, obviously, but he seems to want to see you in all these different situations. He said he finds your company so interesting, that you listen to him so well. He likes how you take charge, and he can be himself when he's with you."

"If that's what he wants, that's what he'll get." It sounded terrible to Danny. A long afternoon with a boring man.

"That is the right answer, my sweet, insatiable darling."

***

Over the following weeks and months, Hugo saw Danny at least once a week, sometimes more often. They played golf together, went to a spa hotel, stayed in country hotels in the Home Counties, had brunch in The Wolsey, afternoon tea at The Ritz and champagne breakfast in the Millennium Wheel.

Sometimes they used the hotel room that had been arranged for them; sometimes it remained empty. Sometimes they sat in the hotel room like a couple who'd been together for years; other times, Danny's libido had an outlet when what Hugo wanted, what he needed, was a session with Danny's tireless sex drive.

But it was always up to Hugo. He was always in charge of what they did, even if Danny gave the impression he was in control. Hugo's detailed instructions for each meeting were followed to the letter, ensuring he booked another session as soon as one had passed.

Chapter 13

Dᴜʀɪɴɢ ᴀ ʀᴀʀᴇ afternoon off work, Danny had gone into town to mooch about the shops. "I'll bring you back something pretty from Bond Street," he'd said that morning.

Meanwhile, Paul was at a large, indoor dog show in Birmingham with Sharon Smith. They'd met when Paul had dog-sat for her years ago, pre-boyfriend and husband, and both rejoiced in well-groomed dogs, nice jewellery and a good slice of salacious gossip. Paul agreed to look after her dogs again, but to make it a bit cheaper, they didn't go through the dog-sitting agency Paul had worked for at the time. Sharon returned from her holiday to a perfectly clean home, four happy dogs and dinner in the oven. From then onwards, they'd been inseparable, both trawling the dog show circuit for eligible husbands or boyfriends.

After a year or so, Paul had introduced Fred Smith to Sharon through an old escort agency contact. Fred had been quite a naughty boy during the eighties but was just out of a divorce from Sloaney Camilla and looking for someone who didn't want children and would be a bit less mumsy, a bit more 'page three'. Sharon had no desire to have anything to do with children, her own or other people's, as she had a pack of furry babies instead.

Now, Sharon had arrived back from the agility competition in which her brown-and-white Papillion, Dusty, had come first. With Dusty on her knee, she and Paul sipped champagne and picked at food in one of the bars at the dog show, agreeing it had been too long since they'd last met up.

"Danny's booked solid," Paul said, and they chinked their glasses together, throwing back their heads in unison. "I've been so busy, I've not had time to spit, never mind socialise."

They both turned to the side and spat, then laughed loudly. zA few people looked at them making a show of themselves and shook their heads or tutted loudly, but Paul and Sharon were completely oblivious, stuck in their own crass, loud bubble and loving every fake-tanned, long-nailed, bottle-blonde-hair moment of it.

Catching her breath and feeding Dusty a dog treat from her pink leather handbag, Sharon said, "I've been that busy too. It takes me a long time to look like this. Six-weekly hair appointments, four-weekly for the nail fill-ins. Spray tan every four weeks. I came home last week cos they'd all come round on the same couple of days, and I'm telling you, Paul, I honest to God felt like a new woman, straight out of the box." She giggled at her unintentional joke. "Seriously though, I do worry he'll want a new woman, you know? He'll go off me. Thing is, I'm quite a bit younger than that old boot, Camilla, so hopefully I'll be all right for a few years yet! I dunno. What d'ya reckon, eh?"

"What about me? He's out there with all these businessmen in bars and hotels, and what's he got when he comes home? This old queen." He gestured to himself, too tightly squeezed into a sleeveless white T-shirt and denim shorts.

"Ahh, but he loves you. The rest is just sex. Isn't that what you always said to each other?"

"It is, and he does, my love."

"Still, rather you than me. I couldn't sit at home all day knowing my Fred was fucking his way around London and then let him come home and sleep in bed with me. No fear. I wouldn't touch it with someone else's." She shivered then sipped her drink, all while absently stroking her dog. "No offence."

"None taken, love, none taken. Anyway, I think men are better at compartmentalising their lives. This time, I'm this person, doing this thing. Then when I go home, I'm this person, doing this thing with this other person. It's all about putting things in little boxes."

"Well, my little box is only for one man." Sharon gave a little giggle. "Sorry."

"Don't be so stupid. If we didn't joke about little boxes, what would we have left?"

"Only thing I want in a little box is a bloody great ring with a whopping big diamond on it. What's that film you made me watch, or was it a story you told me about? Something about a big diamond." She snapped her fingers with her eyes closed. "A ritzy Diamond…"

"*A Diamond as Big as the Ritz.*"

"That's it. I want one of them!"

"And I bet he'll get you one, one day."

"He got me the new Range Rover when the new number plate came out. I said to him, 'What's the point, when it's gonna have my personalised plate on it anyway?' He said he didn't want people thinking he weren't looking after his old lady. I said to 'im, I said, 'Oy! Less of the old!'" She laughed, her mouth wide open.

Paul noticed her silver fillings. "Do you wanna hear some goss?"

She took her fillings off display, shut her mouth and leant forward.

"You know I said it's all sex and love's different?"

She nodded and offered the dog a bit of her burger. He licked it from her hands. She wiped her long nails on a napkin on the table.

"One of the areas we've got the most new clients is the ones who want the love/boyfriend experience."

She sat back and furrowed her brow, still cleaning her hands. "What's that when it's at home?"

He explained the sorts of requests Hugo had made over the months.

She listened, buffing her long, pink nails, pausing every now and then to feed the dog treats from a tiny bag hidden in her cleavage, visible by virtue of her low-cut top.

Paul leant in closer. "And do you wanna hear something even better than that?"

"'Course!"

"You know how much you love your brother-in-law?"

"Stupid wet blanket Hugo. Or should I say Lord Stupid Wet Blanket the Third?"

"The very man."

"What about him?"

"Guess which captain of industry, the man who can do no wrong in the eyes of his dear beloved mummy, has a weekly date with Danny?"

"Shut up!" She put her hand on her mouth.

"Yep. The very same."

"Shut. Up!"

Paul nodded. "He so has."

"Shut! Up! You can't be pulling my leg. Don't tell me this is a wind-up. Is it a wind-up?"

"No, it's the God's honest truth. Not that I believe in God, but—" he spat on his hand "—I swear it's true."

"SHUT! UP!"

"Innit, though?"

"Oh my actual God." Sharon fanned her eyes with her hands. The dog was whimpering on her lap, scrabbling to get more treats from her cleavage. "No, Dusty, stay! Can I tell that snooty cow Isabella? I'd take a picture of her face, and it'd be all over Facebook in seconds. Fucking snooty bitch."

"You really love your in-laws, don't you? It's just *love, love, love* from you today for them. I can feel it pouring off you, straight at me."

"She thinks she's better than us, even though she had the same upbringing as Fred—same parents, same schools, same terraced house in Romford—and ain't nothing wrong with him. I could always start calling her Kylie in front of Hugo. She'd love that. When Fred told me that was her real name, it was the best present he could've ever given me. She'd been looking down her nose at us one time we went round, asking us where we went on holiday, and had we been to The Ivy or The Dorchester? Giving me the Lady Diana sideways head cocked under your fringe look of pity when I told her we was going Benidorm on holiday. I'd always wondered how comes her and her brother were so different. And that's when he told me. It's all put on—the accent, the name, everything. She's just a working-class girl done good, not that there's nothing wrong with being a working-class girl. It's what I am."

"Only you don't work, darling." Paul winked at her.

"Believe you me, I work hard for the money. How do you think that house keeps so clean? My Fred, he's never seen a bill or insurance, anything. I do it all. The dogs, he's not got nothing to do with neither. Even the food I do. Half the time, he don't know I've brought it in from that frozen cook place in Epping. He just thinks supermarket food costs a lot of money. Not to mention the other jobs I do. Know what I mean?" She winked at Paul and opened her mouth wide, flashing her fillings again.

"All right. You're catching flies. I geddit."

"They don't call it a blow job for nothing, do they? And I've even been known, on his birthday, and special occasions, to…you know." She pointed to her bum.

"Don't you have any shame?" Paul sat, open-mouthed, staring at Sharon.

"Lost that at fifteen, as you well know. And you can talk, Mister Married to a Rent Boy."

"Sssshhhh." He looked to either side. "High-class male escort if you don't mind."

"You say *tomayto* I say *tomarto*. So yes, as it goes, I do work for the money, darling." She leant forward and whispered the next bit. "Mind you, there's been a bit less of it lately. I checked me housekeeping account. It's almost all gone, and I'm only two bloody weeks into this month." Back at normal loud volume, she continued, "So I don't have a bloody Scooby what that's about. Never mind, eh." She fished a cigarette from her handbag.

"You can't here."

"They won't mind. Just a few puffs won't do anyone no 'arm."

"They'll chuck us out. Last time, you nearly got us banned from all Kennel Club events. Put it away!" Paul snatched the cigarette from her hand and put it in his pocket.

She reached into her handbag again. "Got one of these e-cigarettes, what d'ya reckon? I can get away with it, eh?"

"Why risk it?" He shook his head.

"All this stuff about Miss Isabella Snooty Drawers—it's better than sex. I need a ciggie."

"You're just gonna have to wait. Put it away. But honestly, you can't tell anyone about this. If we lose this work from Hugo, it'll be so damaging."

"Their marriage is already fucked. I think that ship's sailed, love."

"Not their marriage. Bugger their marriage."

"I thought that's what your Danny's been doing with Hugo." She tipped her head back and laughed.

Those bloody fillings. "I'm on about our escorting business—Danny's clients. They need to be sure he sees them with absolute discretion or the whole thing doesn't work."

"Fair enough, love."

"I'm sworn to secrecy. Swear you won't tell," Paul pleaded.

"I swear," Sharon said, combing her hair with the long nails of both hands and laying it over her left breast.

"Swear on Dusty's life."

"Oh, Paul, come off it, love. This ain't the bloody playground."

"Swear on Dusty's life or I'll never tell you any juicy gossip ever again."

She swore on Dusty's life.

"Truth be told," Paul murmured, "I shouldn't have even told you. But I couldn't resist, knowing how much you dislike them both."

"Dislike? You can take your dislike, gloss it in high-grade acrylic, then reinforce it with another three coats of bastard hatred. That's about how much I *dislike* them. I fucking 'ate the pair of 'em. Two stuck-up snobs, lording it up over us like they're bloody King and Queen of Chigwell. We've got a far more desirable postcode than them two. Where we live, in Wanstead, it's got a village green, never mind your Chigwell Parish Council. Parish council my arsehole. And plenty of nail bars and little coffee shops." She paused to lower her enormous gold Gucci sunglasses from her head to her eyes. "That's better. Gotta protect these babies from sun damage."

"Sharon, behave! We're indoors."

"Same difference. Anyway, if you really *are* rolling in it, you couldn't lend me a few quid, could you?"

"Why? Did your nails cost more than usual?"

"I dunno what's going on, but this housekeeping game ain't no joke. Dunno what I'm gonna do." She stuck her bottom lip out and reached for Paul's hand.

"Sure it's not just that you've overspent? Today must've set you back a fair bit. Petrol, hotel, entrance fees, grooming beforehand..."

"And I did have me roots done two weeks early. You might have a point, actually. It's just…it's not never happened like this before, not the whole time we've been together. Even when, ages ago, I'd gone mad and bought meself another big handbag and new shoes and one of them Juicy Couture tracksuits just for round the 'ouse. Next time I checked, there was more in the account. It just came and came, from the company. I never asked. Never needed to. It was always there. Until this week."

"That's not on. How much we talking?"

"Couple of grand, just to tide me over for the next few weeks. Pay you back, promise." She kissed him.

"OK. You've got to keep your furry babies neat and tidy, haven't you?"

"Thanks, babe." Sharon got her phone from her bag and brought up the calendar. "We must have you and Danny round ours soon. It is our turn, isn't it? We came to you last, didn't we?"

"That's right, we went up west to see that musical with the man that was in the thing on telly, him with the hair. Your poor Fred hated it." Paul laughed.

"Good job he'd enjoyed your cocktail cabinet beforehand. He could 'ardly walk and slept all through that musical."

They laughed for a few minutes, then Sharon waved her phone. "Let's check dates and get it sorted, eh?"

"Definitely! This money stuff's not on. You definitely gotta talk to Fred, find out what's going on." Paul handed her a pile of cash he'd got out the bank, which she immediately slipped into her handbag.

Chapter 14

NEIL LAY ON the bed in his hotel room, this time in Manchester, after another day training and management-consulting his heart out. He'd ordered takeaway using his favourite app, and now he was on the phone to the agency, having requested a specific escort.

"Sorry, sir, but we're afraid we do not have availability for that particular gentleman this evening. We are, of course, able to offer you a number of alternatives at the same or a slightly reduced rate. For instance, we have—"

"I'm not interested in any alternatives. I want him."

"Sir, as I said, we have a number of other gentlemen who match your requirements, all very clean, personable and of our usual standard in terms of their looks. We have…" He reeled off a list of men's names and their essential statistics—height, weight, chest and waist size—ending with their final most vital statistic.

Neil half listened, one eye shut, staring at the picture of Danny on his laptop. "Thanks, bye." He put the phone down. If he couldn't have Danny, he'd just make do with his memories of their last time together and his imagination. He unzipped his suit trousers, hanging them carefully in the wardrobe next to the shirt Charlie had ironed for him to wear the following day. He quickly brushed that thought aside and shut the wardrobe. Sliding off his boxers, he lay back on the bed, allowing himself to be fully immersed in the memory of his last time with Danny and his magnificent cock and libido.

***

Charlie sat in their kitchen, stroking Judy after the morning's walk and veg box delivery round, wondering if Neil had read the little note he'd left in the jacket pocket of one of his suits. He hadn't yet heard from Neil about it, but he would be busy. He worked so hard when he was away so he could continue his version of *The Good Life* in the twenty-first century. *I'm such a lucky man.*

There was a knock on the door. Damn, he'd have to answer it, and it would put him back for the planned start time for the cakes he was baking for the farmers' market the next day. If he sat in silence, maybe the person would go away and leave him in peace.

The knock came again, and this time, a familiar voice shouted, "I know you're in there, Charlie. I saw you come back earlier." With a sigh, Charlie went to the door.

Aaron stood there, a wide smile on his face. "I wondered if you wanted to walk Judy together. Mum said you were alone because Neil's away again this week, and I'm just hanging about, at a loose end, so wondered... Don't worry if not." He tilted his head to one side.

"I'm not really alone. I have her." Charlie looked at the dog. "I'm fine. I've just walked her."

"Oh, well, I'll leave you. You must have things to get on with. Sorry to bother you." Aaron turned to leave.

Charlie wasn't sure why, but he didn't want Aaron to leave so soon. "No, no, come in. I'll make some coffee. As long as I get the cakes in by two-ish, I'll have time to make enough. If it means I'm baking into the evening between TV programmes, I don't mind. It's good to talk, as they used to say in the adverts!"

"Which adverts?" Aaron sat at the table, jiggling his leg.

"The British Telecom ones. In the... Actually, you were probably a little boy then. And that's just made me feel really, really old. Right, coffee!" He set about making some.

"You're not old. I don't think of you as old. Not like Mum, anyway. You're not my age, but if you were, I wouldn't be talking to you. You've got all that extra stuff you know that I can't wait to ask you about. But you're not old-fashioned like Dad and Mum are sometimes. It's the perfect age, just the right combination, I reckon."

"OK, enough. You've dug yourself out of that hole now." Charlie laughed. "Milk, sugar?"

They drank the coffee grouped around one end of the table, having a jokey conversation about their favourite biscuits to dunk into coffee.

"Mum says it's awfully common, but I do it when I'm at Dad's. He doesn't care. It's one thing we see eye to eye on, I suppose."

"How did he take it when you told him you're not interested in working at Lux Sunglasses?"

"Still in denial, I think. It's silly. Tamara's, like, totally gagging to do it, but because he's old-fashioned—" he smiled over his coffee cup "—he can't see how or why she'd be any good." He sipped his coffee, staring at Charlie. "Neil away, is he?"

"Yep, we established that. Your mum evidently told you, ordered you to send out a search party for poor, sad, old Charlie, all alone in the house."

"She didn't tell me that at all. She said Neil was away, but she didn't tell me to come round. I wanted to do that off my own bat."

"Is it bat? I always thought it was back."

"It's a cricketing term, apparently. Learned it in English. There's loads of them, most are sporting or sailing originally. Interesting, really. Useless, but interesting. Like most of the stuff you learn." He looked at the table and played with a biscuit, his mug empty. "Do you use anything you learned at school now?"

"More coffee?" Charlie was enjoying himself, and the cakes could wait. He wanted Aaron to stay a bit longer. How much harm could it do?

"Oh, I mustn't keep you. I'm sure you've got plenty to get on with. It's like me coming to your office, this, isn't it?" He smiled, one of those perfect, genuine smiles, then pushed his strawberry-blond hair from his eyes in that familiar gesture.

One more coffee couldn't hurt, could it? Charlie mentally added up the time for the cakes to bake if he started them at four o'clock. Plenty of time. "No, no, stay. Another coffee. Might as well, it's in the pot. I insist. A shame to waste it." He poured more coffee, and Aaron smiled and thanked him.

They talked about how some of what Charlie had learned at school was useful, some of the maths and the English, but a lot of it, when he thought about it, he'd not used. "Neil's got loads more qualifications than me, and look what he's doing. So they're not all useless."

Aaron agreed, and they talked about practical things he was interested in doing and studying, things he could use in real life.

Charlie enjoyed the time with Aaron. What was this? What was going on here? Why would this teenager want to come round and talk during the afternoon? *It's nothing. That's what it is. It must be nothing.* But he was definitely enjoying Aaron's company.

But then Aaron put his mug down and, after stumbling over his words, said he wanted to ask Charlie something. "Something a bit personal, if you don't mind." He avoided eye contact, twisting a napkin between his hands, tighter and tighter.

Charlie nodded and sipped his coffee, hiding his smile behind his mug. This was wrong. He didn't know why, but he knew it was wrong. What would Neil say if he knew? But was it really wrong, what had actually happened? He wasn't sure either way. "Go on." He raised his eyebrows.

"I was wondering, if you…I wanted to know… What's it like being in a couple, like you are?"

"What do you mean? I don't understand." He did understand, but he wanted Aaron to say the words, to hear him articulate exactly what he was getting at. Charlie had endured plenty of 'who's the woman' or 'who wears the trousers' questions during the years, and he didn't think this was going to be another one of those. But he had to know, to test for sure and hear it from Aaron's own pink lips. And there was that dusting of light stubble on his chin. Charlie shook the totally inappropriate thought from his head and waited for Aaron to reply.

"I mean, it's just…you see. What is it like being a gay couple?"

"In Chelsea? In the twenty-first century? With Neil? Generally? What? It's quite a broad question, and I could talk for hours about what it's like, but if I don't know what you're really getting at, we could be here a while, and I do have to do some work this afternoon."

"All those things. How do people react when they know, like when the postman comes round or when you have a plumber to fix something? But also, how does it work being with another man." Aaron coughed. "Not, like, in the bedroom. I'm not on about that. That's on the internet. I think," he added quickly, coughing again and avoiding Charlie's gaze. "But I mean in the relationship, who does what? Cos all this women's lib stuff, it strikes me, like, all that's, like, happened is women now go to work, but they also, like, do all the stuff they used to do before—looking after the children, the house—and men just go to work. How's that equality I don't know."

"I think that's a bit of an oversimplification. There are plenty of straight relationships where that's what happens. But there are lots of straight men who do their share of the house and children stuff because they have to, because the woman is just as knackered as he is when he gets home from work."

"But you don't have that when it's two men, do you? There's none of that man-woman stuff to get in the way, so what is it like? How's it work?"

Charlie hadn't really thought about it before because he'd not been asked in such a direct way. "I've never been in a relationship with a woman. Neil has, years ago, but not me. I've only ever been in relationships with men." Charlie wondered what Aaron was *really* getting at. Why was he so interested in his relationship with Neil? Was this another of his clever ruses to talk about sex? It didn't seem like it.

"So how *does* it, like, work then?" Aaron pressed.

"If I had to describe it, I'd say you just get on with it. You muddle through. You do things you're good at and the other person might not be so good at. You take it in turns depending on who's home late from work. There's no 'I don't do that because I'm a woman'. You just get on with it." He paused for a moment, mentally ticking off the division of labour within their house. "I cook in the week, but Neil does it at weekends. That's practical, cos I'm here. We choose the car together, but I'm the one who takes it in for its service. Although really, he's more into cars than me. They're a tool, as far as I'm concerned. Stuff for the house—we talk about and agree on it, and someone buys it, depending on who's got the most time that week or a contact for buying it or something." As he continued to describe his and Neil's relationship, how they shared things and played to each other's strengths, Charlie found himself smiling, thinking how lucky he was to have such a perfect relationship, to have found a man like Neil.

Aaron listened as they drank another two mugs of coffee and emptied the biscuit barrel, so Charlie had to resort to the *emergency biscuit supply* hidden in the back of the cupboard.

"When did you realise you were gay? Sorry, that's too much. Don't worry. Don't answer that one. It's not fair. Mum's right. Sorry. Ignore. Fail. Sorry. Abort conversation. Delete."

"No, no, it's OK. It's not the usual one I'm asked, which is what was it like coming out, to which I always ask them to tell me about the most personal, painful, emotional experience they've ever had. That usually shuts them up." He smirked. "But this is different. This is from you, and you're not some bloke I've just met at a wedding, same age as me, having a bit of a poke around at the gays sat at his table."

"If you're happy to tell me… Just what age really, and what made you know, I suppose?"

"I was sixteen. I'd kissed a girl at a school party, and it did nothing for me. She was lovely. We had a right laugh together, talking about music and films and TV shows we liked, but she was all too soft and sloppy for me. Nothing going on downstairs, if you know what I mean."

He and Aaron shared a look of knowing exactly what he meant.

Charlie continued, "So I kept away for the next few years. But that summer, the summer I kissed a girl, Mum and Dad had a patio put in the back of the house, and there were all these builders coming and going, concrete bricks, everything. Cement, sand. All that. I don't know. Anyway, there was this one guy who was early twenties, Irish, with a red sun-burned body and cut-off denim jeans and those big chunky Caterpillar boots. Even when it rained that summer, he still arrived in a little white vest. I spent most of that summer staring at him from my bedroom and…" He looked out the window. "When I did, there was something going on downstairs." Charlie shrugged, feeling a bit embarrassed, although it was a tender, gentle memory he'd not shared it in such detail with anyone before.

"Did you talk to him?"

Charlie noticed Aaron staring at his neck, hovering at the V of his T-shirt where a few hairs showed. He didn't know what to do, how to feel. He turned away, hiding his sprouting chest hairs from Aaron's gaze. "Don't even know what his name was! I was too tongue-tied to even talk to him. But I knew, sitting in that room, with those feelings, that all the other boys in my year wouldn't have spent their summer looking at an Irish builder in their back garden." He laughed. "I even did some drawings too."

"Can you draw?"

He blew a raspberry. "No. They were awful. Total and utter crap. I remember spending hours trying to get his chest hair just right, the way it covered his pectoral muscles, around his nipples, then thinned beneath that and made a thin line from the middle of his chest past his belly button—which was an outy, I can still see it now—into his cut-off jeans."

They both laughed nervously, then sat in silence for a few moments.

Aaron spoke first, slowly, quietly, staring at the ground. "When did you first kiss another man? I take it you didn't get anywhere with this builder?"

"Nothing. They finished the patio, and they were off. I debated about asking for his number but couldn't think of an even half believable reason why I'd want it. Imagine it—*oh yeah, I'm a teenager and won't own my own place for years, but just in case I need some building work done on the house I don't yet own, for ten years' time, I'll take your number.* I don't think so, do you?"

Aaron laughed and shook his head.

"Freshers' week at uni. There was this LGBTQ club meet and mingle, so I went along."

"You spent two years and did nothing?"

"I was terrified. I read all this stuff about AIDS and HIV and didn't really understand it. We didn't do gay sex education at school. Put a condom on a banana, girls have menstrual cycles—which I used to think was a type of bike—and boys have wet dreams, and that was it. Why would I need to use a condom with another man?"

"Didn't you look on the internet?"

"What, in 1997? I don't think so. I'd started to send the odd email, from my college account. There was not much internet then. No NHS resources, or Terence Higgins Trust website. I didn't have my own computer to access it anyway, never mind a smart phone. I'd have had to borrow my parents' computer. You forget, there was a world pre-internet."

"What about libraries? There must have been books and stuff."

"Yeah, go to the library in my home town and ask the librarian, who knew my mum, where the sex education books were. No, I just kept quiet. At uni, I was away from home, away from anyone I knew, so I thought, why not? If I give it a go and it's not for me, I'll just say it was a phase and go back to being straight. None of the people at uni would have known me more than a few months by then. People change their minds about things all the time."

"And did you?"

"What?"

"Change your mind?" Aaron stared straight at Charlie, who turned to face him again.

"What do you think? I've never been in a relationship with a woman. I went to that gay meet-and-mingle thing and ended up seeing the LGBTQ president for the first two terms at uni. At the time, I thought I'd be with him forever. And when it ended, I realised how naïve I'd been, and also, why would I want to be with him forever? Finton, he was called. Dungarees, big high-top trainers and poker-straight black curtains covering his ears, with a wedge cut in the back. It was the nineties. And a…" He stopped himself revealing anymore, knowing that would have *definitely* been inappropriate, as it was something he couldn't have told Neil about either. "Good times. Then there was no stopping me. I couldn't get enough. I had my free johnnies in my back pocket, and I grabbed Nottingham by the shaved, smooth, gay balls and I loved it."

"Christ!"

"Sorry, bit too much. Got carried away there." Had he? Was it too much?

"S'all right. Nottingham?"

"There are gay people outside London, contrary to what Londoners would have everyone believe. Yep, Nottingham, and it was fabulous." Had that been too much? A *fabulous,* some shaved, smooth, gay balls, and a story with free johnnies all in the last five minutes. Charlie swallowed, composed himself, reined himself in. "So that was me. And now look at me. Fourteen years later, here I am."

Aaron stood. "Can I have a bath? There's no hot water at home—something about Dad's money he pays Mum."

Before Charlie could think about whether that was or wasn't appropriate, he said quietly, with a shrug, "Oh, yes, if you want. Do you want me to show you how the mixer tap works? Towels are in the airing cupboard, top of the stairs."

Aaron tugged a towel from his bag. "I've got one." He removed his T-shirt to reveal pale, slightly freckly skin with a dusting of strawberry-blond hair around his nipples and a light treasure trail leading to his very low-slung jeans.

Charlie quickly walked away, suddenly very interested in the recipe book he'd left by the sink, turning his back.

"Your ceiling's low," Aaron said. "All that sitting's made me tired. What did you say about the mixer tap?"

Charlie sneaked a quick look at Aaron, who stood with his arms stretched above his head, revealing the darker hair in his armpits. "You'll work it out. I've got to get on with the cakes."

Aaron walked over and kissed Charlie's cheek. "Thanks."

Charlie jolted at the touch but steadfastly avoided eye contact, stepping away from Aaron and turning his back to him again. "Enjoy the bath, plenty of hot water here. Plenty to enjoy."

Aaron strode up the stairs, two at a time.

Charlie stared at the Victoria sponge recipe he'd made hundreds of times before, yet it took him a while to work out whether he needed self-raising or plain flour, and he weighed the sugar three times before getting it right. It was only when the electric whisk was beating the mixture to a weird consistency that he realised he'd completely forgotten to add the butter...and he had an erection. What the hell was wrong with him today?

Chapter 15

FRED ARRIVED HOME from a long day at the luxury sunglasses coal face to find Sharon pouting, perching, preening on a stool at the breakfast bar. "All right, babes, what's for dinner?"

"Nothing."

"Eh? What's up?"

"I run out of money. The housekeeping account has gone dry. Sorry, *babes*, it's beans on toast tonight." She combed her long, blonde hair with her long, pink nails.

"All right, hands up. I've had to make a few cuts here and there. Sorry, babes, but I had nothing to manage with."

"So you thought you'd take some of my housekeeping and dog-keeping money. And what? Do what with it, eh?"

"The woman's fucking bleedin' me dry. These maintenance payments are taking me to the cleaners. I 'ad to do something, love."

"What about my maintenance? What about my little furry babies' maintenance, eh? Didn't think about that, did you, when you was cutting back." She hopped off the stool and walked into the pantry, reappearing with a tin of beans in one hand and a white sliced loaf in the other. "These do ya?" She noisily started to assemble the dinner, banging plates and tin opener, pushing the bread into the toaster with force.

"All right," Fred said. "Calm down, will you, love?"

"Calm down? I'll give you calm down. How about neither of your kids are actually kids no more? They're both over eighteen, so why you still paying maintenance to her? I'm due my full lot—highlights, tan, nails, eyelash tint, bikini wax—everything. But not if I've run out of money, I can't. And if you think I can give you all those nice dinners on less money, you're wrong there an' all. Just like looking this good, food costs money too. And I'm not skimping on my regime. It's a slippery slope, I'm telling you—eyebrows, bikini wax slipped, and suddenly you're going out with some mung-bean-eating, hairy-armpitted lesbo. Is that what you want?"

"Babe, I shoulda told ya, I know that now. I shoulda given ya warning. Sorry. I think you're right about 'em turning eighteen. You might be onto something there."

"See? I'm not just a pretty face."

"I'll talk to her, get it sorted. Promise."

"Just you remember who you're married to *now*. Not years ago, but *now*. All right?"

"Here." He handed her a credit card. "Order us a Chinese, would ya? I'm not having that crap. I'm gonna have a bit of a lie-down." And he was gone.

Smiling to herself, she pressed four on the white cordless phone which was programmed to their favourite Chinese restaurant.

***

Next day, Fred called Camilla from work and asked her why he was still paying maintenance when both the kids were over eighteen.

She braced herself to go over this familiar territory once again. She removed one earring, so the phone was more comfortable against her ear. "Fred, darling, we've been through this before. It was all agreed in the divorce papers. You were going to pay maintenance for your two children."

"Yeah, but not forever, Cam. At this rate, I'll still be paying for them when they're middle-aged. That can't be right, can it?"

"Don't *Cam* me, please. It is all in the divorce agreement. If you check your papers, I think you'll find it's very clear on the matter. Would you like me to read the particular paragraph?"

"You got it handy, then?"

She coughed and put on her reading glasses. The agreement was always by the phone for instances such as this. Camilla calmly read the relevant paragraph. "'Fred Smith agrees to pay maintenance'—it says the amount here, but I'm assuming you don't need me to remind you how much it is?"

"Go on."

"...'maintenance for Tamara Smith and Aaron Smith, the two children who were born as a result of this marriage, which is being dissolved. Payments will be made to Ms Camilla Constantine'— and then there's details of the account number. It seems perfectly clear to me, darling."

"Don't you *darling* me. I'm not your darling and haven't been for a long time. I'm married, and I've got other things to support, not by paying for you to have Harrods deliveries every week to entertain your bloody gaybours. Why the hell did I agree to that without an end date? I'll get my lawyer on this. You'll have a letter by Friday. This gravy train is stopping, and that's an end to it."

"Well, you can rest assured, I shall be seeking my own legal advice too, but of course, *I* will have to contact the Citizen's Advice Bureau, as I'm unable to afford my own lawyer, since I have two children to feed and clothe. *Your* two children."

"*Our* two children, Cam."

"Camilla to you. Now, is that all? I want to speak to our son, as he seems to have disappeared again. Perhaps he's round Charlie and Neil's." She'd had enough of this conversation and besides, her ear was aching.

"Well, it *was* all, until you mentioned them lot. These gaybours of yours—what sort of crap they spouting in his ear? He mentioned fucking manscaping and poncing hairdressing last time he was here. I've never heard anything like it. Manscaping and hairdressing. If my dad had've heard that, he'd...well, I don't know what he'd've done, but he wouldn't've been 'appy."

"Oh, sorry, my darling. I think I have another call coming through, wait a moment." She paused and sucked her teeth. "Back now. Ahh, yes, it was the 1960s. They would like your homophobic paranoia back. Could you be a darling and send it on to them?" She smiled to herself, sure it would have driven him mad.

"You know where you can stick that an' all. And I am not your fucking darling. Fuck only knows what you've done to him since bringing him up without me. Something's gone on, and I'm not happy. Hairdressing, manscaping. I don't know why I bother paying maintenance for him anyway. It's not like he's even a tiny bit of a chip off the old block. In fact, sometimes I wonder if he wasn't the bloody milkman's."

She felt a chill across her heart, then took a breath, composing herself for the next round. "Are you quite finished, darling?"

"How many times...I'm not your darling! Or are you deaf as well as stupid?"

Camilla bit back with all her will the urge to tell him to be a dear and kindly fuck off, knowing in the long run it wouldn't do her any favours. "Force of habit. Everyone's *darling* to me. Noted. You're not my darling." She heard the front door closing. "I think that's him now, returning from another afternoon with our lovely neighbour, Charlie. Have I told you about him? He's the one who lives with his marvellous boyfriend, Neil. Such a darling, wonderful couple..."

Fred had put the phone down.

Aaron flounced through the door, an enormous grin on his face, his hair wet and a damp towel resting over his shoulders.

"Where have you been, darling? I've been trying to find you all morning."

"Only over at Charlie's. Not been long."

"What happened to your hair? Why's it wet?"

"He was showing me how to water his garden, and the hosepipe slipped."

"But your T-shirt's dry. And the towel, why...?"

But he was gone, up to his room, two steps at a time.

Camilla called after him up the stairs, "Darling, I need to talk to you and your sister. Daddy's being beastly about money. It's awfully tedious, but we need to work out a plan of attack. Oh dear, not attack. Anyway, we can talk about it later, as a family, together?"

Where had he been all afternoon? Why on earth would he be spraying a hosepipe with Charlie? He'd never shown any interest in gardening before. And what was with the towel? How many times had he been round theirs this week? This must be the third, and it was only Thursday. It couldn't possibly be, could it? Charlie and Neil were happily married! Well, not quite married, but very much together, weren't they? She put her earring back on and stared at the ceiling where Aaron was banging around in his room.

Chapter 16

THAT NIGHT, AT the kitchen table, eating soup Aaron had made—would wonders never cease?—from a recipe Charlie sent out with his veg boxes, Camilla recounted the phone call with Fred to her two children. They listened in companionable silence, quickly eating the homemade soup.

"That was delicious, darling," Camilla said, finishing her last mouthful. "Bravo for making it. Most you've made before was cheese on toast. It's not much to ask, but your father's getting a bit anxious about paying all this money, and look at how you two behave towards him. Just humour him a bit. Aaron, can you at least *pretend* you're interested in the business and maybe lay off the hairdressing talk? If you want to do that, or whatever it is you want to do, we'll tell him gradually. It's simply too much to go from putting uni on hold to being a hairdresser and talking about manscaping all in one step. Too much for your father, anyway. I'm a bit more of a woman of the world." She tucked a stray hair back under her Alice band and hoped she was a woman of the world.

"He, like, doesn't listen, Mum," Tamara said. "I've tried to tell him what I can do, but he, like, won't listen."

"Darling, he's—" Camilla coughed "—*like*, a man. He takes time to get used to things. You've got to drip, drip, drip the idea into his head until he eventually thinks it was his."

Aaron said, "If I want to be a fucking hairdresser, I'll *be* a fucking hairdresser. If I want to be a pastry chef, I'll *be* a fucking pastry chef. I might even be...I don't know, a make-up artist or a costume designer. If I want to be those things, I will, and there's nothing he can say to make me change my mind. It's my life, and I'm sick of people telling me who I should be." Aaron stood. The chair made a scraping noise as it slid on the tiles.

"No one's telling you who you should be, darling." Camilla gestured for him to sit.

He remained standing, arms folded across his chest. "What then?"

"OK, darling." Sensing the electricity coming from him, Camilla paused, careful to assemble the next sentence in her head before letting it free from her mouth. "I'll be happy whatever makes you happy, of course. So, do you want to be a make-up artist or costume designer, darling?"

He shrugged and slowly sat. "Dunno, but I might."

"OK, darlings. If we want to continue with this little life we've created for ourselves, skiing in Val d'Isere, designer trainers and Harrods deliveries because poor Mummy can't cook for toffee, then we'll have to look sharp and play along with Daddy for a while. OK?"

Tamara started to clear the table.

Aaron stood again, swiping his hair from his eyes. "We done?"

Camilla stared at her son's beautiful hair, then glanced to her own bottle-platinum-blonde with mousy-brown roots, much like her and Fred's natural colours. "Yes, darling, we're all done here. Where are you off to now? It's awfully late."

"Charlie's gonna show me another recipe. Blueberry muffins. They're meant to be a piece of piss. When he explained the soup one it was, like, waaay easier than I thought it would be. He's well good at cooking. So can I?"

Camilla knew how the balance of power had shifted, now her two children were young adults, but couldn't stop herself worrying about them, just as she had when they were babies, toddlers and young children. "Have fun!" she replied, a bright smile fixed on her face as he left. Once the door had slammed, Camilla met Tamara at the sink, next to the piles of crockery. "What's going on with him and Charlie all of a sudden?"

"All of a sudden? Mum, like, where've you been all your life?"

"What, darling?"

"They've been friendly for, like, ages. Ever since he told you he was having a pause from uni." She rolled her eyes and left the room.

How was it possible that after living with and bringing up these two children, she found herself, as they both became adults, feeling more and more like she lived with two gangly, loud strangers?

***

Twenty years ago

Camilla walked quickly to the garden, then stood, her arms folded. "I'm pregnant."

Henry, the gardener, stopped digging her tulip bulbs into the ground and leant on the spade. "Congratulations, Mrs. Constantine."

"No, not congratulations. That is not the right response." She bit her lip as she remembered the afternoon they'd spent together on the picnic blanket in the shed in her back garden.

"You wanted children. You said you and your husband were trying for a family, now you're married. That's what you told me. Look, I don't know what this has to do with me. Can I get on with this? I've got loads of bulbs to plant still. So if you don't mind, Mrs. Constantine." He turned, wiping the sweat with a freckly arm from his light brow and pushing his strawberry-blond hair back from his face.

"It's yours." She stood in front of him, in the garden of the beautiful workman's cottage she and Fred, her husband of a few months, had moved into shortly after they'd married.

"It can't be. We only did it once." He walked towards her.

She pushed him away. "Not here, not in the garden. People can see." She stared into his eyes. "It only takes once, you know. One stupid fucking mistake, and now look at the mess I'm in."

107

"But, but…how do you know it's not his? How can you be sure until it's born?"

"Because Fred and I didn't have sex for the whole week I was ovulating. At the beginning of that week, he was home so late from work I didn't see him. In the middle of that week, we had the most almighty screaming-blue-murder row, about what I can't remember, but the next day, you found me crying in the shed. And then…" She pulled a handkerchief from her sleeve and wiped her eyes. *"That bloody, bloody job. If only he hadn't been working so late earlier that week. Or if we hadn't had that row. But he didn't, and we did. And now this is the mess I'm in."*

He tried to comfort her, but she pushed him away. *"How can you be sure, totally sure?"* he asked.

"A woman knows. I know when I did and didn't have sex with my husband. Christ, the second man I sleep with and he gets me pregnant while I'm married to the first. It's like some bloody soap opera storyline, isn't it? Only it isn't. It's my bloody life now, the life I'm living and will have to go on living forever."

"You could tell him. Come clean. I'll help, bring up the baby with you."

"Where did you come from, one of those soap operas too? Run away to join the circus, shall we? I don't want that."

"Why not? I'm all right. I'm a bit of a toy boy for you. Plenty of women would love it."

"Well, it seems, unfortunately for you, I am not 'plenty of women'. I am married to Fred. I love Fred. I want to be married to Fred. I want to continue being married to Fred, and I want to have children with Fred. You, I'm afraid, do not really fit into that picture."

"I'll finish this bed and you won't see me again."

"I think that would be best."

That had been the last time she'd seen Henry in the flesh. But every single time she looked at Aaron, with his strawberry-blond hair, freckly light skin, his smile, his blue eyes, she saw Henry the gardener again.

Chapter 17

A MONTH AFTER THEIR Chinese meal, Fred Smith walked into the dining room where Sharon Smith stood at one end, next to two silver metal food covers. Her normally blonde hair had dark roots showing, and her skin was much lighter than its usual orangey hue.

Fred rubbed his hands together. "What we got tonight, babes? You all right? You look a bit...different."

Sharon, with a flourish, removed the metal covers to reveal four pieces of cheese on toast. "Dinner...is served." She sat and helped herself to a piece of toast.

"Is this it?"

"I told you before. I ran out of money in the housekeeping account. And you said I wasn't to use the credit card for normal, everyday things like that, didn't you?"

He leant across the table and grabbed two bits of toast, nodding. "What's up with your hair, babe?"

"You wanna see the dogs! They look even worse than me. Rough as arseholes."

"Lovely."

"I've gotta tell you, love. It ain't pretty." Sharon held a carving knife next to one of the plates of cheese on toast. "Shall I carve?"

Fred took the knife from her. "What's all this in aid of? You trying to make some kind of point?"

Sharon pushed the plate to one side. "I've had this out with you before. You seem to have cut the money going into the housekeeping account. With what I've got left, I can't do the same dinners you usually want. Not to mention my own routine's gone right out the window." She bent her head forward, showing her dark roots.

"What's this about the dogs?"

"Well, my furry babies have to look their best, as you know, for the shows I do with them. And it's not something I can do all on my own. I do try. I try to do as much as I can, but with four of 'em and running this place, it's just not possible. But I've had to let that slip too lately, cos I've not had the money. I wasn't going to complain to you. I know you've got enough on your plate at the moment, with work and the kids. In all honesty, I thought I could sort it out, make it work, and you'd never know. I did try, love. But I just can't stretch it. So—" She picked up the last bit of toast from the silver tray. "—this is what we've got." She shrugged.

A black-and-white Papillion dog trotted into the room, its coat dirty and matted. It hung its head as it walked towards the water bowl by the patio doors.

"Leave it with me, love." Fred picked up the cutlery and started on his dinner.

Sharon picked at the beans with a fork. "Want mine? I'll have a fag instead." She walked out the patio doors and smoked three cigarettes one after the other, stroking her dogs with her free hand.

Chapter 18

FRED AND CAMILLA had been discussing arrangements for child maintenance in her living room for most of the afternoon.

Camilla held her copy of the divorce papers, containing details of the maintenance payments. "It is for *our* children. The children as a result of *our* marriage. Isn't it fair you continue to support them, since they are still *your* children?"

"I'm not denying that. 'Course they're mine. But children? Not any more really. If it's for the children, why does the money go to you, not them?"

"Because they're children, and they can't be expected to manage money themselves."

Fred waved his copy of the divorce settlement papers. "Ahh, *then*, maybe, but now, they could, I bet."

"What exactly are you proposing? Haven't you got somewhere you could be? I'm awfully busy and need to get on." Camilla could see where this was going, and she didn't like it.

Fred looked at the Harrods bags in the recycling box next to the Aga. "It's not for you. It's for them."

"But who feeds and clothes them, eh? Who does that, I wonder."

"Harrods, by the look of things. You've never cooked. Look, I don't see why I should pay you to have Harrods delivering, while me and Sharon are living on cheese on toast. It's just not fair."

"Beans on toast, you say. It's a complete meal I read somewhere." Camilla leaned at the sink, willing herself not to cry and only just winning.

"Come on, let's not split hairs."

"I think, sadly, we're far too late to be avoiding that."

"I want it to be fair."

Camilla turned from the sink, blinking quickly to clear her eyes. "Who said anything about fair? Are you saying your wife's little dogs are more important than your own children? Is that what this has come to?"

"No. You're twisting things around. You always do that. You always do. I'm saying I think there's gotta be a way to keep everyone happy. Some sort of a compromise."

Camilla turned away to make a cafetière of coffee. "I object to that. I do not always twist things. If you're going to continue like this, I shall have to ask you to leave, and we can do this through solicitors." She took a deep breath and collected a mug.

"I don't want that, an' neither do you, I reckon. I've already spoken to my solicitor, and he said an open-ended maintenance agreement like this one is very unusual. He doubts it would stand up in court. They're legally not children any longer, ipso whatsit, they don't need maintenance payments."

She put a hand on her mouth and finally, losing completely her battle not to get upset, started to cry. "What about me? What am I supposed to do to keep this place, eh? I've not worked since the children came along. I'm qualified for precisely nothing. I've experience of doing exactly nothing except bringing up your children. Where does that leave me? Where does that leave us, with this home? The home your children have lived in all their lives."

Fred walked to Camilla and held her shoulders from behind. "Cam—"

"Don't you bloody well Cam me. I simply cannot believe you're doing this. It's the most awful, beastly thing you've ever done. Apart from the divorce in the first place, of course."

"Come on." He gently turned her to face him. "We can come to some arrangement. It won't be sudden. I'm not going to just stop payments. The solicitor suggested paying the children directly, since it's to help them. It'll also give them experience of managing their own money."

"Would you stop all payments to me?"

He nodded, still holding her shoulders. "Not straight away, but eventually, yes. The money's not *for* you. You got the house and everything in it. And the car. There's no mortgage left, hasn't been for years."

"You paid fifty per cent deposit."

"I remember—a few years' bonuses from the city. They really were the good old days!"

"That car's long gone. I've bought a few of my own since then, you know. I'm not totally reliant on you." She had been. She'd used Fred's money to buy the cars, but she didn't want to admit that to herself right at this point, her lowest ebb in a long time.

"Come on. We can't let this turn into a big thing. At the end of the day, it's all about the kids."

"An unfair term, your solicitor said?" Camilla asked curtly, biting down the urge to dissolve in a big, blousy, uncontrolled heap of tears.

Fred nodded.

"And you won't stop payments straight away?"

"Let's sit down, work out something staged and agree realistic money for me to pay the kids directly. Of course, if they're still here and working, you could ask them for housekeeping money, which they could pay from my money."

"That sounds awfully convoluted." She paused and got another mug from the tree. "Coffee? If we're sitting down to work this out, you might as well have something to drink." She knew she was beaten, no hope trying to hold out any longer. The best option was to sit down like two adults and work it out together.

"What is Aaron doing with his life at the moment?" Fred asked.

Camilla hid her bitten lip behind her coffee mug. "It seems to change daily when I ask him. Why?"

"He's mentioned hairdressing, cooking, some crafts—all sorts. Has he made any actual steps towards any of these airy-fairy notions?"

"I think he's still at the ideas stage. He's unwilling to rush into something again, after making such a big hash of uni. He said he felt swept into it, without us really asking him. He wants to think properly about what he wants in life. Our neighbour, Charlie, is being most helpful. Aaron's round there at the moment, I think. He comes home bursting full of ideas—he even made a soup recently."

"Found the tin opener, did he?" Fred laughed.

"Homemade. From scratch. Carrot and coriander soup. It was a triumph. It was delicious. Well, he didn't make the chicken stock, as we didn't have any chicken hanging about. We never have any uncooked chicken hanging about. Anyway, he used a stock cube, but the rest—that was made by him, your son."

"I don't know him at all, do I?"

Camilla shook her head slowly. "Neither do I, and he's been living with me since he was born. Now look at me. I couldn't tell you where he is, what he's doing or what his hopes and dreams are. I used to think I knew all that, which is why I persuaded him to go to uni. It made sense."

Fred said quietly, "Don't be so hard on yourself. You know he's at this Charlie's at the moment, cooking or something."

Camilla shrugged. "Suppose I do."

"And uni did make sense for him because he was always going to go. After that school, that's what was expected."

Camilla tidied her hair under the Alice band, checking her reflection in the window. "*Expected*. See, that's the problem. He simply wasn't consulted."

"Consulted...do you think I was consulted about going to work in the city and doing fifteen-hour days five days a week? Or how about was I consulted when I bought the business and built that up to what it is today?"

"Your choice to buy the business. Fred. It's not like when you were his age. They're all Generation Y or something. It's all about portfolio careers and meaning and social contribution. They don't just want a job and a pay cheque at the end of the month. They want meaningful work. Charlie was explaining it to me, all this Gen Y and Gen X business."

Fred rolled his eyes. "Don't make me laugh. He wants a clip 'round the ear. That's what my dad would have done and told me to get down the Job Centre sharpish."

"I don't think that approach would quite wash nowadays. It needs to be more of a conversation than an order. I think you'll find that will go down better. I'm happy to talk to them about the money changing and us having to make adjustments as a household and some money going to them directly. But you have to listen more to them—really *hear* what they're saying. Do you know what Tamara's studying at college?"

"Secretarial college, isn't it?"

"See, I knew you hadn't listened. They both said so too. Business studies. She's dying to be more involved at your work. She's got loads of good ideas. She's a bright, young graduate. Companies fight for people like her."

"So I shouldn't give her filing and typing to do next time?"

"No. I think that would be best." Camilla poured them both another mug of coffee from the cafetière.

"Thanks. You live and learn."

"With children, you certainly do. Now, have you got a calculator? I'll get a pen and paper and we can work this out, like two mature adults. For the best of the children." She stood and searched for the pen and paper.

"For the best of the children."

They talked and number-crunched for almost two hours, going back and forth over figures until they reached an agreement. Fred would continue paying a reduced amount of money to Camilla and an increased amount to Tamara and Aaron for the next two months until, by month three, he would give a reduced amount overall, split between the children, and Camilla would receive nothing directly from him.

***

Later, Camilla summoned the children so she and Fred could explain the change to them.

"What if I need new trainers?" Aaron asked. "Who pays for them?"

"You do," Fred said. "From either the money I give you or your own if you're earning."

"What about supplies for college, stuff like that?" Tamara asked.

"Either me or Mum."

Camilla played with her wedding ring, which she'd kept on since the divorce because...well, it was so pretty, and somehow being unmarried at her age had seemed a bit undignified then. After the divorce, she'd told herself she'd keep it on for a few weeks, which had become months, which had become years, and so it had stayed.

116

"I won't have an awful lot of cash floating about," she said, "since I don't work. I'll need to sort out a plan for some money for things like that, food and running the household generally."

How was she meant to manage? How had she got away with it for so long? Now in her mid-forties, she found herself looking for work with precisely no skills and no experience to carry her through. She had no idea what to do but couldn't let it show to the children. This was a mature, adult agreement she'd arrived at with Fred, so she would bloody well stick to it.

"I'm sure we'll muddle through." She smiled brightly and put the gas bill in the drawer of the wooden cabinet.

Chapter 19

Hugo lay against Danny's chest, playing with his chest hair and kissing his nipples. They had finished the second go that afternoon, and Hugo had said he didn't want another one yet; he wanted to talk.

Hugo looked up at Danny. "I simply must see you later this week. I know the paperwork has all been used up for this month, but I cannot bear it otherwise."

"I'm sure that can be arranged." Danny smiled to himself, then quickly looked down at Hugo.

"I have nothing else. My wife hardly talks to me, except about her work and when we're with Mummy and Daddy. She just swans around the house, ignoring me whenever we pass."

"What about your work?"

"It's hardly diverting or taxing. I'm barely there at all. All I have to do is sign a cheque here or a contract there. Rifle through the board papers to check they're all in order. If they have a board meeting, I turn up, nod through whatever schemes the other board members or general manager propose. And of course, I have advisers, managers and such like to tell me if I need to worry about anything. As quick as I'm in the building, I'm sitting at my desk playing Solitaire or clicking those silver balls. It's crushingly boring. Have you ever tried to look busy in an office? It's like a slow death of the soul as you watch the vim leave your body."

"Isn't there more you could do for the business? Any new ideas you could work up? Any problems to be resolved? Changes that need to be implemented?"

"Oh, hang all that bloody nonsense. I barely know what it does, the silly business. I'm just keeping the seat warm, really, so Mummy and Daddy can say I'm doing something, but I have a wonderful executive board and team of divisional managers who are running the whole thing without my input at all. I'm the family chief executive, a sort of figurehead for it being a long-established family business. I think they like it that way."

"So what do you want to do with your time?"

"This?" Hugo grinned.

"What would your parents think about *this*?"

"Daddy was in the army, so I'm sure he's met a few...you know. But Mummy, she'd be heartbroken. She has awfully old-fashioned ideas about this sort of thing. Thinks two men together is unnatural, unhealthy. Besides, she wants a grandson. This would finally spell out to her why she hasn't yet got one." He shuddered, then sat up. "Let's not talk about them or that silly business any longer. It's all so terribly dreary and depressing. I'm here to get away from all that, not dwell on it."

"What would you like us to talk about?" Danny asked.

"I would love us to have another weekend away in the country together. I can sort out the paperwork with Paul, to ensure it's all above board if you're free."

"When would we be talking about?"

"ASAP, really."

They knocked a few dates about, finally agreeing on one in a few weeks' time.

Hugo said, "I can make up an excuse for my wife. She hardly notices I'm not there anyway."

"Not meaning to pry, but what does she think you're doing these weekends with me?"

"Golfing weekends. Work-client entertainment. Sometimes I tell her I'm staying in a hotel to write."

"Do you write? I didn't know that."

"'Course not. I've never written anything more than an email or the odd report or board paper. And most of the time, someone else writes them. I just cast a quick eye over them. She didn't question it, and I knew she wouldn't want to see what I'd written, wouldn't be in the least bit interested, so that was that."

***

A few weeks later, Hugo stood next to a small suitcase by the door as Isabella left for work.

She looked at the case. "Where are you off to?"

"Golfing weekend with chums. I did tell you."

"But you don't have any chums." She smirked to herself at her little, accurate joke.

"Daddy suggested it, and I thought, since you've been so busy at work, you might like to unwind and relax in the house on your own. No need to fuss and worry over me." He smiled sweetly.

Fuss and worry—since when had she done that over him? "Well, have a wonderful time, darling. You can tell me all about it when you're back. When is it you're coming back? I'm sure you told me, but these things do slip my mind somewhat." Because she didn't care one iota about them.

"Sunday sometime. Depends how the games go and how late we stay up drinking on Saturday night."

She gave him the briefest of brief kisses on the cheek. New aftershave? No matter. Who cares?

On her way to the office, she listed all the things she would be able to do without him hanging around. She could have a spa day with the girls or meet someone for a drinky-filled lunch on Saturday. She could settle down in her nightdress, with a face mask on, paint her nails and watch one of the films he didn't like while gorging herself on chocolates. Blissful.

***

Isabella returned from work that evening, opened a bottle of wine and drank it in the bath. Saturday was spent shopping in Bond Street with a friend who lived that side of town and who'd been asking her to meet for a while. They filled their bags with gorgeous little expensive things and shared a long, boozy lunch at Quaglinos, followed by a bit more shopping around Harvey Nichols, including a few cocktails at one of the bars inside the building.

Sunday, she lounged in bed, with no guilt about him lying next to her, asking if she would get up. She spread the *Sunday Times* across the duvet and waded through it until lunch, sipping a big pot of black coffee. She spent the afternoon covered in an expensive serum she'd bought the day before—it had said something about royal jelly and revitalising tired lines, so she slathered it thickly over her whole body and shuffled about the place in her fluffy pink bathrobe.

By the evening, she started to think about work so put in a few hours. She drafted a couple of board papers and called her friend Verity, the marketing director and the only other woman on the board, first talking about her marketing proposal and then drifting onto their weekends. Verity said she'd also sat about all day swathed in special royal jelly face cream. They said their goodbyes just as Hugo returned.

"Good weekend, darling?" she shouted, not turning from the TV.

"All right. Bit tiring, actually. You?"

"All right." She watched him carry his suitcase upstairs, noting the absence of his golf clubs as well as his crumpled demeanour. "Good game?"

"Oh, yes. Good game."

"You do look awfully shagged out. Red and exhausted."

"Do I?" He straightened his back and continued on his way upstairs.

***

A few days later, Isabella called Danny Traviati. She tutted loudly when it went straight to voicemail. *What's the point of giving someone your business card if you don't want to be contacted again?* She lay on the bed, trying to remember the last time she felt a man's body against her own. The vision of Hugo's back flashed through her mind, curved on his side of the bed. She flicked through her phone and called another man from *that* section of the phone's address book.

"I'm at a bit of a loose end this Saturday night. Poor me." She put on a slightly babyish voice. "I was wondering if you were free to keep me company."

The man said, "Yes, poor you. And you're hoping I'd be able to help you out in this little fix you've gone and got yourself in?"

"Well, if it's not too much bother, that would be marvellous."

"*You* must pay for the hotel this time. After last time, *she's* scrupulously going through my credit card statements, so I can't risk it again."

"What perfect synchronicity. I've the house all to myself the weekend I'm talking about. He's seeing his chums or playing golf or working—some such tedious engagement anyway. It means he's gone, and I know I won't hear a thing from him until late Sunday evening. So..." She smiled then giggled as he began to describe what he would do to her, given enough time.

He had the most extraordinarily long tongue, if she remembered correctly, and a real enthusiasm for cunnilingus.

Such fun.

They talked for a while, gradually raising the stakes about what they wanted to do to each other in the few short days when they'd be together. She put the phone down and jumped into a long, hot shower to relieve the excitement and anticipation.

Chapter 20

PUSHING THE BUTTON for the folding hard top, Danny parked his silver BMW on the yellow crunchy gravel at the front of the large, sprawling country hotel deep in rural Buckinghamshire. It was a short hop off the M40 yet not a town or main road anywhere nearby. "Far enough for you?"

"I say! This is the best one yet. Your Paul's a great asset. He's organised all this. It's like having my own personal virtual butler."

"Talking of which." A porter arrived by the driver's side and offered to carry their luggage.

They stood in the plush reception, full of low-slung leather sofas and coffee tables, with people milling about, sipping champagne and wine.

Hugo's stomach felt like a bowling ball, gurgling loudly at the same time.

A group of white-haired women selected dainty sweet things from a three-tiered silver plate between mouthfuls of champagne. A man in a light-brown safari-type suit and a woman in a skirted safari suit drank wine while leafing through the leather-bound hotel information folder.

Danny gave the names of Mr. Smith and Mr. Jones, as arranged, leaning on the reception desk.

Hugo looked at the safari-suited couple. Definitely not husband and wife—too much public touching without consciousness. Anyone their age wouldn't still be in the first flushes of youthful romance. He'd been looking forward to this weekend for weeks.

Ever since he'd suggested it, he'd been counting down the days. And Isabella had seemed so pleased when he confirmed he was going away. It had all been so easy, yet again, to keep this part of his life separate from the other part of his life.

He wondered how long he really could carry on with this particular *carry-on*. Did he want to make a go of it with Danny, or was he going to always keep this side of himself hidden for affairs like this?

It had been so much more than just sex, once he'd got to know Danny. They talked and laughed together like a proper couple. Of course, the sex was wonderful. Every time they did it, he couldn't quite believe how much he enjoyed it and how it contrasted with his soft, damp squib of a performance whenever he felt obliged to perform for *her*.

Yet even now, standing at a hotel reception, checking into a double room with another man, he couldn't quite see himself as *one of those people*. He still couldn't imagine introducing a man to his parents as his partner, like he had Isabella years before. He knew it would never be well received. After all, his parents were from another century, from another upbringing, from the country estate stock from which he tried to distance himself. He also knew even if he were to be one of those people and to live the life— *openly! brazenly! unashamedly!* Mummy would call it—it certainly wouldn't be Danny with whom he'd share it. Their 'relationship' was built on exchanges of paperwork and the detailed emails he sent to Paul about what he wanted each and every time he saw Danny.

For now, he was able to push those thoughts deep down, away from his consciousness, and enjoy the smile as Danny ushered him first after the porter as they all walked towards the room that was theirs for the whole weekend. He could feel himself stiffen at the mere thought of being in that room with Danny and his inexhaustible sexual appetite, endless creativity and imagination and gymnastic sexual skills.

Danny tipped the porter and closed the door behind them. His grin said all Hugo needed to know. "What shall we do?"

Hugo looked around the room, picking up the phone, the notepaper, the expensive-looking crockery with the tea and coffee making facilities, slowly walking around, inspecting their den for the weekend. He shrugged and smiled. "Don't mind."

Danny walked to him in the corner and kissed him, hard, on the lips with his mouth open. He pushed against Hugo, closer and closer, pulling at Hugo's clothes until both of them were naked and having sex like dogs, Hugo kneeling on all fours, Danny kneeling behind him, thrusting away energetically on the four-poster bed.

Afterwards, Danny ordered champagne and strawberries from room service, and Hugo cuddled up against him, playing with his nipples. "Must we leave this perfection tomorrow? Must we really go back out there?" He pointed to the closed, black-velvet, floor-to-ceiling curtains.

"We've only just got here, and you're already thinking about leaving. Why? Can't you just enjoy now and worry about later... well, later?"

"Problem is, the more I have this, the more I notice how unlike this my real life is. It makes going back to her and the big empty house that much harder each time."

Danny smiled and bit into a strawberry, allowing the juice to drip down his chin before licking it with his long, dexterous tongue.

"Don't you find it hard to separate this from your home life?" Hugo asked. "Paul's your boyfriend as well as your manager, isn't he?"

"He is, yes."

"What does he think about you having sex with all these men? Doesn't he get jealous?"

"*All these men*—what do you think I am? Some cheap whore plying my wares from a window in Amsterdam? I have a small and select client base. He's only ever known me doing this work. And that's how I see it—work."

"Oh, so I'm just another job to get done in the day. Another chore to endure before going home. Thanks so much." Hugo pouted and sat up a few feet from Danny.

Danny leant forward, but Hugo shrugged away. Danny sidled closer, whispering softly to him, all his skills working overtime. "That didn't come out right. This is why, normally, I don't talk about other clients. I'm here, and when I'm not with them, I don't exist as far as they are concerned. One of my little rules."

"Why break it with me?"

"Because you asked. None of the others asked. They don't want to talk about it. You asked, so I'm talking about it. Which now, I realise, was wrong. I'm sorry. It's a rule for a reason." He kissed Hugo's shoulder, working his way up his neck, lingering on his ear, licking inside, then returning to Hugo's neck, where he nibbled ever so gently, gradually biting harder and harder.

Hugo knew he'd opened a box he shouldn't have opened. He knew that by straying from the instructions in the email, he'd caught Danny unawares.

Danny pulled back from kissing and said quietly, putting his hands up in a defensive gesture, "OK, cards on the table. This is work, and at home it's home. Doesn't mean I don't enjoy my work, enjoy being with my clients. If I really didn't enjoy it, I wouldn't do it. This way, I'm working and doing something I love. If I wasn't in this line of work, I'd be in an open relationship because I am highly sexed. Paul knows this. He knows he would never be enough to satisfy me."

127

Hugo's eyes sparkled, and he moved closer to Danny. "I bet I could."

"Do you really?" Danny kissed Hugo.

"I'd give it a bloody good go."

They had sex one more time that afternoon before they went to the hotel's spa, where they spent the early evening having a range of treatments side by side. Hugo particularly enjoyed the massage, as his masseur was a large, wide, blond Swedish man. He enjoyed the moment, yet afterwards, he wasn't quite clear if that did make him *one of those people* or whether he was a straight man who happened to prefer particular activities in bed which his wife could not perform.

Over a candlelit dinner that evening, they talked about plans to walk along the footpaths nearby. Hugo had enthusiastically read the brochure in reception when they'd arrived. "Or we could go antiquing. I hear there's a marvellous selection of shops open on Sunday, just a short drive from here. Do you like antiquing?"

Danny smiled and nodded and asked the waiter to bring over the wine list.

Hugo stared into Danny's eyes, leaning on his elbows across the table. "Do you know, I don't think I've ever felt happier in my whole life."

"I aim to please."

"I...I...I love you."

Danny continued to stare at Hugo. "That's very kind of you, but I think you'll find you're—" he leant forward, whispering "—in love with my cock, not me!"

Chapter 21

As Charlie served his and Neil's dinner, Neil left the room to take a call. It was Paul.

"Hello, Mr. Bingham. How are you? I'm doing a customer satisfaction survey. How satisfied would you rate your last session?"

"Can you get to the point? I'm just about to eat. This isn't a good time. What do you want? I've settled my account. I don't wish to speak to you until I am ready to rebook."

"At home with your wife, are you?"

"Wife? I don't have a wife?"

"Ahh, you're one of those, are you? I see. Is he the little homemaker while you gallivant all over the country doing your own thing? Always the obedient husband to return to at the end of the week?"

"What do you want?"

"I thought you'd be interested to know I have some pictures of you and Danny, and I wondered if you'd like to see them?"

"How have you got those? You could be making it up. I don't believe you."

Charlie's voice from the kitchen carried through to the hallway where Neil stood on the phone. "I'm dishing up now."

"Look, can you get to the point? I want to go."

"I'll email you a photo from the selection we have in our possession. If you'd like us not to send any more to your home

129

address, for the attention of a Mr. Charlie Frost, you should call me back as soon as possible to discuss terms."

"Blackmail is a crime carrying a prison term of fourteen years. Goodbye!" Neil put down the phone and dismissed the nasty little man. He'd never book that particular escort again. Surely the whole point of these agencies was their discretion and confidence, and that call gave him very little confidence in their discretion.

Over dinner, Charlie asked who Neil had been talking to.

"Oh, nobody. Work, very boring. This is marvellous. I'm so lucky to have you. What is it?"

"Chicken chasseur. It was very simple to make. Nothing special, really." Charlie smiled and took another forkful.

"Well, it's delicious. I don't know what I'd do without you. What have you done with this sauce? It's perfect!"

"Red wine and some chicken stock. Nothing out of the ordinary. I cooked it all slowly for a couple of hours, that's why the chicken falls off the bone."

"It really is delicious." Neil proposed a toast to them, and as they began to talk about holidays they could go on with Judy, he felt a buzzing in his pocket. As soon as he could without rousing suspicion, he made his excuses and left the table. Checking his phone, he saw a picture of himself, sitting on a hotel room chair, his eyes shut and his hands above his head, while Danny knelt on the floor and gave him a blow job. There was no blurry outline, nothing covering part of the frame; it was a perfectly set up shot.

Set-up. That's the best way to describe it.

He stared at his closed eyes and remembered Danny suggesting he do that, and how he'd obeyed easily. As there had been some activity, he'd assumed Danny was getting undressed, but it was obvious he'd been setting up the camera like an expert spy. Maybe that was a one-off. Who knew if there were more? He'd have to deal with it later. He needed to get back to Charlie.

His phone buzzed again, and another picture appeared. This time, it showed Neil with a rolled-up ten-pound note up his nose, halfway through sniffing a fat line of white powder. His face was clearly visible with Danny's hand partly in shot. *The crafty cunt.* Danny had offered it, saying it was all part of the service— "Something to spice things up, make us last longer." And Neil had agreed, greedily snorting the free coke all night, thinking how life didn't get much better than that. What was it they said? No such thing as a free lunch—or a free snort. He couldn't possibly take that photo to the police as evidence of blackmail. He might as well hand himself in now and close up his business. *Fucking smart phones.* It had all been so much more innocent in the nineties when no one had a camera in their pocket at all times.

As he tried to work out what to do, a text came through: *Sex, drugs, shame you couldn't fit in some rock and roll too... maybe next time.*

Charlie smiled as Neil entered the room. "Finished?" He looked at Neil's nearly empty plate.

"Yes. I can't eat any more." Neil's stomach churned as he thought about the picture. "Let's talk again about holidays this year. I'm sure if we put our heads together, we can come up with some ideas. I can block out some weeks where I won't take work, make sure we get a good break together. As I said, I'm busy at the moment, but I will have some gaps later in the year. It's always the same. January and February are usually quiet, but April it picks up when people get their budgets, and they're always eager to start spending it. What's going on with you? What of the baking business, the veg boxes?"

"They're going well. Nothing much to report really. I've a few more farmers' markets lined up. I'm having to juggle it, with being an unofficial mentor for someone." He pursed his lips. "Dessert?

It's gooseberry fool, from our own garden. Well, the cream isn't, but the gooseberries are."

Neil nodded. "Yes, please. Who are you mentoring? Anyone I'd know?"

"It's a bit embarrassing, actually. I feel guilty for not telling you. I mean, it's not as if anything's happened. Of course, it never would, but it's one of those situations where I've not felt quite comfortable, not quite clear it's above board."

"Who is it?"

"Aaron."

"Camilla's Aaron?"

"The very one." Charlie blushed, then went for the cream and gooseberry compote, lingering with his head in the fridge, willing the redness to subside.

"Does Camilla know?"

Charlie set out the bowls, cream and gooseberry mix on the work surface, his back to Neil. "Of course! It's not that clandestine. She suggested he speak to me, or they did together, I think. Anyway, he's been coming round. He's at a bit of a loose end, it seems. Dropped out of uni and doesn't want to have anything to do with the sunglasses business, which, by all accounts, does sound deathly boring. Wants to do something a bit more..." He looked around the room at the pile of veg boxes in the corner and the stack of recipe books on the shelf. "Crafty, using his hands."

"And that's where you come in?"

"Exactly."

Charlie whisked the cream until it was thick, then folded it in with the gooseberry, finishing it with a little dusting of icing sugar. "To take away some of the sharpness." He put them on the table. "Dessert is served. Tuck in."

Neil noticed the churning feeling in his stomach return, only this time harder. What was going on with Aaron, and why was this the first he'd heard of it? He remembered the picture on his phone; he had far from the moral high ground. But Aaron was a boy, hardly a man at all. And why did Charlie want to tell him this now? Neil took a small spoonful of dessert and wedged it in his mouth, willing it to go down as he chewed and played with it, a smile masked on his face.

Charlie wolfed back his dessert, smiling while he told Neil about the afternoon when Aaron had asked to have a bath at theirs.

Neil listened and asked Charlie to describe what Aaron had looked like, standing in the kitchen, wrapped in only a towel. He noticed himself stiffen. Maybe Aaron wasn't a boy. Nineteen is really a man, after all. "And then what? He didn't come on to you, did he?"

"He said he needed to get clean, and he'd be in the bathroom. I think he's confused, doesn't know what he wants. Why else would he ask me all those questions about coming out and my relationship with you? I left him to it, didn't go into the bathroom. He went upstairs, and next thing he's back here, dressed and with damp hair. I had to get on with my baking—he'd made me very behind from all the talking." Charlie spooned another mouthful in.

"I wouldn't mind giving him a helping hand to get clean." Neil's eyes twinkled, and he took Charlie's hand across the table, stroking it gently. "Poor lad. I think you're right. He sounds confused. Why doesn't he just go to that gay pub off the Kings Road? Or better still, go to Soho or Vauxhall, check out the bars there. Surely he'd meet someone then. Or the internet. I hear there are all sorts of phone apps now."

"Yes, I hear that too."

Neil forced down the last mouthful and stood behind Charlie's chair. He kissed Charlie's head and massaged his shoulders.

"So a teenager's flirting a bit because he's confused and you're helping him get unconfused. No big deal."

"I suppose not." Charlie looked up to meet Neil's kiss. "Don't know why I didn't tell you before. It's not like anything's happened."

"And is he interested in what you tell him about your work, how you changed, what he could do—all that?"

"Oh, yes. Very much so. Since that time with the bath, it's been all about the cooking and hairdressing and that side of things."

"No more armpits being flashed in the kitchen?"

Charlie looked Neil straight in the eye. "None." He reached behind himself on the chair and squeezed the bulge in Neil's trousers.

"Leave this, we'll do it afterwards." Neil pushed into Charlie's hand and leant forward to kiss him.

The chair clattered to the floor as they ran to their bedroom and rolled about on the bed. Neil made love to Charlie in exactly the way he loved it, slow, sensual, long strokes, while staring into his eyes and bending to kiss his mouth. Neil loved to watch the pleasure build on Charlie's face as they locked in that position, Charlie on his back, his legs held up by his head as Neil knelt over him, his strokes matching him pulling Charlie, stopping to lean forward and kiss Charlie before building and building to the ultimate. They tried to match their rhythm, nodding to each other to speed up or slow down, both ending at the same time in a crescendo. Neil collapsed, resting his head on Charlie's sweaty, sticky stomach as they held each other, waiting for their breathing to return to normal.

Afterwards, Neil kissed Charlie and handed him a glass of water, then went to the bathroom to shower. As he waited for the temperature to be just right, he absent-mindedly checked his email on his phone. Another picture from that nasty little cunt

Paul. He opened it and saw a photo of him and Danny fucking on a hotel bed, with 'Charlie Frost' and their home address at the top of the email and a message saying there was more to come. This would kill Charlie. He couldn't allow his mistake to mess up what they had. After all, it was only sex. It was just fucking. It was nothing like what he and Charlie had, making love to each other.

Neil locked the bathroom door quietly, turned the shower up and angled the nozzle to the glass screen so it made as much noise as possible, then called Paul to discuss terms.

"Ahh, it's so lovely to hear from you so soon. To what do I owe this pleasure?"

"Cut the crap. How much, and I want all the pictures on a USB stick."

They discussed terms, Paul first naming a price he didn't think Neil would match, but he bit immediately.

"One-off or regular?" Neil spat. Whatever it was, he could find it, and it would be worth the money to keep this away from their home. He thought of Charlie lying exhausted, smelling of that slightly musky but sexy scent only he exuded, and he knew he had to do whatever he could to keep this from him.

"Let's see how we get on with one payment, and we'll take it from there, shall we?" Paul said.

They discussed how the money would be transferred and when, and Neil thought they'd agreed this would be a one-off payment to end this transaction.

"I want the pictures, all of them. I don't want any of the files to be left."

"I'm sure you don't. Tomorrow midday, if the money's not in the account, I will start printing the pictures. Isn't it amazing the quality of home printing nowadays?" He put the phone down.

Neil stared at the picture on his phone, deleted it, then jumped in the shower.

***

Charlie turned over in bed. He had heard voices coming from the bathroom. That wasn't like Neil at all. He normally just went to the next room for any work calls. He didn't like taking his phone into the bathroom because he was worried about condensation getting inside and damaging it. And he said the noise of the water was distracting. If ever Charlie answered the phone from the bathroom, Neil made him call back afterwards. Every time. He brushed that thought away and revelled in the memory of their love-making and the way his whole body, inside and out, ached and remembered the pleasure it had felt not ten minutes before.

Chapter 22

ISABELLA LOOKED AROUND the large, wood-panelled boardroom. The long table was now empty. She was pleased with her performance; the board papers had done their job, and her presentation had shown them where she was going to take the business, with their support. She reminded herself it was her and Fred's business but that she needed the board's approval for certain decisions. It had all been part of the checks and balances the old board had built into the sale contract when she and Fred had bought it years ago. It kept them on their toes and meant she couldn't become too power-hungry and would run it like a small family business but with much higher stakes. She enjoyed the politics and factions that appeared in the boardroom, and now, in her fifth year on the board, she relished the challenge it provided.

She scrolled through the list of men in that part of her phone's address book, her thumb hovering over one particular name. She'd give him one last chance, and if he didn't come back to her, she would give up. After all, a woman had standards and couldn't be seen to be running around like a lovesick teenager.

She sent a short text to Danny Traviati asking if he wanted to meet.

He called her immediately, apologising profusely for not managing to see her before. "I've been very busy. But you now have my undivided attention."

She giggled coquettishly and chided herself for it. This wasn't her. This wasn't the woman she was, so why did she behave like this where Danny was concerned? She could hear his smile, feel his charm oozing from the phone. It was so easy to fall into that with him, wasn't it?

***

Camilla and Charlie walked Judy around Battersea Park. Camilla had called saying she was in a terrible fix, and Charlie knew he needed to leave the house, having been cooped up with two days of solid baking for a cake sale later that week.

Camilla had explained how she now had no money from Fred and all the 'significantly reduced, mind you' money went straight to the children.

Charlie threw a stick, which Judy ran after to collect. He assembled the words carefully in his mind before saying them, knowing with one slip he'd both lose her attention and come across as a bit of a bastard. "I do think you've had it very good, up to now. You should look at this as an opportunity to build a new life and to create something for yourself."

"Cut out all that new-age mumbo jumbo. What should I do? You're always so practical. Tell me."

"It's not mumbo jumbo. And you have to admit, you've been pretty cushy so far."

"It was all I knew. We agreed it, when the divorce came through, and ever it has been thus. I didn't think anything else about it. It's all because of that awful orange, blonde woman, with her bloody dogs, her bloody nails and her bloody long blonde hair."

"Nothing wrong with dogs." Charlie threw the little ball again, and Judy ran off to fetch it.

"Oh, sorry, of course. Honestly, if you'd ever seen her..."

"Relying on your ex-husband for money forever is not right. You need something for you. What will you do when they leave home? Then where will you be?"

"Chelsea, still, I hope. I hadn't thought about that. I just sort of assumed they'd always be there, popping in and out, dropping in on Mummy, bringing boyfriends and girlfriends to meet me."

"Since when did you live in a Richard Curtis film? Look, Aaron went to uni, and Tamara will move out eventually. If she gets a boyfriend, they're not going to want to live with 'Mummy' forever, are they?" Bless her, but she really was pretty clueless sometimes.

"It honestly hadn't occurred to me, not one jot. What can I do? What is to become of me?"

"How much do you need every month to keep the house running as it is with a few cutbacks?"

"What do you mean?"

"You can't get catered food from Harrods every week. It's not sustainable. This isn't Knightsbridge, you know, and Harrods is not your local corner shop." He paused, wanting to test something. "How much is a pint of milk and a loaf of bread?"

"Ooh, well, it could vary enormously, of course. Depends on where you buy it. I mean to say, it might be as much as...or it could be as inexpensive as..."

"You have no idea, do you?" They had reached the peace pagoda and sat on a bench overlooking the Thames. It was worse than Charlie had feared.

"Twenty pence and four pounds. There. I've had a go. How wrong am I? Come on, hit me with it." She closed her eyes in anticipation.

Quite a lot worse. "Not quite. A pint of milk is about sixty pence, and a loaf of bread is a pound or so. I feel like one of those civil servants having to prepare the prime minister for general cultural knowledge. Could you name a character from any one of the main soaps?"

She shook her head. "I'm terrible, aren't I? I honestly don't know what's happened to me."

"You've lived in a little Chelsea bubble all this time. Now it's burst, it's time to live in the real world, and I'm here to help you."

"But I don't want to live in the real world. I like living in my little bubble. I like just calling for food and it all magically arrives, and not having to worry about how much things like…milk…and eggs or bread cost."

"Have you ever bought eggs or flour?" He was pretty sure of the answer.

"Why would I want them? Scrambled eggs are repulsive, and I can't do boiled eggs. They always end up grey and powdery. Hideous little things."

"So you literally can't even boil an egg?" He shook his head, remembering the boiled-dry kettle on her Aga the first time he'd been there years ago.

She laughed nervously. "No, it seems I cannot." She adjusted her white Alice band and folded her hands in her lap.

They talked about how to budget and what skills Camilla had that she could build on. She had an awful lot of experience in charities and committees, organisational, fundraising and bookkeeping skills. Every time she explained what she'd done for one of her events or committees, Charlie named the skill it represented, and they agreed to work on her CV later that week, so she could get herself *out there*.

Camilla folded her arms. "Out there. It sounds so frightening, doesn't it?"

"There's a whole world, and you've not experienced it yet." He was on a bit of a roll now, gathering a head of steam.

"It's easy for you to say. You've still got Neil's money pouring in every month."

That stung, but she was vulnerable, so he cut her some slack. "I do my fair share. Besides, if you want to help Aaron with what he does with his life, you'll need to take a bit of an interest in his choices."

She bit her lip, then turned to face him. "Yes, I was wondering that. He said he's been seeing you an awful lot about things, and you've been such a great chum to him."

"Not really." Charlie stroked Judy, who sat at his feet, then gave her a dog treat. "He's not the one we're talking about here. This is about you. You as a person separate from being their mother or someone's wife—"

"Ex-wife."

"Yes. You, doing things for yourself." *The Camilla Project.*

"Quite." She turned away and looked across the park. "I'm sure there's something I can do. Out there. I mean, quite honestly, it's only food, utilities and clothes I need money for. How much can the odd Alice band from Whistles cost? It can't be that hard, can it?"

"Not with a little practice. I've always wanted to speak to you about your penchant for Alice bands." He put his hand on hers. "I'm sorry to break this to you, but it isn't 1985 any longer. You really do have to bring your wardrobe up to date. It's for your own good."

She nodded slowly, adjusting the Alice band again, smoothing along its length with her fingers. "Part of the bubble, I suspect."

"I expect." They sat in companionable silence for a few moments as Charlie tried to assemble his thoughts clearly. This would be the first time he'd said out loud his concerns, and that somehow would make it real rather than something in his head. "Can I ask you something? You're more experienced than me. Is that OK?"

"Golly, is there anything I'm more experienced than you at? You're not thinking of having children, are you? Honestly, the first few years until they're a toddler are the most awful, crashing bore. Babies can't do much except shit and cry. I don't know why everyone is so fascinated by them. It's not until they can talk that they become of any real interest. That's marvellous. Then they seem to go back again, once they turn into teenagers. They stop talking, communicate only through grunts and banging things. That's pretty challenging too. But when they give you a hug, a hug you've not asked for, that makes it all worthwhile." She turned to face him again. "You're not thinking about adoption, are you? Or surrogacy? I would offer to help, but I think I've shut up shop in that department years ago." She tapped her stomach playfully.

"It's about affairs. You said Fred cheated on you, and that's why you divorced."

"I did say that, yes." Her eyes widened as she turned to him. "You're not having an affair, are you? I simply couldn't bear to keep it secret. I'm friends with both of you. I can't take sides, I'm afraid. It's between you two. I really don't want to know. I could never condone that sort of thing, I'm afraid. I know how terribly hurtful it is. Sorry." She stood, her hands clamped over her ears. "We must get back. Haven't you got some vegetables to peel or deliver or something.

He gently removed her hands from her ears. "It's not me, it's Neil. I think he's cheating on me."

Camilla sat again and listened without interruption while Charlie told her about the conversation on the mobile in the bathroom, finishing with, "So what should I do?"

"Oh, you poor darling. I am so sorry. And there was me going on about children. That's the least of your worries. I suppose that would be a blessing—that there are no children involved—if he is having an affair. It makes it all so much more complicated and beastly overall, I found."

Charlie smiled weakly and wiped a tear from his eye.

"Right, concentrate, Camilla, old girl. This is serious. I have been in exactly this situation before. I asked Fred after a month of late-night working and coming home smelling of perfume. I said, 'Are you having an affair?' And do you know what the little shit of a man said to me?" She paused as Charlie shook his head, allowing himself a little smile in anticipation of Camilla's story. "He looked me in the eyes and said, 'No, I am not having an affair.'"

"And was he?"

"What do you think? Of course he bloody well was. Lying little shit."

"How did you find out? What evidence did you have? You have to give evidence as a reason for divorce, don't you?"

"Yes, and you still do."

"How did you find out?" Charlie asked. "Do I have to become very sneaky?"

"Sneaky isn't the word for it. You have to become your own little Miss Marple, a Hercule Poirot in your own home. But it's for your own peace of mind and your own good. If there's nothing going on, he's nothing to hide, and you'll find nothing. Check his jacket pockets for receipts. Do you have a joint bank account?"

Charlie nodded, took out his phone and started typing.

"Am I boring you? Do you want me to stop?"

"I'm not texting. I'm writing a note on my phone. This is very helpful actually."

She laughed and punched him playfully on the arm. "Oh, darling, I am sorry. I didn't realise. Me and technology. You are sweet. Now, let me see..." She continued with a variety of techniques, ranging from mobile phone checking, noticing if he always took his phone everywhere with him or whether he left it out on display, if any normal behaviour had changed, like phone calls in the bathroom. Any strange smells or eau de toilettes, anything in his suitcase when he stayed away. "You pack for him when he goes away, don't you?"

"I iron his shirts and put them in."

"OK, have a root around, see if he's bringing presents or... I don't know, any sexual things a man alone in a hotel room wouldn't bring if he was going to be on his own." She looked at him, smiling. "I don't know. I'm not going into details. Use your imagination."

Charlie eagerly continued typing notes into his phone.

Chapter 23

HUGO AND ISABELLA were halfway through a dinner party. Hugo had felt it was their turn to host his parents, and he had invited Isabella's brother and sister-in-law too.

They'd had a relatively easy conversation about Hugo and Isabella's work, during which Hugo had avoided giving away any details about Reece Jones Instruments and how much he'd been there, since over the past few months, he'd seldom been there at all.

Isabella was happy to talk about her recent idea to use customer feedback at her and Fred's Lux Sunglasses company, which had interested Lord and Lady Reece Jones somewhat less.

Isabella refused wine on a number of occasions, which caused a raised eyebrow from Lady Reece Jones. "Anything the matter, Isabella? Anything we should know about?" She patted her stomach gently.

"No. I've a very busy day tomorrow, and I don't want my head fuzzy from wine. Best to stick to this." Isabella smiled, holding up a glass of sparkling water.

Later, she rushed from her main course to the bathroom and was heard by everyone being loudly and violently sick. She returned to the table, slowly sipping water and dabbing her mouth with a napkin.

"Are you sure you're all right, dear?" Lady Reece Jones enquired, more from a family interest than out of concern that her daughter-in-law was really OK.

"I think I've overdone it at the office. I'm doing some very long hours, aren't I?" She looked to Fred for support.

He nodded emphatically before explaining how great Isabella's ideas had been and how they were planning to take on new staff in the next financial year if the growth continued. "I'm trying to find something more permanent, a bit more interesting for Tamara." He noticed his parents-in-law's eyebrows furrowing. "My daughter from my first marriage to Camilla. And I have a son too—Aaron..." There he trailed off.

Hugo cleared the plates and noticed his wife wiping her mouth and cradling her stomach under the table. *It can't be, can it? It's not possible.* They'd not had any physical relations in...not just weeks but months, if not years. Unless he'd forgotten one time. Unlikely. He returned to the dining room, distributing glass bowls of lemon sorbet.

Lady Reece Jones stared at Isabella as she took tiny spoonfuls of her dessert.

There was a lull in conversation as everyone ate and found there wasn't much more they could discuss with the others, until Fred broke the silence with, "My ex, Camilla—I've managed to get my way out of a totally unfair maintenance agreement for the kids. Open-ended it was, see. And my lawyer said that's not fair, so I'm paying the kids some and her none. It's saving me a bloody fortune, isn't it, love?" He patted his wife's hand. She smiled at him around a mouthful of sorbet.

Isabella dabbed her forehead with the napkin. "Isn't that a bit harsh, Fred? Just cutting her out like that. The poor woman."

"She'd 'ad it for years—years longer than she should've done. She's had it cushy, and now she's got to live in the real world, like the rest of us. It was leaving me short at the end of each month. It weren't sustainable."

"Well, it all seems a bit much to me. Will she have to leave the house, where she and the children have lived? Are you making the mother of your children homeless?"

"It was very amicable, a staged retreat from the payments. Worked it out together, me and her did. She'll be fine. She always is. She's a resourceful woman. She'll sort it out."

Sharon smiled to herself. "So, Hugo, what sports and hunting or shooting have you been up to lately?"

He screwed up his face. "What do you mean?"

"Have you done any particularly manly things lately? Your family are into hunting and fishing, aren't they?"

Lord Reece Jones nodded and said, "Hear, hear."

"I thought you enjoyed it too. I keep wondering if Fred will get into it one day, but it's not really his thing, is it, love?"

Fred shook his head. "Prefer a bit of footie on telly, me."

"I've always thought of you as a real man's man." She stared at Hugo, smiling without blinking. "So those man's man's things— are they up your street? Or what else do you do to unwind after a busy day at work? You have been busy at work, haven't you? Only you didn't mention Reece Jones Instruments much, did you?"

Hugo stuttered a bit and played with his napkin. "Well, of course I've been keeping it all ticking along at RJI for Mummy and Daddy. They know this. After all, they've entrusted it to me to look after, so look after it I must." He smiled at his parents.

Lady Reece Jones leant forward and squeezed his cheek as if he were a little baby. "He's such a good boy, isn't he?"

"Thank you, Mummy." He turned to Sharon. "I'm not as into the country pursuits as Daddy, I'm afraid. And Reece Jones Instruments seems to have taken up an awful lot of time lately. I've not had much chance to squeeze in these…manly activities you talk of. It's been very much all work and no play, makes Hugo a dull boy." He smiled but continued to play with his napkin.

Isabella dabbed at her mouth. "I do think you may have confused my husband with another man." She stared at Sharon. "He's never really been into those sorts of things, not since I've known him anyway. Perhaps he was into them when he was a little boy?" She turned to her mother-in-law, who took it as a prompt to give a detailed account of the games Hugo had liked to play as a child and how once he'd grazed his knee playing hockey at school, after which he'd been forced to stand it out for the rest of the term, among other long detailed stories about her darling son.

Halfway through this account, Isabella left the table, retching into the napkin once again, then was loudly sick in the nearby toilet.

Soon afterwards, in the absence of conversation and the desserts having been cleared away, they all said their goodbyes and thanked Hugo and Isabella for 'such a wonderful evening' even though not one of them meant a single word of it.

Fred asked Isabella if she'd be OK for work the next day. She waved him away, nodding that of course she'd be OK.

***

Once in their car, Fred said to Sharon, "See, I told you she'd be all right for work. Don't know what you're on about."

"She's pregnant. That woman is up the duff. No two ways about it, darlin'."

"She'd have told me. I'm her brother. Wouldn't she have told Hugo, surely? He looked surprised when she refused wine, didn't he?"

"Your dozy wet heap of a brother-in-law don't know about it either. And I'll tell you for why. Because he's had nothink to do with it. Nothink at all." She folded her arms and pursed her lips, checking her make-up in the vanity mirror.

"What is that supposed to mean?" He looked at Sharon.

"Get going, and I'll explain it all to you. I've got a little theory, and I think you're gonna like it."

Fred pushed the car into drive, and they glided the few miles back to Wanstead through country lanes and the back end of Leytonstone, where Sharon locked the doors at traffic lights, all the while explaining to her husband, enjoying every lasciviously gossipy moment about her theory of Hugo being gay. She enjoyed it as much as she'd enjoyed her last mani-pedi and facial. She was careful not to share the actual news Paul had told her. Instead, she skirted around the issue, saying how Hugo had to be gay. It was the only thing that made sense when they thought about it.

Chapter 24

Aaron met Tamara at her college refectory to get away from the house and his mother's endless prying on where he was, who he was seeing, and why he was spending time at their neighbours' house, alone with Charlie. Aaron wasn't sure of the answers to the last set of questions, so he hadn't given any. If he couldn't explain it to himself, he sure-as-damn-it wasn't going to tell his mother anything. He'd felt it was wiser to meet his sister here, away from Charlie and his mother.

With a tray of food for them both, Tamara joined Aaron at the table he'd saved for them. "What's this about, that we couldn't say it at home?"

"I'm not doing the sunglasses thing with Dad. I'm going to do something at college instead."

"Did you, like, talk to somebody here this morning?"

"Yep. Very helpful. Some of the courses are interesting—the sort of thing I want to do. Others, not so much. But I know it's something in this area, and I'm definitely not going back to uni again. That's really gonna piss Dad off too, I suppose."

"You don't know until you tell him. I think he's different. He's not like I thought he'd be. Things change. Look at what he did with the money to Mum."

"Yeah, that was hilarious. *Not.* Poor Mum. I thought she was going to cry when she told us."

"But she's all right now. She's like, totally sorted it, and we're still in the same place."

"For now." Aaron took a bite of the sandwich on the tray.

"What's that supposed to mean?"

"Dunno. I don't think it's that simple. Anyway, I want to talk about me—what I'm gonna do, or not do."

"Tell him. Just come out with it and tell him, straight up, you're not working for Lux Sunglasses, you're doing something else, and that's it. He'll get used to it. He has to. Mum's been supportive, hasn't she?"

He nodded.

"She's been, like, OK with Charlie helping you, hasn't he?"

He shrugged.

"Look, while it's just, like, us, what *is* all that about, you suddenly spending time round his? Is there something going on?" Tamara stared hard at him.

"What like?"

"I don't know. Do you, you know, *like* him that way?"

"What way?" Another bite of the sandwich.

"You know exactly what way. Fancy him. Honestly, I don't give a shit if you do. I've got loads of gay friends at college. It's, like, quite *in*, actually. There was a bit of competition to get the best gay best friend out of the guys in the class who'd come out. So are you?"

"What?"

"Are you, like, my gay brother?"

"I dunno." He avoided her eyes.

"You so are! And that's a whole different thing to tell Dad. Once he knows that, he won't give a shit either way about the college stuff."

"I dunno. It's difficult. It's complicated, confusing." Aaron paused, trying to assemble his thoughts and turning the rest of the sandwich over in his hands, as if it held the key to his problem. He looked up at his sister. "It's complicated."

Chapter 25
Early Spring 2014

ISABELLA SAT IN a three-star Michelin restaurant in central London. She knew she was pregnant, almost twelve weeks, and she knew it was Danny's, but she couldn't tell him, or their quiet little affair would become something very open and real, in the form of a child. *Have the affair, just don't get caught out,* one of her girlfriends had told her years ago, when she was thinking about dating a married lecturer at university. She needed to consider her options before telling Hugo, but she wouldn't tell Danny; it was nothing to do with him. Her body, her baby, she'd tell whomever she wanted.

Danny held her chair for her and then pushed it under the table as she sat. He ordered a bottle of wine.

"Sorry, none for me, just water."

"Why?"

She waved her hand in front of her face. "Nothing serious. I've felt a bit sick the last couple of days. Had to take a couple of days off work, which is so not me, but I'm feeling better now." Should she tell him? Maybe she could and claim she didn't know which man she'd slipped up with.

"It's not…? Is it?" He looked at her stomach.

She nodded slowly.

"Whose is it?"

"That's the thing. I'm not a hundred percent sure. Well, I'm sure it's not *his* because we haven't had sex in years, but I'm not sure who else's it could be. It may be yours, but probably not." That was enough to see what his reaction was without telling him the truth. She was still keeping to at least part of her original plan.

Danny's eyes widened. "And there was me, thinking we were exclusive." He smiled and took her hand, stroking gently with his thumb.

"I never thought that for one moment. Just a bit of fun. No strings attached. That's what we were always to be." But she had cooled it with the other men lately. Since she'd started seeing Danny, the other men had paled to nothing in comparison. She'd been through her diary for the little secret initials she used to signify the different men she'd seen, and during the last window when she could have got pregnant, she'd only seen Danny. But she didn't want to tell him that, not yet. She wanted to consider her options, work out if she did want him to know the baby was his.

He leant back, still stroking her hand. "You look beautiful tonight. The dress, the necklace, your hair—you're a very well put together woman."

She smiled bashfully. She could get used to this. She *had* got used to this. It was such an antidote to her marriage.

"But you don't look your normal happy self," Danny added. "Tell me all about it. I really want to listen and help."

She'd carefully kept the details of her life away from her interludes with other men, Danny included, but his smile seemed so genuine, encouraging her to share. So she explained how she and Hugo were obliged to present the perfect image of the perfect power couple to the outside world when really they lived separate lives.

"I love my job. I'm good at it. But it's not enough. I return home every night to his back facing me on his side of the bed. I thought I could sate my hunger for physical contact with other men, but after a while, that stopped working too. They were all only into one thing, and once they had the physical aspect, that was it. Men are like burst balloons once they've come, I've found." She laughed quietly at her description, and Danny joined in.

"Of course," he said, "I've never met your husband. You've been very careful not to tell me his name, but I agree. He does sound like he's not giving you all you deserve and need *as a woman*. But that's what I'm here for. For you to forget the daily issues and worries and escape them into our own world."

She talked late into the night about the pressure from her parents-in-law to provide a grandson. She talked about the pressure she felt from her job, how she had to deliver what was required of her and couldn't just call in and say she didn't feel up to it. She told him about her niece and nephew and how, although they had caused some issues with his ex-wife, she could see how proud of them her brother was, how much he got from them, and how she wished she could have some of that. She talked about her biological clock ticking and not knowing what to do with it, as she was nearly thirty and may not have much more time to have children, not naturally at any rate.

Danny listened, pouring sparkling water for her at regular intervals, holding her hand and staring into her eyes. He made her feel she was the only other person in the room and his only consideration that night was to listen to her woes.

When the waiter asked if they would like anything else, Danny asked for the bill, and Isabella noticed they were among the last people left in the bar.

"Oh, I am sorry. I've talked all night. I'm so silly."

Danny paid and said there was still another part of the evening she was very welcome to avail herself of. "A hotel room has been booked very near here. Or if you're exhausted, I can put you in a taxi bound for home."

She saw his smile and felt her body go limp with tiredness. She remembered the last time they'd been together, how he'd made love to her and insisted she lie back and enjoy it without pressure. It was enough to convince her she was only going to the hotel to rest her head.

In the hotel room she lay on the bed, and Danny undressed her gently. He made love to her with his mouth, soft kisses and licks from her head to her toes, then moving upwards again to linger *there* with his mouth, blowing gentle puffs of air, lapping away at her with his expert tongue until she was arching her back and moaning in pleasure. Then, when she called out for him to do it, he was inside her, deeply thrusting, and she felt pleasure coursing through her whole body in waves, building then soaring, building and soaring.

He made her come three times that night before finally allowing himself to finish in one long, last thrust and collapsing on top of her, both of them panting and sweating together.

**

She woke to the sound of him in the shower and checked her watch. It was almost one in the morning. She must get home; Hugo would want to know where she was. She couldn't push her luck too far, or he would find out what she'd been doing all these years with all these other men.

Danny emerged from the bathroom, wrapped in a small towel. "Are you staying or going? I think I could go again. It's been long enough." He smiled and brushed his hand over the bulge behind the towel.

"I've got to go," she said. "Now." She quickly showered, washing off the smell and feeling of his body and their sex. Yet it seemed to linger on her in the taxi on her way home, as she remembered the feeling of him, the tiny licks and pokes of his tongue and fingers, teasing her until she was begging for more, and the delicious feeling of him coming inside her.

Chapter 26

A FEW DAYS LATER, Hugo called his wife's secretary to check where she was that afternoon. That familiar itch needed scratching, and he had a few ideas where he could spend the afternoon. The possibility of seeing Danny was always there. He was within his quota for the month still. But first, he needed to ensure he had enough time without bloody Isabella being around, so he could make the necessary arrangements.

"Mr. Jones, I'm looking at her calendar at the moment," her secretary said, "and the appointment for this afternoon is marked private."

"Can't you see it? You do manage my wife's diary, don't you?"

"Yes, but she made this appointment."

"No clues to what it might be?"

"All it's showing is private, I'm afraid."

"Oh, well. Thank you." He put down the phone. Maybe it was something to do with the awful stomach troubles she'd been having, no doubt due to the stress of the long hours she'd been putting in at the office lately. Long hours that stood in stark contrast to the average fifteen-hour week he put in at his office. Reece Jones Instruments was lucky if he did two or three hours a day, five days a week, these days. It had become embarrassing, as Isabella left for her work first thing while Hugo was still lolling around in bed, half awake. And every night he'd be home, having arrived mid-afternoon, to greet Isabella when she walked through the door at seven or eight o'clock. There were only so many times

Hugo could say, "A quiet day again," when Isabella asked what he'd been up to, and he'd switched to telling her was bringing work home with him—"To work in peace and plough through it"—when in reality, the only ploughing through had been his and Danny's hotel exploits during those exquisite, illicit afternoons.

So there was no guarantee where she'd be, and he couldn't take the risk. It was quite short notice to book Danny, who was very much in demand and often booked well in advance, Paul had explained on a number of occasions. Plus, there wouldn't be time to send the email instructions as he liked. No, it was best he didn't see Danny this afternoon when it would be tinged with worry in case Isabella found out where he was.

Hugo spent the afternoon at home, browsing through other male escort sites, never quite finding anyone who measured up to Danny. From there, it had only been a hop, click and jump to the other websites Hugo often found himself inexplicably viewing and amply able to relieve the tension on his own. A short nap was followed by a little walk around the gardens to inspect the progress their gardener had made, as he quietly made a note of things he'd like the man to do next time he came. Hugo always so enjoyed talking to their gardener, a young man in his mid-twenties, who'd studied horticulture at the technical college nearby in Loughton. He was so keen to please Hugo and Isabella and was easy on the eye in his torn denim shorts and little white vests, which he often had to remove due to the heat. Hugo would make excuses to speak to him during the long days alone in the house. Nothing had ever come of it, of course. The gardener talked enthusiastically and fondly about his girlfriend and their new baby, but that didn't stop Hugo going back to his bed after their conversations and fantasising what *could* have happened.

The gardener's note completed, Hugo took a tour of the house, jotting down extra jobs for their 'woman who did' to pick up next time she was there. He enjoyed ticking off each room as he moved about their house, adding jobs to the list, knowing she would do as he'd asked the next time she read the note, which he left under a magnet on the fridge. Of course, he could speak to her, but really, it was so much easier if he just left her a note. She was so efficient and preferred it that way, avoiding any awkward face-to-face interactions.

Later that evening, exhausted from his little chores, Hugo played the violin for a while in the music room, ensuring the door was closed to the sound-insulated room. Mummy would have sat for hours, listening to him practise, praising him on how marvellous he sounded, but Isabella insisted he keep his musical expressions to himself, and he went along with it.

The front door banged. Hugo put his violin down.

***

Hugo greeted Isabella in the hallway. "Busy day, darling?" He kissed her cheek.

She automatically kissed him back, also on the cheek. "Board meeting."

"All day?"

"Yes. Why?"

He told her about the conversation with her secretary.

"Why would you do that, darling?" She put her bag by the coat stand, then removed her coat.

"I wanted to surprise you with something this afternoon."

"Oh? What was that going to be?" *Surprise me? He's never done anything like that before. I smell rubbish, with a sprinkling of lies.* She walked into the living room and perched on the sofa to rub her feet. Hugo followed her in.

"Oh, darling, it was to be so perfect. Afternoon tea at the Ritz together. I know how much you've always wanted to do that."

Have I? Maybe she had mentioned it once, but she couldn't remember. "Well, I was busy. We'll have to do it another time." Her body ached and longed for a bath full of hot water and bubbles instead of this tedious conversation with her usually tedious but suddenly and inexplicably attentive husband.

"I've had such a busy afternoon." He recounted at length the chores he'd done and added he was keen to know what she'd done at work that afternoon.

"I told you. I was at a board meeting. Hugo, I am absolutely fagged out. I simply want to flop in front of the TV."

"Yes, but, darling, that's not what your secretary said. She said you had a private appointment in—"

"Are we back on this private appointment business again? I keep some appointments private, and that is my business." She studied her husband, who stood with his hands clasped in front of his groin, his shirt hanging loosely on his thin frame. Her mind darted back to Danny's biceps pressing in on either side of her. He'd been on top of her for most of the afternoon.

Hugo blinked. "So, I'll ask you again, darling, what have you been up to?"

Fuck it. She'd made a massive, inexcusable mistake. *Stupid bloody secretary, she has no idea.* The first time she'd made an appointment in her diary—a quick swipe and click from her phone after a call with Danny—and now here she was, having this conversation with her husband. "What do you want me to say?"

Hugo smiled. "I want you to tell me the truth, darling."

That was when Isabella knew she couldn't continue with this marriage—couldn't continue with this life as it was. She'd had a good run of it, though. It had, no one could deny, been terrific fun. And she'd become complacent. She'd allowed her greed for the next afternoon of delight with Danny—a man who'd managed to knock all the others into touch—to get the better of her. Perhaps her subconscious had wanted her to get caught, and this was it, the opportunity to change things in her life, in her marriage.

She stared at Hugo, took a deep breath and said, "I spent the afternoon with a man who made me come three times. It's all the rage. It's called the six-oh-one diet. You have no sex for six days a week, none whatsoever, and then you have a mammoth session once a week."

"All that…*exercise*, yet you've put on weight?" He looked at her slightly expanded stomach. "How is that possible?"

She rubbed her belly. "Don't know." How much more of a hint did she have to give for her stupid husband to realise she was pregnant? She needed it out in the open, to have the truth spoken about, because she felt stuck, blocked in this situation. Having this conversation now would surely unblock this.

"Who is he?" Hugo asked.

"A man I met at a bar in London." She told him about how she'd met Danny, omitting his name from the story.

"How long's it been going on?"

"A few months. Off and on." And the other men, but she didn't think it was wise to mention them. Not yet, anyway.

"What am I meant to tell Mummy and Daddy? They'll think me awfully weak, such a cuckold." He held his face in his hands and began to sob quietly.

"Then don't tell them. We'll keep it between us two. I'm sure we can work things out." She paused, holding her breath, wishing with her whole being he would agree. It would make everything easier for both of them. Then, thinking she'd succeeded, she threw in, "Haven't you ever been tempted to stray, not even once?"

"I never look at women. Not since I've been with you." He wiped his face with his sleeve and left the room.

"Where are you going? We were having a conversation." And she thought she was doing jolly well persuading him to keep all this mess quiet.

He shouted from the hallway, "What's there to discuss? The conversation's over."

Exhausted, she stayed where she was a moment longer, but curiosity got the better of her. She went to the door and saw Hugo hunched over, talking on the phone and wiping his eyes and nose with his sleeves.

"But Mummy, I don't know what to do. She's literally just told me. I am all in a tizz. What should I do, Mummy?"

Straight to *Mummy*, without passing her, without collecting two hundred pounds, pulled back by some sort of umbilical whiplash. Isabella sighed and stormed past, up the stairs and into the bedroom. If there was any way of making this situation worse, that surely had done it, well and truly. Hugo and his bloody *mummy*. Isabella lay on the bed and closed her eyes.

Chapter 27

AFTER LADY REECE Jones told him to calm down and to not be in such a tizz, Hugo sat at the phone table at the base of the stairs and listened to his mother's advice.

"I knew there was something wrong, my darling. I could tell. There has to be a problem if you two healthy individuals have been married for five years and you've still not produced any offspring. It can't be anything to do with you—it's what I always say to your father. If there's a problem with the puppy, it's due to a problem with the bitch. And that's what you have here, a problem with the bitch."

"Oh, Mummy, please don't call Isabella a bitch. I can't bear it. She is still, after all, my wife." But she *had* put on some weight recently, and there was all that business with her being sick at dinner. She'd have said, wouldn't she? No, tackle one problem at a time. Best not to muddy the water with conjecture when she hadn't told him directly.

"Darling, I wasn't saying she was a bitch. It's a metaphor. You have a problem with children, and now she's confessed she's been with another man. It's simply this one isn't working out. You need to find yourself another b...wife and make sure that one works out. I always thought you'd married beneath you, darling. She's ever so *new money*, and I did say that at the time. It's all very well having your power suits and smart office to visit and play powerful business woman, but it's all a bit distasteful. You can see it in the way she wore her clothes and how ghastly her

163

brother is, with his Essex barrow-boy ways, flashing his money about. It's all a fluke, the new money. It's different from our sort of money. That's due to breeding, class, inheritance and lots and lots of time. How many generations of Smiths have been in their fortunate situation, financially?"

"Including Isabella and Fred?"

"Yes. Of course, darling. Go on."

"Two. It's just their children too." Hugo looked over his shoulder and was relieved to see Isabella had left the doorway. His mother had that curious effect on him, enabling him to forget all that surrounded him and concentrate on her voice alone.

"And what sort of a comparison is that with our family? Generations and generations of Reece Jones living in this wonderful estate, looking after the interests of the family business. Sunglasses are hardly an enduring industry, are they? Musical instruments—that's a timeless craft, a skill that's been passed through the ages."

Hugo began to cry once again.

"Darling, please do stop that. I have a marvellous idea. There are a few unmarried women scattered around the various committees and charities I work with, some of them daughters of friends of mine. Why don't you meet one of them? I could set it all up with a quick phone call. Would you like that, darling?"

Hugo nodded in silence.

"Darling, I asked you a question. A few short telephone calls, that's all. You wouldn't even need to cast a backwards glance. She would be gone. You must remove her from the house as soon as possible. It won't do for people to know what *she's* done and that she's still reaping the benefits of living in the family home. No, you must cast her out, start afresh. Would you like that, darling, if Mummy made a few enquiries for you?"

He felt like a deflated balloon. Quietly and slowly, he said, "Yes. That would be very helpful, Mummy." He put the phone down with a loud click and went up to the bedroom to tell his wife she had to move out. *Just for the moment, until things are sorted. Mummy thinks it's for the best.*

Isabella was already half-packed when he arrived. She threw a few more items into her suitcase, closed it and carried it downstairs to the front door, turning to wave at Hugo, who sat at the foot of the stairs, looking like a little boy left at boarding school for the first term, all alone.

Part 3
Spring 2014

Chapter 28

CHARLIE AND CAMILLA were busying themselves in her kitchen, the work surfaces covered with ingredients for a beef casserole. It was the second week of the informal cooking lessons Charlie had agreed to give Camilla so she didn't have to rely on catered food any longer...since she couldn't rely on it, as she didn't have the money.

Camilla closed the door on the middle oven of the Aga and looked at Charlie. "All that food from that cheap cut of meat. Are you quite sure it'll taste all right? Will the children eat it? They are terribly fussy, I'm afraid. I have spoilt them somewhat. It won't be chewy or fatty, will it? Or they won't eat it."

"It's going to cook for almost three hours. All the different flavours and the meat will gently mix to form a perfect, slow-cooked dish."

"Yes...about all the flavours. You're quite, quite sure it's meant to have those little fish—"

"Anchovies? You can have them on pizza too." Charlie smiled and started to clear up the kitchen.

"Yes, and the black, gluey stuff. Treacle, did you say? And all those little black pickled things. Nuts, I think you said they were."

"Walnuts and black treacle."

"Quite. Those flavours do actually go with the meat, don't they? It did seem like an awful lot of meat for not an awful lot of money. There was some of the white fat in it as well, which does worry me somewhat." Camilla bit her lip and grabbed the cloth Charlie held out to her.

As they cleared the kitchen together, Charlie explained the recipe was from a very well-known but sadly departed TV chef with decades of experience. Accordingly, it was a recipe Charlie made at least four or five times every winter, and everyone who tried it had only compliments to pay it.

With the cleaning done and a cafetière made, they sat at the table. "What's next on the cookery lessons list?" Camilla asked, pouring the coffee. "I can't feed them beef stew and dumplings and toad-in-the-hole forever."

"I think you'd find you would have two pretty happy teenagers. You could do beans on toast between times. Next time, I'm going to show you how to make a roast chicken dinner with all the trimmings, which will mean you're basically set for doing your own Christmas dinner with a turkey, as long as you jazz it up a bit, as Delia always says. And I'm doing cakes and puddings too. Do your lot like puddings?"

"Jam roly-poly, spotted dick, Sussex pond pudding, treacle sponge—all those are our favourites. The catering service does such a good selection. I worry mine will fall short."

"Trust me, homemade will not fall short on those."

"Harrods, darling, you do know that, don't you?" Camilla sipped her coffee.

"Even them."

They sat in companionable silence for a few moments, sipping their drinks and enjoying the satisfaction of a productive session in the kitchen. It was a new feeling for Camilla but one she was growing to enjoy.

She leant forward conspiratorially. "How's things on the home front?"

"The same. I don't know if I have something to worry about or if it's all in my head." Charlie tensed.

"Any more phone calls in the bathroom with the shower running?"

"Not that I've heard."

"Keeping his phone with him at all times, guarding it with his life?"

"Now you mention it, yes. Quite a lot of that."

Camilla put her hand on Charlie's arm. "Do you know his phone pass code?"

"I used to, but he's got one of those whizzy new ones that uses your thumbprint to unlock."

"Interesting. Very interesting."

"Is that suspicious, do you think?"

"Not on its own, it's not, but with the phone guarding, it may well mean something's going on. What else have you uncovered?"

"I went through some receipts in his suit pockets and suitcase, and it was all takeaways he'd picked up or room service from the hotels. Nothing interesting there."

"What does he say when you ask how his trip has been? You do still do that, don't you?"

"I do," Charlie said. "He's less committal about what happened. All very vague and broad. Talks about where he's been, not much more really."

"Darling, *are* you still suspicious? You don't have to continue with this palaver, you know. If you're satisfied it was nothing, you can simply stop."

"I know, but I can't shake this niggling feeling that I've let him do his own thing for so long with nothing from me that he really could be doing anything he wanted, and I would never know. And since that little seed of doubt was sowed, I can't get rid of it. I have to carry on until I find out one way or the other. Make sense?"

"Makes perfect sense. In that case have you tried…" Camilla went through a range of other tricks she'd picked up during her marriage to Fred after numerous denials on his part about his cheating, until she'd been forced to take it into her own hands and turn home-spun detective on him.

***

It wasn't long after that when Aaron arrived in the kitchen, and they had to stop talking about Neil.

"What's for dinner, Mum? I'm starving."

"You'll have to wait. It's beef stew and dumplings, but it won't be ready for another—" Camilla looked at Charlie then the clock. "—hour or so. Why don't you sit here and tell me what you've been up to?"

Aaron sat next to Charlie, opposite his mother.

"How did you get on at your sister's college?"

He screwed up his face and mumbled something no one could hear.

"What was that, darling? I'm afraid I don't speak surly teenager. You'll have to translate to English."

"Was all right. Some things they do are pretty cool. Others, I'm, like, not bothered." He shrugged. "Maybe I could work with Dad. Maybe it wouldn't be *so* bad. Depends what I'm doing, I suppose."

Camilla clapped. "Marvellous. Daddy will be pleased. I am so relieved."

Charlie put his hand on hers but turned to Aaron. "Whatever work you do, you're going to be working for forty years before you can get any sort of pension. Forty years of doing something every day, eight hours a day or more. Now, what makes you smile when you think of doing it? Is it sunglasses, working with your dad… or something else?"

Aaron stared out the window, but then his eyes lit up and he nodded. "Hair. That's interesting. That's what I want to do. I want to create things for people that make them smile when they leave."

"Bingo!" Charlie said. "That's what you need to look into in more depth. You can't do something for your dad. You've got to do something you want to do."

"But what about Dad? I've thought about this, and if it's so important to him, I'll do it. If it means I can spend time with him, then I suppose it would be OK. I could get used to it."

"You can't spend forty years doing something you could *get used to*. Trust me, I tried it before. You reach a wall after ten years. You see the endless days stretching out in front of you and realise you can't carry on doing it. That's what happened to me anyway."

"But what about Dad?"

Camilla said, "Half of it is him seeing you or doing stuff with you. As long as he knows you've got some sort of a plan, he'll come round to whatever it is. It's the lolling about he's not so keen on. If it's not work, then you can do other things together. You'll make time to see him. Imagine if you didn't live here and you came home and asked me to iron your clothes for you as a way of talking to me, a way of us having something in common."

He shrugged. "Sounds pretty sensible to me."

"But wouldn't it be much nicer if we were to have lunch together or go shopping for something you needed? That's proper time together, rather than me shouting at you from an ironing board. Isn't it?"

"I suppose so."

Charlie smiled at Camilla, then said to Aaron with a wink, "So if it's hair you're interested in—and it's always hairdressers who seem to have the worst hair—then I'd say you're at least halfway there."

Aaron grinned and pushed his hair from his eyes, then combed through the whole strawberry-blond mane with his fingers. "Whatever."

"That's what you should look into," Charlie repeated. "Talk to the students, talk to a hairdresser to see what it's really like."

Aaron combed his hair again, with his other hand, this time leaving his hands above his head so his belly button and its darker ginger-blond hair poked out above his jeans. "I'll do it tomorrow, OK?" He looked around the kitchen. "When's dinner ready?"

Charlie concentrated on not staring at Aaron's belly button. "I'll be round to check you've done it, and if you haven't, I'm going to nag you until you do. It's that or call your dad, and he'll have you talking about customer feedback and profit and loss in sunglasses. Your choice."

"Fuck's sake, it's like having two mums," Aaron muttered and stood, stretching and yawning, his T-shirt rising further to reveal a good six inches of his pale, hair-dusted belly. "Call me when it's ready, Mum, OK?" He left the room.

Charlie tutted and rolled his eyes. "It's a hard life, isn't it?"

Camilla chuckled and looked at her watch. "All my fault. I've spoilt them both terribly. Now look who's picking up the pieces. Thank you. He listens to you. Not sure why, but he does. And that's worth its weight in gold when it comes to surly, disinterested teenagers. It really is. Another coffee before we serve?"

"I'd love to, but I've got to get back. I need to check the veg box orders for tomorrow and walk Judy before he gets home." Charlie kissed and hugged Camilla, and as he left, mouthed, *Thanks*.

Chapter 29

ISABELLA WAS STAYING with Verity in her flat on the Mile End/Shoreditch border. As Verity had ushered her in on the first night, she'd offered Isabella a glass of wine, the sofa and a sympathetic ear. Isabella had refused wine and asked for water, and Verity had said, "How far gone are you?"

"Oh, I'm just tired. I don't want to drink at the moment."

"Yeah, right, pull the other one. It's got Mothercare-plastic-safe-for-baby's-mouth bells on it. Come on, how long?"

Isabella had crumbled and said she'd been very silly and hadn't taken precautions but didn't think she could fall, since she hadn't so far with Hugo.

"But you don't have sex with Hugo. You generally need to have sex to get pregnant, I've found."

They had both laughed at that, and Isabella told Verity about Danny, the sex sessions, the pressure for a child—everything.

"Hugo doesn't suspect?" Verity asked once Isabella was done.

"Why would he? We've not slept together in years. And he's a bit dim. He has no idea how women work, physically or emotionally. Never has done. He thinks we're all like *Mummy*, and fortunately none of us, or very few of us, are." She shuddered at the thought and took a generous glug of water.

Verity poured herself another glass of wine, crossed her legs beneath her and settled into the squashy white leather sofa. "Then I think we can come up with the perfect solution to everything, for everybody."

And so, on that first night at Verity's, they had hatched the perfect plan for Isabella to get her home back and keep the child.

***

Fred and Sharon were digesting the latest part of their family story as it unfolded in front of them. Fred sat in their Jacuzzi next to Sharon, who had her hair covered in foils and wrapped in a towel while her home hairdresser prepared the next stage of its treatment regime in the kitchen.

Fred ducked then reappeared, spouting a jet of water from his mouth to say, "It's not a big surprise she's had enough of that bloody brother-in-law of mine. Hugo's a fucking great wet blanket and a mummy's boy to boot. I never understood what she saw in him."

Sharon surveyed her nails. "Fair enough. He's a bit camp, but you never know what goes on in someone else's marriage, love. Still waters run deep. Or something."

"If she was so happy with him before, how comes she was always off with blokes left, right and centre?"

"How'd you know, love?" Sharon sat up, allowing her perky, cosmetically enlarged breasts to poke above the water line.

"Everyone knew. You can't tell me you didn't."

"Well, I might have had a little inkling." Sharon giggled.

"Inkling my arse. She might as well have taken a full-page ad out in the *Daily Mail*. She never actually told me, but it doesn't take Sherlock fucking 'olmes to work it out. She was always off for long business lunches and so-called business dinners, entertaining clients. None of them was anything to do with me or our business, I know that much."

"Why didn't you say nothing?"

"Nothing to do with me, love. It's her marriage. If that's what she wants to do, why should I get involved?"

Sharon shrugged. "Want me to do your back, sweetheart?"

"Please." He turned his back to her, and she started scrubbing it with a four-foot-long loofah. Fred groaned in pleasure. "'Sides, she never said nothing when I was putting it about a bit when I was married to Camilla."

"So much for sibling support or whatever it's called." She was still scrubbing away, really putting her back into it now.

"Oh, that's good, I could get used to this. You bin practising, love?"

"No."

"Anyway, it didn't affect her work, or I might have said something to her. I just turned away. If she wanted to use Lux Sunglasses as an alibi for the husband I've never much liked, no skin off my nose. If you wanted to pick a man who is less like me, you couldn't have got anyone better than him. I put up with it for Isabella's sake. He's my brother-in-law, so... But now this has happened, I'm not gonna cry myself to sleep or nothing."

Sharon stopped scrubbing his back.

"What's up? What you stopped for?"

"You know my friend Paul from the dog shows?"

"The poof what lives in that posh flat in Canary Wharf? Dragged us to that shit musical and got me pissed on cocktails? Thinks he's better than he is?"

"He's gay, and yes. He don't think he's any better, he just likes nice things. What's wrong with liking nice things, eh?" She gestured around the home steam room, sauna and Jacuzzi complex she'd insisted on having installed as soon as they'd moved into the house, and then at the Molton Brown and Clinique toiletries filling three glass shelves on the far wall.

"Is there a point to this little story, Shaz? Only there's a match I wanna watch in a couple of hours, so if you don't mind..." He made a winding motion with his hand.

"I'm getting there, my sweetheart. His partner—"

"Boyfriend? Partner sounds like they're running a company together or something."

"Well, as it goes, they do. They run an exclusive male escort company. His partner, Danny, is the escort, and Paul does all the bookings and money side. Didn't I tell you that's how we met? He introduced us through an old contact of his."

"Nope, never mentioned it, love."

"Probably didn't want to at the start. Anyway they're doing very well out of it, thank you very much. Danny tells people he's an exec assistant for one of the big accountancy firms or something, but I've always known what he does." She laughed. "Didn't you wonder how they could afford that apartment and car?"

"No kids, rich gays. That's all I thought. They're everywhere. So, this Paul, then…"

"Swear you won't tell no one. I swore on Dusty's life. Swear too."

"I swear." Fred shook his head and chuckled.

"Say it properly."

"All right, I *swear!*"

"Paul said one of Danny's clients is a certain *effete* man. A man's man but not that sort of man's man. The other sort." She giggled.

"What you saying to me? Are we still talking about Hugo?"

"Who else we bin talking about, love?"

"Hugo's been booking this rent boy—"

"Exclusive male escort, don't you know. He's quite a few steps above a blow job in a doorway in Soho."

Fred put his fingers in his ears. "All right, love, no need to get graphical." He took his fingers out. "You sure this ain't a wind-up?"

"Why would he make it up? It's his boyfriend who's sleeping with Hugo. It's hardly an unreliable source. Says he's come back again and again—had Danny on a retainer at one point. He just couldn't get enough of it."

"Blimey, love, I think I'm gonna be sick. Just thinking of Hugo and Danny in bed together's making me gag." He put his hand in front of his mouth, controlling the sick feeling rising up his throat.

"Funny though, eh?"

"Amazing what people get up to, innit?" He coughed then chuckled to himself. "Suppose it's not that much of a surprise, now I think about it."

"I knew you'd enjoy that bit of gossip. But you can't tell no one. Paul's sworn me to secrecy. It's not the done thing, apparently, sharing details of clients, and that sort of thing. He's only told me cos I'm his bestie, and he knows how much we both hate Hugo. He's nice like that, is Paul."

"Yeah, he's all heart, isn't he, love?"

***

Lord Reece Jones wiped his moustache and threw the serviette on the table, leaning back to rub his large stomach and allowing himself a small, under-the-breath belch, since his wife was at the far end of the table.

"I heard that, Richard. Don't think I didn't!" Lady Reece Jones peered over her glasses at him.

"Any news from dear Hugo, the old fruit? I was so surprised he threw Isabella out. It all seems so undignified and from nowhere."

Lady Reece Jones rolled her eyes and wiped her mouth with the napkin. "He did not throw her out. He politely asked her to leave, as was appropriate for the situation at the time."

"Sorry, old bean, sorry." He waved at her and bowed his head.

"Anyway, that's all rather academic now because he said she's moving back in." She let out a voluminous sigh and coiffed her large hair, waiting for her husband to ask why.

On cue, he said, "Why, what's happened now?"

"Well, it really is true what they say. Every cloud does indeed have a silver lining. And this particular silver lining is in the form of the little bundle of joy she's carrying. Isabella is pregnant. Isn't that wonderful?"

"Rather! I say, what a jolly good show. What perfect timing. We must have them round and throw a little party to celebrate."

"Early days still, Richard. She's not had the twelve-week scan yet. It's really only the size of a walnut, but all the same, it's our, I mean, *their* walnut, so isn't that marvellous?"

"What was the reason he asked her to leave? I never did quite work that out. It was all so confusing."

"Hugo wouldn't go into any of the details, out of respect for their marriage, which of course, I respect, absolutely. All he said was another man was involved."

"Oh, well. All's well that ends well, old bean!" Lord Reece Jones clapped to himself, like a well-amused child given a new toy.

"It's far from the end yet, darling. Far, far from the end." And it was far from simple. If she couldn't free Hugo of that blasted woman, this was a close-run second best, all in the interest of the family, and it would simply have to do. There was time to sort out any other loose ends regarding her daughter-in-law, but for now, Lady Reece Jones would join in the celebration of the news, like the proud grandmother she would soon be.

Chapter 30

CHARLIE SAT AT the kitchen table, surrounded by neither baking nor vegetables but by bank statements. Bank statements were not an area of household management Charlie had much to do with, but having listened to Camilla, he'd turned into something of a sleuth in his own home.

He noticed a series of large cash withdrawals from their joint account going back, as far as he could make out, to soon after they'd opened the account and moved in together. All that time, and Charlie hadn't so much as opened a bank statement or a credit card bill for their joint account. He'd left all that to Neil in complete trust, as that had been, in a sort of unspoken division of chores, given to Neil to deal with.

What were all these £500 withdrawals, and what did they coincide with?

Checking the calendar in the kitchen, where Charlie marked nights that Neil was away—for dinner purposes more than anything—he noted these withdrawals always happened when Neil was away on business.

Feeling more uncomfortable by the minute but also compelled to find out more, Charlie looked through Neil's suit jackets and the small, wheeled suitcase he took on business trips. At first, he found only a few more room-service receipts and used train tickets, but then, at the bottom of the suitcase, was a black business card with red writing. It was for a *Danny Traviati* who offered *personal services*, whatever that meant. Charlie put the card in his pocket and replaced all the jackets and suitcase in the wardrobe. Neil would be home soon. He was in central London meeting a client…or was he? Charlie didn't know what to believe anymore.

He checked the list for the following day and began mechanically putting vegetables in the boxes ready for the deliveries, all the while turning over what he'd found out and biting his lip as his stomach churned. There was sure to be a normal, simple explanation, and he was making a meal out of nothing. But he had to hear it from Neil to be sure.

***

A few hours later, Neil arrived home, put his bag by the door and held his arms out for a hug from Charlie as usual.

Charlie didn't come to greet him and stayed at the table, flicking a card between his fingers.

Something wasn't right. Something had happened to disturb the perfect relationship he and Charlie had together.

"What's up, sweetheart?" Neil asked.

Charlie wouldn't look him in the eye. "Oh, nothing much. I'm just interested to know who—" he turned the card over and read it aloud "—Danny Traviati is and what his personal services are. That's all."

Neil grabbed the card from Charlie and stared at it, his mind racing. He glanced up at Charlie. "Funny story," he said. "Danny's a client. He wanted some advice and consultancy about his… his…work flows, client bookings and that sort of thing. Standard consultancy work, really. It was very boring." He smiled and put the card in his pocket, wishing it would disappear, shortly followed by himself.

"Right. And what exactly *are* these personal services he offers? Cos it sounds like they're sexual or something. The dark card and red text has a touch of the Soho sex scene about it. Is that what this Mr. Traviati is into, or am I reading something into nothing?"

Neil wiped his sweaty hands on the back of his trousers. "Well, so there's a funny story to that too." Neil took a deep breath to give himself time to think up an explanation, funny or otherwise. "He is a male escort, yes. That's what he does. A high-class escort. He doesn't always have sex with his clients. That's not what the service is advertised as. It's about company for the evening. And if the clients want more, then that's something between Dan—I mean, Mr. Traviati and them."

"I see, although I don't see why that's particularly funny. And there's one more thing I'd like to know, and then we're done, we can eat dinner. Why is there a withdrawal of five hundred pounds in cash about once or twice a month when you're away on business?" Charlie was staring at Neil now, making complete eye contact.

Neil's eyes widened, and he stuttered slightly, wiped his brow with the sleeve of his suit. "That's the cash for incidentals when I'm with the clients—if they want coffee, or taxis to get from the hotel to the client, that sort of thing. It's all tax-deductible. I keep the receipts, and it all goes through the books."

"Five hundred quid, every time you're in a hotel for a few days. That's a lot of taxis and coffees."

Neil continued to look at Charlie but said nothing.

"I think I'll call Mr. Traviati. It would be nice to speak to one of your clients, who you've helped so much, get the praise straight from the horse's mouth, as they say." He began dialling the number on his phone.

"The card's here." Neil tapped his pocket.

"I know. I put his number in my phone earlier." He smiled as he put the phone to his ear. "It's ringing. Still ringing. Oh, here he is. Ahh yes, Mr. Traviati? I was wondering if—"

Neil snatched his phone and cut the call off.

Charlie folded his arms and said quietly, "Now are you going to tell me what's really been going on?"

With a sigh of defeat, Neil handed Charlie's phone back to him. "What I said is true. Danny's a male escort, and…"

"And?"

"I've used his services."

"Just to be clear, so there's no pussyfooting around, you *have* slept with Danny?"

Neil hung his head and nodded. He might as well get it all out in the open.

"Is that what the cash was for?"

More head nodding. No sense hiding it now.

"And again, to be clear, when you say you've slept with him, we're not talking sharing a bed with him, pyjamas on, like a slumber party? You've fucked him."

Neil looked at Charlie, then out the window. He swallowed, but his throat felt like it was full of sand. He put his hand over his mouth and nodded slowly.

"Right. How long have you been doing this? Are we not having enough sex for you? I didn't think we were doing badly, not for a couple in a long-termer who aren't teenagers anymore. But I guess I was wrong. One big performance fuck at the weekend and maybe another squirt and sleep or a blow job in the week. I didn't think that was too bad, really. So how long's it been going on?"

Quietly, so it was only just audible, Neil said, "Few years."

"Always with this Danny, or others?"

Neil was crying now. He'd never meant for anyone to get hurt. It had been his little secret, nothing to do with his and Charlie's love. If he could get Charlie to understand, it would all be fine.

"Depends where I was." Slowly, between tears and Charlie asking questions, Neil told Charlie about his routine when he stayed in hotel rooms all over the country.

"Why? That's what I don't get. If you were going to cheat on me, OK, that's one thing. But paying for it, with prostitutes. Thousands—no. *Tens* of thousands of pounds of…well, I suppose it's *your* money. But actually, not really. It's from our account, so it's *our* money. So I was paying half for you to fuck other men while I ironed your shirts and packed your bag. Fucking hell, you must have thought you had it made. All that money…we could have done something with that—a holiday, the house, a newer car, something. But—"

"I did it once, and that was meant to be it. I just wanted to try it out, see what it was like, whether someone would really come round, like ordering a takeaway. It was a buzz. That's what it started as. A bit of a buzz."

"And what was I? A bit of a bore? Safe, dependable Charlie, ready to iron your shirts at home and make you dinner while you fucked your way around the country."

Neil had no answer to that because Charlie had summed it up pretty well on his own. He hung his head.

"Why didn't you stop? Once, OK, that's a mistake. But what has to be at least a hundred times over years, that's not a mistake, that's a…a…"

Neil clutched at straws now, in a desperate attempt to excuse his behaviour. "An addiction. I got addicted. I couldn't stop myself. It was a compulsion. I knew it was damaging to me, to us, to our bank account, but I couldn't stop myself, I had to get that hit—that exhilaration of meeting a new…" He trailed off, aware of who was standing in front of him.

"You can say man if you want, unless there were women too. Actually, I don't want to know. So why keep the card of this one?"

"I don't know. I guess…he was more than the others. He talked to me, and he listened." He stared out the window, remembering some of the sessions he'd had with Danny. "Sometimes I could almost believe we were together. It made being away—"

"Yeah, cut the crap, Neil. I bet he's hung like a donkey and goes like a train, doesn't he?" Charlie wiped away a tear. "You can't tell me for five hundred quid you sat and watched TV with a pizza all night."

"No."

Charlie made a rewinding motion with his hands. "Hang on. You said it was like you believed you were together, so it was like you were having a relationship with this Danny. Is that right?"

"Yes."

"Jesus. I don't know which is worse. The mindless fucking or the emotional cheating. You know what? It's all fucking terrible. You are disgusting. I can't even look at you anymore. I don't know who you are."

Then Neil remembered something. Something that might just save this whole situation. "He blackmailed me. Some of the money went to paying them to keep quiet. Paul—Danny's partner—had pictures of me and Danny together, and of me snorting coke. He threatened to send them to you, so I paid him not to…to protect you from what I'd done."

"How considerate of you! And you did drugs with him too. Lovely." Charlie smiled a fake smile Neil had never seen him do before. "I fucking hope you were careful with him. Who knows what he's got, fucking his way around. He's bound to get something. Makes our tests and decision not to use anything a bit of a joke, doesn't it? If you're out fucking with a whore, who knows what you've got and given to me." He held his head in his hands and cried.

Neil put his arms around Charlie's shoulders. "I was careful, I promise. I knew I had to be, to protect us both. Of course I didn't forget our tests and what we'd agreed."

"But the whole closed relationship slash we don't want to have an open relationship conversation—that conveniently slipped your mind, did it? This amnesia, you should go to a doctor, get that seen to."

"It somehow felt different because they weren't just any men, they were escorts. Like it wasn't properly cheating because it was their job and a business thing."

"A business thing? Did it feel like a business thing when you had your dick in his mouth? Or maybe when you fucked each other, did that feel like a business thing, like your little spreadsheets and workflow charts? Was that the same as when you felt one of these men inside you, or when you watched yourself going in and out of his arse? A business thing. Don't make me fucking laugh. You make me sick. All I can think of is you with these men and coming back here, telling me you love me and pretending it's all normal."

Charlie shook out of Neil's embrace and walked to the door, then broke down in tears again.

"I do still love you, Charlie. Why do you think I paid the blackmail money? I wanted to protect you, to protect us."

Charlie turned, wiping his eyes with his sleeve. "So much protection that you carried on going back to Danny and the others after the blackmail. Am I right?"

"It was only Danny. I stopped the others six months ago. Only him."

"Oh, well, that's all right then." Charlie left the room, then reappeared at the doorway a few moments later. "Pack. Put it in that little suitcase and go. Cos if you think I'm leaving, you can think again. I'm not the one who's done anything wrong. You're the one acting like a one-man fuckathon."

"Can't we talk about it?" Neil pleaded.

"What do you think this little performance was? What more is there to talk about? You fucked a load of prostitutes, and that wasn't in the relationship rules we agreed. There was no 'no cheating, but if it's with a prostitute that doesn't count' clause. Hmmm, funny that. Fucking hilarious, I'd say." He walked back and stopped, his face inches from Neil's. "You've broken us. You took our relationship and you ruined everything we had together. Broken. You're a nasty cunt." And then he was gone, upstairs to their bedroom with a slam of the door and a heavy thump as he either threw something or threw himself onto the bed.

Neil stood in kitchen they'd fallen in love with when they'd first viewed the house years before. Charlie had said he had to have that kitchen, in that house, because it would be perfect for the business he wanted to set up. And Neil had said if that's what he wanted, that's what they'd have, and he'd kissed Charlie right there in the kitchen, in front of the estate agent, who'd looked away with a smile.

That kitchen, where on the day they'd moved in, they'd fallen in a pile at the bottom of the stairs leading up to their bedroom, unable to make it that far, and ended up having slippery, slidey, slow sex and laughing how it was good it had a tiled floor, as it would wipe clean.

That kitchen, where he'd just revealed the ugly secret he'd always hoped would never come out. The ugly secret that had broken Charlie's heart and their relationship into a thousand pieces. In the silent aftermath of their argument, all he heard was the muffled sobbing of Charlie, his boyfriend, the love of his life, whom he'd thought he would grow old with, in that kitchen, in that house, in Chelsea, who'd just called him a cunt.

Chapter 31
Late Spring 2014

I SABELLA HAD MOVED back in with Hugo, with much fanfare and preparation of the nursery. She had called him from her friend Verity's house a few nights after she'd left. That was when they'd hatched their plan.

"But, but, darling, I thought we couldn't, you couldn't...we'd tried for so long..." Hugo had said, racking his brains for the last time they'd slept together in anything other than the literal sense.

"I know! It's such a surprise, but people's bodies can change, and the conditions can be right when they weren't right before. I've read so much literature about couples who adopt because they can't have children, and once they have an adopted child, they fall pregnant naturally. Just like that."

"But I don't understand. It can't be mine," Hugo said quietly. "Unless it's an immaculate conception."

Isabella said, "Fine, I'll tell *Mummy* you couldn't provide her with an heir as you weren't man enough, and she'll carry on nagging you to have one with whichever poor wife she saddles you with next. Or...we play along with this little charade, carry on with our separate lives, and bring up baby together. Mummy will be so pleased you've done the manly thing, won't she? It would be such a shame to disappoint her, don't you think? Unless you'd like to try for a baby with another woman?" She let that hang in the air between them.

He knew this made him weak, but in his parents' eyes, it would make him the perfect, strong son, and it would allow him to continue with his trysts with men while having an heir. Isabella was right; Mummy would do exactly what she'd said. She wouldn't allow him to remain childless after Isabella had gone, and what was it they said? Better the devil you know than the devil you don't. "This is your final offer?"

"I think it's a fair deal. You get an heir and no hassle from Mummy, and I get my half of the house back. Or it's wife-hunting and baby-making for you, and I know how much you love those."

Hugo sighed to himself. "Righteo. I'd better start decorating the nursery. Come back when you're ready. I'll tell Mummy it was all a mistake, and once I realised you were carrying our baby, I couldn't bear to be without you both. She'll be so overjoyed by the baby news she won't dwell on the rest."

"I'll be back soon." She paused before saying goodbye, and Hugo *knew* she was smiling to herself, but what choice did he have but to go along with her charade?

He stood in the hall next to the phone, convinced he'd been played for a fool and unsure what to do about it, if anything at all. Well, there was *one thing* that would take his mind off his wife's return. He texted Danny to see if he was free to meet that evening.

The reply came seconds later: *Last-minute cancellation, see you later. D*

***

Mummy and Daddy were so relieved when Hugo told them the next day.

"But what about the nasty business with the other man and the infidelity?" Lady Reece Jones asked. "What are you doing about that, darling?"

"Mummy, please don't go on about it. She said it was a mistake and only a few isolated times. It was all to do with how she hadn't felt close to me because we were having problems in the...with the baby department. And this...well, it proves we weren't having any problems. It seems such a shame to simply write off all these years of marriage when the thing we've been waiting for so long has finally happened."

"Quite. Well, we're very happy for you, darling. And neither of us shall mention the other issue, the—" she whispered "—affair. Not a word. Our lips are sealed."

"Must go, Mummy, do tell Daddy. We're off to Mothercare shortly, to pick up some non-gender-specific essentials. It's so exciting how it all rolls from the one miracle."

***

As time passed and Isabella grew larger and larger, and Hugo tried to think of ways to back out of the charade, he realised he couldn't possibly do anything but go along with it. He couldn't deny Mummy and Daddy a son and heir, not now the nursery was all decorated with blue sailor motifs, as they now knew it was a boy.

A boy.

Mummy and Daddy had been so, so pleased, like their Christmas and birthdays had all rolled into one. How could he tell them it couldn't be his because he didn't sleep with his wife any longer and was instead having the most wonderful, mind-bending, body-contorting sex with a man? And actually, when he thought about it, the baby was the perfect cover for all that mind-bending, body-contorting man sex. No one would suspect a thing. Hugo had got his wife pregnant, against all odds, and if that didn't prove his virility and stock as a man—a *real* man's man—then he didn't know what would.

So he went along with the baby shower, the decorating of the nursery, the plans for Isabella to take maternity leave while he continued at Reece Jones Instruments. He went along with all of it because denying it would reflect so badly on him, worse than it would on Isabella, and then it would be open season on Hugo bashing, about all aspects of his life, and he simply couldn't allow that.

***

Once Verity had explained how Isabella could use the pregnancy to her advantage, it had seemed like the perfect solution.

"He won't admit to anyone it's not his because what would that make him look like? An effete, dubious on the sexuality front, useless son and husband. And even Hugo doesn't want people to think that about him. Can you imagine him saying to Mummy and Daddy he's not slept with you for more than a year? He will go along with your proposal, I'm sure of it, because he hasn't anywhere else to go. Mummy won't leave him alone otherwise."

Verity's eyes had sparkled with the excitement of a plan all coming together so well, and when Isabella told her she was having a boy, Verity squealed with delight.

"Bel, you are untouchable! The carrier of the son and heir— that snooty bitch of a mother-in-law won't be able to touch you. You're doing exactly what they wanted."

At first, Isabella was unsure. "Do you really think this will stick? I've been back a while, and I can't believe he hasn't said anything. He knew it couldn't be his before I told him." She shuddered at the recollection of Hugo's sloppy kisses and quick painful little stabs, all delivered with his eyes screwed shut.

"We know he won't say, for all the reasons we've gone through. He's agreed to go along with the lie. It will make his life easier, paint him as the perfect son. If he backs out now, he'll look even worse than he did before. You're back, it's stuck."

Isabella nodded.

"And you're not going to tell him anything else," Verity said. "You've got the affair out in the open. That's more than enough brow-beating and hair-shirt-wearing on your part. No need to add the baby's father into it. It's a perfect get-out for Hugo to forgive you because all along, you did love him, as you were carrying his baby. Any other reason and he'd look weak, useless."

"I suppose. Why would I tell? If it means I get the house back and all the rest, why spoil the ship for a ha'porth of tar?" She smiled mischievously. "It means we get to carry on with our detached marriage—that's what I told Hugo I wanted. He gets to do what he wants, I get to do what I want, and Mummy leaves us both alone now we've bred."

"Darling, the father—he's not black, is he? I think you'd have a bit of a job explaining that, don't you?"

"Dark-haired, blue-eyed, olive-skinned. A bit Mediterranean-looking."

"He sounds delicious."

"He was, and he has the longest, most agile tongue I've ever known!" They giggled together.

***

So although Hugo knew it couldn't be his baby, and Isabella knew that he knew, neither of them spoke about it to each other or anyone else. Complicit in the security and cover the lie provided, they continued to act out the perfect family, the proud devoted wife and virile father-to-be.

Chapter 32

CHARLIE STAYED IN one of Camilla's guest bedrooms. He'd visited her a few days after the row in the kitchen with Neil and explained Neil wasn't leaving, it was he who had to leave.

"He's told me to fuck off. My name's not on the mortgage. It's just him, and my money doesn't count, apparently. I was between jobs when we bought it. I'd left the bank and was setting up the veg boxes and baking business but not actually up and running. So we put him on the mortgage. He was earning more than enough. It seemed very sensible at the time, and we never got round to changing it."

"But you're married, or civilly thingummy-whatsit, aren't you?" Camilla asked.

Charlie shook his head. "We talked about it. I didn't want a big fuss or to spend lots of money, and Neil couldn't agree who from his family we'd invite, so we never did."

"What about common law? Is that a thing?"

"As far as the law's concerned, we're just two housemates in a house that's legally his."

Camilla put her hand over her mouth. "Oh."

Charlie nodded. "I've got no legal right to that house. Never have done." His eyes filled up with tears. "So if you wouldn't mind, could I squeeze into one of your spare rooms?"

Camilla hugged him. "Don't be silly. We'll sort something out. Fred was the most terrible shit when we were married, having affairs all the time. So I know how painful it is. I know exactly what you're feeling." She tugged Charlie tight to her bosom, stroking his hair as he cried yet again. "Once a cheating little shit, always a cheating little shit. It won't feel like it now, but you're far better off out of it."

Within a few short days, Camilla's family had absorbed Charlie as if he'd always been there. He helped with the cooking as well as continuing his sporadic cookery lessons not only with Camilla but with Aaron and sometimes Tamara. He kept up his businesses, delivering veg boxes and baking cakes as necessary, the only adjustment being that he had to use Camilla's Aga instead of his all-bells-and-whistles electric double oven. He was delivering to more farmers' markets, farther afield and into the southern Home Counties, sometimes baking for six or seven hours a day before doing a late-night veg-box delivery.

He didn't allow himself to mope in their home, but he did a fair bit of crying in his little van, which fortunately had been in his name, not Neil's, so he'd kept it. After an initial refusal to take any money from Charlie, Camilla had been persuaded of the financial sense it would make, and it gave Charlie a more equal stake in the running of the house, rather than feeling like a long-term squatter.

Aaron was very pleased to have Charlie around, often spending entire days hanging about the kitchen while Charlie worked and offering to help deliver veg boxes or go to the markets to sell the cakes with him.

Charlie found Aaron's presence an enormous comfort, particularly as he was missing Judy. Neil had waved the adoption papers from the dog rescue under his nose, which named Neil, not Charlie, and then pointed out who paid for the monthly insurance premium and the vast majority of vet bills. Charlie pointed out he walked, brushed, loved and comforted Judy every day while Neil was out at work, to which Neil said he'd been advised the paperwork and finances would be taken into account in any division of property, at which point the act of him referring to Judy as *property* had proved too much for Charlie, who had suppressed the tears as they bubbled up, kissed and hugged Judy goodbye and then left her with Neil.

Whenever Charlie asked Aaron who was looking after Judy while Neil was away, Aaron said it wasn't for him to worry. "I've seen a van pull up outside your old place, and someone walks her, if that's any help. But I think it's best if you don't talk about it now."

Charlie would nod and say, "At least she's being walked," and they would continue in easy discussion about baking or hairdressing or all manner of other topics.

Charlie soon felt like he was really one of the family, sitting around their table, dishing up dinner he'd cooked, talking to Tamara and Aaron about their days, asking Camilla how she'd got on with her latest job interview or CV-posting spree around businesses on the King's Road.

But the thing Charlie really loved—the thing that made him want to get up in the morning and made his heart sing and flutter a little, despite all that had happened and that he was sleeping in a single bed in his neighbour's box room—was seeing Aaron every day. Talking to Aaron every day, driving him to local hair salons to see if they had any work experience placements available, encouraging him to talk for himself beneath his floppy, strawberry-blond fringe, Charlie felt like a mixture of an encouraging uncle and a friend.

Aaron told him about personal, private, sensitive things he couldn't or wouldn't tell Camilla and had more questions about Charlie's coming out, his previous relationships and generally what it felt like to be an out gay man.

One morning, Aaron asked Charlie, "Why would Neil do what he did when he had you?" On another occasion, Aaron said, "If I was Neil, I would have been so proud to come home to you every night. I'd have married you years ago. If I was Neil, and if I was gay, or course."

Aaron's crooked smile and a squeeze of the shoulder had given Charlie goosebumps and a little flutter of the stomach. He wasn't sure what that meant, if he was reading the signals from Aaron correctly or it was wishful thinking on his part, combined with a deep, physical longing for intimacy he'd not had since leaving Neil. Whatever it was, it made Charlie able to plough through the sadness that often threatened to swallow him whole.

***

One morning, after working herself up into a lather of worry, Camilla said to Charlie, at the kitchen table, "I thought I could manage the household with less money. Well, with no money, and it all going to the children. But it turns out, I can't." She waved a pile of bills at him. "These simply keep coming and coming, and I don't have anything to pay them. No cash. And unless British Gas and British Telecom will accept a few dozen homemade blueberry muffins or a casserole or maybe a roast beef dinner, I'm going to have to do something."

Charlie took the bills from her. "I'll pay these. Part of my housekeeping. No problem."

"I'll pay you back." Camilla smiled weakly. "And I wasn't telling you as a womanly, wily way of getting you to pay them. Honestly. I need to get a job to bring in some money of my own."

"How's the CV dropping at shops going?"

"Nothing. Nada. Rien. Not one has got back to me." She smoothed her sky-blue pleated skirt on her lap and adjusted her pearl necklace. She was so clueless about all this sort of thing.

Charlie put his hand on hers. "I think we might have to update your clothes if you want to work in fashion. I hate to say it, but that look is about thirty years out of date."

She looked at her clothes, pulling the creases from her white pie-crust blouse. "What look? I don't know what you mean."

"How long have you had those clothes?"

"I bought them not long after Fred and I married, so that would be…eighty-four, eighty-five."

Charlie nodded. "Thought so."

"I was rather pleased I could still fit into them. That's impressive, isn't it?" She puffed her chest up slightly.

"It is. It absolutely is. And that's something we can celebrate by getting you some new clothes, in the same size, which are from this decade—this season even. Nowadays, people only wear Alice bands if they're being ironic. Are you being ironic?"

"Why would I be ironic? What's there to be ironic about?" She took in what she was wearing, compared with Charlie's dark-denim, thin-legged jeans, leather boots unzipped halfway, and a pink polo shirt. "It is rather—what's the term everyone says nowadays? Oh, yes, retro. In comparison with yours, maybe it is a bit retro."

"When was the last time you worked in an office, or worked at all?"

Camilla thought for a while, mentally flicking through the years. "Eighty-four, I think. Maybe eighty-five."

"It all becomes clear." Charlie smiled. "How are you with a computer?"

"Well, Aaron and Tamara can practically make one sit up and beg, whereas I'm not great once I'm beyond the on switch."

"But you did the CVs, didn't you?"

She sipped her coffee and avoided eye contact. Her little workaround to avoid technology was coming back to bite her.

"I Tippexed out the dates from my last CV and used my typewriter to update it. It was a bit squashed, I'll admit. Then I took it to the post office to photocopy."

"When was the last time you used a computer?"

"The last time I typed, before my CV, was when I worked in a solicitor's office, with an old electric typewriter, in…"

Together, they said, "Eighty-four, eighty-five."

Camilla laughed. "How did you guess?"

"What about the internet?"

"I leave all that nonsense to the children."

Chapter 33
Summer 2014

WITH A COMBINATION of a local college course on basic computer use—to which Camilla said, "Oh, I couldn't possibly do that," then, after the first class, "I think I'm getting into the swing of it now"—and Charlie's patience, Camilla was confident that no matter what she did, she wouldn't 'break the computer' or indeed 'break the internet'. A couple of months later, she was using her children's laptops as easily as she now used the Aga—once again, thanks to oodles of Charlie's patience.

Camilla's updated CV and dress sense got her two part-time job offers, one at an exclusive women's wear boutique on the King's Road and the other as an administrator at Chelsea Library, where she was by then a familiar face, having asked the staff enough times at the beginning of her quest to conquer technology to help her with 'the spinny thing and the egg timer' on her screen.

"Two job offers. Who'd have thought it!" she said, then asked Charlie which one she should accept.

After much deliberation and comparison, despite the hefty staff discount, the women's wear shop was felt to be too exclusive and a perk she would rarely make use of, so she went for the library. With a reason to leave the house three days a week and dressed in modern clothes and make-up, Camilla's confidence outside the home grew, and of course, the money was useful to pay the bills, since British Telecom and British Gas still didn't take baked goods in lieu of payment.

***

Neil had at first enjoyed the space he gained after Charlie moved his things from their...well, strictly speaking, *his* house. He allowed himself to spread out within the wardrobes and fill the gaps from removed kitchen implements with electronic gadgets to mount and project music from his various small devices. But he couldn't escape how empty the house was. There were still large gaps where Charlie's belongings had been, which only reminded him of what had happened and how he couldn't go back.

Neil called Danny to ask him round the house. "I don't have to hide things now, so you can come to my place—no more hotel rooms. How does that sound?"

"Yes, it could be interesting. You can book and sort out the paperwork with Paul."

The paperwork. Every time, he always came back to the paperwork. This was escort code for money without saying it and highlighting that the whole transaction was cold and business-like.

"But I said I loved you. I told you I'd left my boyfriend to be with you. It's more than just sex. I want to get to know you, to be with you, maybe." Because it had been more than sex, hadn't it? He wasn't just kidding himself, was he?

"Paul can handle all that side of things."

Neil didn't know much about this Paul and didn't dare ask lest it uncover a whole other side to Danny. But he knew Paul was part of the seedy underside of being an escort—someone Danny would surely be keen to get away from.

They met for a cocktail in a medium-range gay bar in Soho. The go-go dancers in little feathery jock straps gyrated and thrust their groins in customers' faces over loud music as Danny ordered the first round of drinks.

Neil was determined to get his point across, to explain why he was really there and to put the blackmail behind them. "I don't blame you, you know."

"For what?" Danny chinked their glasses and kissed Neil on the lips, lingering slightly and reaching forward to squeeze his thigh.

"All that nasty blackmail business. Not one bit."

Danny raised his eyebrow and sipped the cocktail. "That's good."

"I blame that Paul. He's obviously controlling you. He must have something over you, so you go along with his plans. I know how it works. I watched a documentary on Channel 4."

Danny put down his drink and went in for a proper big snog—all tongues and teeth and biting lips. Resting one hand on Neil's thigh, he used the other to gently tease him through his trousers. Danny pulled back from the kiss with a wide smile and continued to tease and squeeze Neil.

Neil twitched with pleasure as Danny brought him closer and closer to the point of no return. He put his hand on Danny's to stop him reaching that point. He was determined to have this conversation, to get it out in the open. "I had to get out of the house. For the moment. You can come there after if you want, but I thought it best to have this conversation on neutral ground. Although most of his stuff's gone now, so that's good. Anyway, I wanted to make it clear that we don't have to carry on like this, in this way. I love you. And I know you love me. You've pretty much said as much already. I can support you to get away from your pimp, to lead a life free from all that. We can be together as a couple. What do you think?"

Danny leant forward and whispered into Neil's ear, "What I do know is there's a hotel room booked just round the corner from here, and if you wanted to relieve some of the stress and tension of what you've been going through, I know some very effective techniques. Would you like to try that out with me?" And then he started to whisper about some of these techniques in more detail while gently stroking Neil's thigh and a bit higher up towards his erection.

Danny kept Neil hovering around the point of no return for the short taxi journey to the hotel, then in the room, he fucked him so hard, Neil could hardly remember his name and the day of the week as he lay dripping with sweat, all spent, laughing shakily when Danny offered to go again.

Neil sipped some water by the side of the bed and gathered his thoughts about what he had been saying in the bar. "Have you seen the film *Pretty Woman*?"

"Yeah, a couple of times. Do you want me to put on some high-heeled boots and a wig? We could arrange that for next time if you want."

"No, no, no. What I'm saying is, I'm Richard Gere and you're Julia Roberts. I have enough to support both of us. You wouldn't have to work—not that sort of work anyway. You could stay at home, be the homemaker for me. Get away from evil Paul and his controlling ways."

Danny looked at the clock on the TV. "I've to leave in just under an hour. What would you like to do? Go again, or sit here and chat?"

"I'd really like to bottom out this thing I'm offering you, get it signed off and agreed, and we can move forward on a different basis, without all this paperwork."

"You want me to bottom this time?"

"No, no, I want…" Neil repeated at length his offer for Danny to move in with him, as his boyfriend/homemaker, while Danny nodded and remained noncommittal until his time was up, at which point he jumped out of the shower and put on his clothes.

"It's all paid. Enjoy the room. I've got another appointment." Danny kissed Neil's forehead and left.

Danny was obviously in a rush, but Neil was sure he could make him understand how they needed to take their relationship to a different level. It was the most obvious thing to do after all they'd shared together. Maybe next time, he'd insist that Danny come to the house, make it more homely, set it up like he meant to go on. Yes, a bit more persuasion and he'd soon have Danny where he wanted him.

***

Danny checked the details of his next appointment on the phone with Paul, then said, "We've got another fucking love job this end."

"Who, what? What's wrong? Are you OK? Has anyone hurt you?"

"Calm down. It's that bloody Neil. He wants to bloody rescue me from you. Thinks we're gonna make house together now he's split up from his boyfriend cos he found out he was fucking rent boys."

"Male escorts."

Danny jumped into a passing cab and gave the driver an address in The Strand. "Whatever. I wasn't the only one, apparently. Turns out Neil had a bit of a taste for takeaway cock when he was…away on business. Turned into a bit of an addiction. Poor man. He poured his heart out to me the last two times I've seen him, but this time it was more serious. A bit scary, actually."

"Oh, shit. What do you want me to do? Refuse bookings or what?"

"It's standard. I'm surprised you don't have a handbook for this sort of thing by now. Every time they're drawn in through the blackmail or the love route, they fool themselves they're in love and want to be with me cos they've lost everything else. Standard."

An interesting acoustic sound came down the phone, which Danny knew was caused by Paul waggling a pencil between his teeth before he asked, "So what now?"

"I dunno about you, but I'm going to The Strand to fuck the brains out of a married senior civil servant who likes to call me Daddy."

"Have fun."

"An escort's gotta do what an escort's gotta do. I'll be home after this one. Do we need anything while I'm in town?"

"Nip into Clone Zone and see if they've got any decent porn DVDs and a large dildo with a suction-cup base. The old one's broken. Some lube too—the big tubes. And some milk."

"What's the milk for, some kinky request?" He rolled his eyes.

"We've run out. If you want tea when you get home, we need milk."

"Fair enough." Danny had arrived at the hotel on The Strand. He said goodbye to Paul, paid the driver and went up to the agreed room number, giving the arranged name.

Chapter 34

FRED AND SHARON Smith were at their favourite pub in Chigwell, the King Edward VI. The chandeliers glistened, and the white leather sofa had moulded comfortably around their bodies, as they'd been there a while, discussing Isabella moving back in with Hugo. Sharon's bright-blonde hair contrasted with the deep-purple fleur-de-lis with gold edging on the wallpaper behind her head.

"Why would he take her back?" Fred asked. "If she's cheated on him, why do that to yourself? He's made us think he's less of a man." *Much less of a man.*

Sharon chinked her champagne glass on the bottle, and a waiter glided over to fill it. "Camilla did, when you cheated on her all those years ago."

"That's different."

"How's it different?"

"Cos it was my 'ouse. And anyway, I never meant it. I just couldn't stop meself. It was never a thing, not an affair, just a quick—"

"Oh, charming. So when you cheat on me, I'll be well comforted that it was just a quick in and out, and nothing romantic, not an ongoing affair of the heart. Great. I'll remember that one." She pursed her lips and turned away, sipping her champagne.

This wasn't going as he'd wanted. "That all come out wrong. I'm sorry. What I meant was, Hugo knew it was an affair, not

206

just a one-off, and he still took her back. I wouldn't do that, is all I'm saying."

"Yeah, but love, you're not Hugo, are you?"

"Thank fuck for that." He leant forward and said, quieter now, "What I don't get is why he'd have her back if he's a, you know, horse's hoof."

"Gay. That's what we call them now, love. Gay."

"All right. If he's gay, then they're not having much going on in the bedroom, so why?"

"It means he can play happy families with her, be the good daddy, and his parents are happy. No one suspects he's actually a gay. I mean, that he's gay."

"He must think we're fucking stupid, going along with that pantomime."

"It's only that cos you know the truth. And remember, we can't say a thing to anyone about it. Besides, it's their marriage, and who knows what goes on in other people's marriages? I know how much you love Hugo-bashing, but can we talk about something else?"

"You ordered yet?" Fred looked at the menu.

"I was just gonna have something light. I'm on a *two* day today. Do you think they'd do me a boiled egg if I asked?" Sharon felt her stomach.

Fred rolled his eyes at his wife's latest faddy diet. There was always something food-wise with her. He returned to the menu. "It's not down here, but I can ask. Why you're on this diet, I don't understand. There's nothing of you as it is."

"And don't you think that's because I watch my weight, my love?"

"If you'd have said, we could have gone out tomorrow, and you could have eaten normal. Sorry."

"Don't apologise. It's for me to fit it round my life, and this is my life. If they can't do a boiled egg, then I'll just have a bowl of soup, no bread and butter. I can't only go out on my *five* days. This is fine."

***

A while later, tucking into their mains, the conversation had moved on to other matters. Fred was telling Sharon he'd heard from Tamara that Charlie, one of the gay neighbours, had moved in with Camilla and the kids, and what did Sharon think to that?

She took a small spoonful of her soup and ate it in three tiny sips while staring into the distance out of the window. Eventually, soup spoon emptied, she said, "I'll tell you what I think. I think you've got some sort of a problem with gay people." She let it hang there in between them.

"I ain't got a problem with gay women, lesbians, whatever you're meant to call 'em now. In fact, I'm quite interested in them in a lot of ways…" He trailed off and stared into the distance.

Sharon snapped her sparkly blue long-nailed fingers in front of his face. "Get those filthy thoughts out of your head. *That* is not what I'm on about. I'm on about gay men. You've got a problem with gay men."

Fred shushed her and made a down motion with his hand. He looked around the pub to see if anyone else had heard. No one had, it seemed. "I dunno where you got that from. When I was in the city, I used to be friends with all sorts of men—black ones, Asian ones, white ones… There was a bloke from Latvia too, and yes, some gay ones. Mind you, there's not many of them left cos they all died of—" he whispered "—the AIDS in the eighties. But I don't wanna talk about that. We're still eating." He looked at his plate of food and rubbed his stomach. "I'm not racist, I'm not sexist, I'm not anything-ist. I told you before, I don't see people like that. People are people. That's it for me."

Sharon called a waiter over to collect her half-eaten bowl of soup. "Can I have 'alf a grapefruit, please?"

The waiter nodded.

Fred said, "What's that about?"

"They say the grapefruit digests the calories from the meal I've eaten, or I digest the grapefruit and it makes me digest the calories without absorbing the fat. Something like that. It was on *This Morning* a few weeks ago. I got the gist of it at the time, but since then, it's gone. Anyway, if you don't see people like that, why is it all you can talk about is Charlie being their *gay* neighbour? Why not that he's a cook or a businessman or a friend of your bloody Camilla's? They're all true too, aren't they?"

"Yeah, they are. It's just they don't…it doesn't…I'm not…"

"What, love? Spit it out, will ya?"

"I ain't worried about my son living with a friend of Camilla's, or a cook or a businessman, but I am a bit worried—only a little bit, mind—about him living with a gay man old enough to be his dad." He sat back and put his napkin on the table. "There, I said it. And if that makes me something-ist, then OK. I am something-ist, but when it's my son, I think I'm entitled to be a bit something-ist about who lives in his 'ouse."

"Right, we got there in the end, didn't we? So what exactly is it that worries you? Camilla has known him for years, since him and his boyfriend moved in. They're friends, not just neighbours."

"What's that got to do with it? I bet that's what Fred and Rosemary West's neighbours said too, when it all came out. 'Lovely couple, you'd have never known it!' Or what about that geezer who met gay blokes in the West End, slept with 'em and chopped 'em into bits. He was a civil servant or something."

"Dennis Nilsen." Sharon turned away, examining her nails in the light.

"That's the one. What did his neighbours think about him, eh? You never know what goes on behind closed doors, do you?"

"If you compare those houses with this Charlie and his boyfriend's house, I think there's a big difference. Camilla's always round theirs—or she was when he lived there. These other people, they're psychopaths. Their houses looked like crime scenes, weird shit all over the place." She paused. "Do I have to say it? Are you really worried about what I think you're worried about? Because there's a big difference between a gay man and a... you know what."

He shook his head and made dismissive signs with his hands. "No, no, not that. I know that. I just wonder, is this Charlie *influencing* him, putting ideas into his 'ead about...you know, helping him with college stuff, and Aaron thinks, that's a nice idea, I wouldn't mind some of that."

Sharon laughed.

"What's so funny?"

"You, thinking you can persuade someone to be gay by making it look like a nice idea. That is amazing. Wait till I tell Paul! He's gonna piss 'imself!" Sharon checked her make-up in her small compact mirror.

"You don't know, do you?"

"Do you think if a gay man—say this Charlie, as we're on about him—if he came to you and told you all about 'is life with 'is boyfriend, how great it was, and how they had lots of great friends, and they had lots of sex together... Do you think you'd go, 'Oh, yeah, that sounds like a laugh,' and you'd *go gay*?"

Fred shook his head quickly. "No amount of rich with no kids, expensive holidays, double income could make me do that."

"Well, then." She clasped her hands in her lap.

"Well, then, what?"

"That isn't how it works, love. You can't persuade someone into a different sexuality unless they're already going that way themselves. Everyone knows that." She rolled her eyes.

"But what if he *is* gay?"

"Who?"

"Aaron! That's who I'm on about! I couldn't give a monkey's if this Charlie is gay, as long as he doesn't do it in front of me or Aaron."

"Same as anyone wouldn't have sex in front of friends or children."

"Yeah, suppose so." Fred shrugged.

"I spoke to Tamara. She said Aaron was all over the place since he stopped going to uni. Didn't know what to do with 'imself. This Charlie's been helpful, telling him to research colleges, courses, things your Camilla's a bit useless at."

"She's not my Camilla anymore. That's what I'm worried about."

"If he's gay, he's gay. It won't be anything Charlie has or hasn't said to him."

"Aaron *has* seemed a bit more chatty lately when I've called." Fred tapped his hands on his lap, lost in thought.

"You had a proper conversation with him when you last called, didn't you?"

"Yeah. He was on about going to the college and some course about hair styling. And he said he'd talked to the local barber—only he didn't call it that—about some placement or something."

"He said quite a lot then?" Sharon raised one eyebrow, only just.

"He did mention this Charlie too—how he'd made some suggestions, and how he's helping Camilla around the house now he's living there full time."

"And was there anything he said that made you worried about Aaron?"

Fred thought for a moment. "Nothing specific. Nothing he said, no. It was just generally about that man living with 'em."

"In that case, I think you're just gonna have to put your little bit of an -ism aside and be supportive, my sweetheart."

"I am supportive! I want 'im to do something with his life. Whatever that is. If he wants to be a hairdresser, then I support him."

"Even if he's a gay hairdresser?" Sharon smiled as she put the dessert menu down.

"One thing at a time, love, eh?"

"Right. A hairdresser is one thing, but a gay hairdresser is a whole other thing. What about my friends Paul and Danny? You like 'em, don't you?"

Fred nodded. "I mean, yeah, they bicker and all that, and have their own in-jokes, but they're like any other couple we know, aren't they? But this Charlie—I don't know nothing about 'im, and it worries me."

"Ignorance is the fear of not understanding something you don't know."

"Yes, thank you for the English lesson, love."

"They talked about it on *Loose Women* last week. The universe has brought Charlie into your Aaron's life at just the time he needs the guidance and support. You can't argue with the universe. It's crystals or lay lines or energy. It's something anyway."

"We'll see." Fred turned back to his food, his brow furrowed. Clearly, he'd had enough of gay son talk for one day.

Chapter 35

Charlie sat at the roll-top writing desk in Camilla's study, looking through papers Aaron had shown him about hairdressing—a letter of recommendation from a local salon explaining Aaron had completed an eight-week placement there and the college prospectus. He leant back and wondered how Camilla had managed to function with a study like this for so long. He put down Aaron's papers, his fingers wandering to a pile of utility bills, a copy of Camilla's will, her old CV—pre computer course and covered in Tippex—her birth certificate, and finally a letter to Camilla from the mid-nineties. Before he could think about the appropriateness of reading it, he'd picked it up.

July 1995

Dear Mrs. S,

I know you told me not to see you again, which is why I am writing instead. I know the baby has been born, because I heard from one of your neighbours when I was working in their garden. A boy, they said, with a head of red-blond hair. I had to find out to be sure if he was mine or F's. And now I know for sure he's mine.

I understand why you didn't tell F, but I will always know he is part of me and a part of you, whoever brings him up. It was a mistake what we did, but I don't regret it. F wasn't

*treating you right, and if I was your husband, I would never
do that.*

I will go now. I don't expect a reply to this.

*Yours sincerely,
H xx*

Charlie put the letter back with the other papers.
Bloody Camilla and her filing skills. What did she think she was
doing, leaving personal papers out like that? But she'd been good
to him. She'd taken him in when he had nowhere to live, and now
they were a family—of sorts—rubbing along nicely together.
Why would he want to do anything that would jeopardise that?

But didn't Aaron have a right to know? Or did he? Did *anyone*
have a right to know? Or was that another of those new modern
obsessions about always getting to the truth? Weren't there some
things best left unsaid? Wouldn't he himself have been better off
not knowing about Neil's outside interests? He would certainly
still be in their home, making dinner for Neil, none the wiser.
But was that really better, living in ignorance?

He couldn't make that decision for Aaron, however close
they'd grown since Charlie had moved in with the family.
First, he'd speak to Camilla. It could, of course, all be a terrible
misunderstanding, couldn't it?

Chapter 36

SUNDAY WAS TRADITIONALLY a quiet day for bookings—clients tended to have to stay with their wives and boyfriends—so Paul was catching up with some paperwork. Checking his account, he saw Sharon had paid him back that two grand he'd lent her a while ago. She'd told him Fred had much more money now he'd sorted things out with Camilla. Paul had been confident Sharon would pay him back, but he was glad it hadn't affected their friendship.

It had been such a busy few months, and he'd not had a chance to check business and personal finances much, barely having time to take new bookings, ensure Danny was briefed on any specific client requests, and process payments. Paul checked through Danny's diary and made sure it tallied with the income for each week. He noticed some private appointments, ones which he didn't think he'd added. Why would he have made them private? It was only he and Danny who saw it. There were also some cash deposits that didn't link to any bookings. Danny was resting from his run earlier that morning, lying on the sofa with a face pack and cucumber slices on his eyes. It was a day for maintenance for him too.

"Babes?" Paul shouted over the TV's noise.

"Yep?"

"There are some private appointments in the diary. I never put anything private. Did you?"

Without moving or removing the cucumber from his eyes, Danny said quietly, "That's for an extra client."

"One I don't know about?" Paul was standing now, next to the sofa where Danny lay.

Danny nodded.

"And why haven't you told me? I know all your clients. I book all your clients. I process the money you take from them. It all has to go through the books. We've been through this—anything that's not a gift has to be recorded. I'm not having another fucking audit from the fucking tax man again. Don't you remember what happened last time?"

"Yes, I remember. I meant to add the money, but it's been so busy. You know how it is."

"Right, but why keep the client from me?"

"I think we need to diversify a bit. Widen our client base."

"And you didn't think of talking to me about this first?"

"I wanted to try it out, see how it went. Think of it as research. Then we can formalise it. After all, it's me who's got to perform with them. You're just sorting out the details." Danny removed both cucumber slices from his eyes and sat upright. "Not that that's not an important role, of course." He smiled.

Paul sat again, fingers poised on the laptop. "What's the details of the new client? I'll put him into the database."

"Here's the thing."

Paul bit his lip, fingers still poised. "Right?"

"It's a bit complicated. There's the person I see, and the person who pays."

Paul cracked his knuckles over the laptop. "And these are two different people?"

"Yes."

"Jazzy. Interesting. Some of these people do like to mix it up a bit, don't they? The name of the client first, we'll get to the money next."

"Isabella."

"It's a woman?!" Paul was back on his feet, hands on hips.

"Generally, people called Isabella do tend to be women, yes."

"And you didn't think of discussing this with me?"

"As I said, it was an experiment. If it didn't work out, then nothing to discuss. As it happened, it went very well."

"But...a woman. How did you, with a woman? You are gay aren't you? You've never even mentioned women before, not when you were younger. You said after your first time as a teenager, you knew you liked cock and never looked elsewhere." Danny had said that, but somehow this changed the whole situation. It made Paul feel uncomfortable, insecure, as if all he knew was shifting.

"That was all true. It still is true. But it turns out, I'm such a professional I can put my mind to anything. I reckon I'm actually bi. More leaning towards men, but a little towards women too."

"*Anything*, anything?" Paul motioned to his groin. "Even..."

Danny nodded. "Yes, even." He smiled.

Paul put his hands over his mouth and felt the need to be sick. He ran to the bathroom and threw up in the toilet. As he walked back to the living room, he said, "This is too fucking weird. You, with a woman?"

Danny sighed. "Maybe you'll change how you feel when you know how much money I've made from the person who pays during this little experiment." He patted the sofa, and Paul joined him.

They talked about the money side of the deal and quickly segued into what they could buy with it. Paul gradually felt less like he was carrying a bowling ball in his stomach.

"I can just about get my head around that it's a woman because it's work, and here, it's pleasure. Like you always said. Even so, it's not something I could do, I'm sure."

Danny shrugged.

"What I can't forgive you for is the lies. We said the only way we can do this together is for there to be no lies between us, and now you tell me this, which is a big, huge, whopping, great lie." He paused, waiting for Danny to respond. He didn't, so Paul continued, "I have to know there aren't any more lies other than this. That this is it. We're done with secrets."

"I knew it'd be a shock to you. Of course, it's a different sort of business, but I also knew once you realised it could almost double our income, you'd get over the shock—once I'd done my little bit of market research, just to check I was up to the job, so to speak." Danny's eyes glinted, and he leant forward to kiss Paul.

Paul felt himself respond to Danny's kiss in anticipation of that tongue darting all over his body. Danny undressed Paul, then kissed his whole body, starting at his chest and working his way down, down, slowly, until Paul stood with his eyes closed, his arms against the wall as Danny made love to him.

Chapter 37
Autumn 2014

C HARLIE SAT AT the kitchen table, feeling the letter in his pocket. He'd tried to talk to Camilla about it that morning over his veg boxes and while she grabbed a slice of buttered toast he'd made her before she left for the library. But between the children running about, grabbing sandwiches and eating cereal, it hadn't felt right then.

He was determined to confront her when she came home from work. He'd spent the day rehearsing how the conversation would go in his head.

***

The key clicked in the door, and Camilla walked into the kitchen. "Can you be a dear and put some coffee on, please? I am absolutely shattered. I must admit, I do enjoy getting out there in the world of work again, putting on clothes, doing my hair, having some responsibility and decision-making above what colour underwear to put on and what to eat for lunch. And the camaraderie—I don't remember anything like it."

"Right," Charlie said.

"It was one of the girls—well, she's a woman really, a bit older than Aaron, but she looks like a girl to me—it was her birthday today. We had cake and cards, and later in the week, they're going for a drink at some wine bar on The King's Road. I said to them, I said, it felt like the eighties, when I was their age, off to Annabel's—wine bars and high heels and birthday cakes.

When I told them how old I was in the eighties, *then* I felt old. I hadn't until that point, but I did then."

Charlie smiled.

"But no matter. One of them is going to teach me all about being on the social media. She's going to set me up with one of these Facebook things, and she did try to explain Twitter, and what I should be twittering about, but I somewhat lost the thread of that. And I had to leave." She looked at Charlie.

He stood holding the cafetière and milk. He swallowed so hard she heard it.

"Whatever's the matter?" Camilla frowned.

"I want to show you something...well, ask you something really, but I don't want to spoil everything. You've been so kind to me, letting me stay. But this is bigger than that, it's about..." He trailed off, then turned to put the coffee in the cafetière and the kettle on the top of the Aga.

"Come on, quick as you like. Spit it out, will you?"

He took some crumpled papers from his pocket and held them out to her.

A shiver raced down her spine—like someone had walked over her grave, her mother used to say. "What were you doing snooping around in my paperwork?"

"I was going over Aaron's stuff about college, which he'd left in your study, and I came across this. It was out. It wasn't like I was going through your drawers or anything."

"I should bloody well hope not." *What a bloody cheek*. And she'd thought Charlie was a friend. Still, she chided herself for being so careless. "Out, you say?"

He nodded.

It was a risk, but she thought she had a good strategy to deal with the letter. "Well, it's quite obvious, isn't it? It's all just a joke, all made up. It's nothing to discuss or worry about." She put it in her jacket pocket. "So where has Aaron got to with his choices and research? I've heard bits and pieces, but it seems you've been doing a marvellous job helping him. Which, of course, I'm so grateful for."

Charlie stared at the pocket where she'd put the letter. "He was a bit clueless at first, because no one else was helping him. Neither of his parents. So he turned to me."

"Yes, well, I'm not good at that sort of thing. I barely knew how to turn a computer on, never mind the internet. And Fred...well, he was dead set against this whole college vocational thing. He wanted Aaron to go back to university or to help him with Lux Sunglasses, so as soon as he started talking about manscaping and hairdressing, he lost his father too." She shrugged. "Which is why it's been so marvellous having you here, to..." She picked a hanky from her sleeve and wiped her eyes. "So you see I'm so grateful for your help."

She paused, staring at Charlie. It was like the letter was burning through her pocket lining and pulling at her insides. Reconsidering her earlier strategy, she took the letter out. "Don't you think he's had enough upheaval lately? Do you really want to add this to what he's having to deal with?"

"Is it upheaval? I think it's about giving him the knowledge of where he's from, *who* he's from. It'll help him understand who he is now, who he wants to be in the future. At his age, that's all important stuff."

"I'm sure it is." She sat at the kitchen table, trying to weigh up the pluses and minuses of telling Aaron. "Are you making coffee or what?"

Charlie set to it.

"Have you ever found something out you wished you didn't know?" she asked. "Because the thing is, darling, once you know something you can't un-know it. You can't go back. It's a one-way street. Nineteen years, Fred has been his father, brought him up, changed his nappies... Actually, I did all that, but he went to sports days—some of them—had the awkward sex talk when he was a teenager because heaven forfend schools do it, taught him how to shave, played sports with him—the whole nine yards. And now you want to tell him all that wasn't his father, that he's from someone else, from a man I knew for two weeks and never saw again?"

"I...I thought he'd want to know. Fred will always be his dad, the man who brought him up, but this other man is his biological father." Charlie turned away. "But what do I know?" He shook his head.

Camilla understood his point but really wanted to close this conversation off and move on. "And what about Fred? Don't you think it would destroy him too? And don't think he wouldn't try to take back all the child maintenance payments because I'm damned sure he would. Do you think Henry's going to suddenly turn up in his little van, spade and fork in his hands, offering to be Aaron's daddy and my husband? He was only just a man then. He couldn't have done anything at the time. He was still living with his parents—he was younger than Aaron is now. So what's he supposed to do now, almost twenty years later?"

Charlie opened his mouth as if to respond, but then closed it again and handed Camilla a coffee, exactly how she liked it. He sat next to her at the table. "*You* could get in touch with him. Use Facebook, the internet. I bet you could find this Henry."

"For what, though? To do what?" Camilla was irritated this conversation still happening and annoyed at Charlie for throwing in Facebook and the bloody internet. Even so, she hadn't meant to shout. She lowered her voice slightly and went on. "He's already got a father, and you seem to be doing a marvellous job filling in the gaps. Why spoil all that? Why throw another thing into his life? He's a fragile boy, sensitive to what's going on around him. When Fred and I were splitting up, he was only young, but he *knew* what was happening. He kept asking me if I was all right, and why did we keep shouting. He even offered to do something to help. He wasn't even six then."

Charlie put up his hands. "OK, you win. We say nothing. He is really getting into this hairdressing, and who knows what this would do to that."

Camilla took a slow sip of her coffee. "It's not a matter of winning and losing, darling. It's about what's best for Aaron and Fred. You carry on doing whatever it is you're doing to help and encourage him, and I'll see what I can do with Fred. He's old-fashioned and has a set view of the world. Hairdressers and men, and his mind jumps to one conclusion. If you really care for Aaron, you know this is the right thing to do."

"I do. You know I do." He nodded, and they drank their coffee in silence, waiting for the house to be filled with the noise of the two teenagers.

Camilla had to protect her son. Since Charlie had been involved, Aaron had grown and blossomed so much. Whatever it was Charlie had been doing and saying to Aaron, she wanted him to continue, even if it riled one of Fred's -isms. She knew there wasn't anything to worry about with the relationship between Aaron and Charlie. Charlie was a kind and thoughtful man, and Aaron was a normal teenage boy. She dreaded the moment he would bring home a girlfriend, asking if she could stay the night like it was nothing at all. It would happen one of these days. She knew that. But she envisaged it would still take her by surprise when it did, and she would have to put aside all of her old-fashioned upbringing be a cool, modern mother, casually mentioning precautions and shaking the girl's hand, when inside her head she'd be screaming, *But he's my baby, my little baby! What are you going to do to him?*

***

Isabella put her baby down in the newly decorated nursery, staring at little Thomas's deep-blue eyes, knowing where they came from. She'd been impressed at how Hugo had jumped into action as soon as she'd returned home from Verity's. He'd organised the nursery to be decorated, bought supplies from Mothercare and had constantly asked her if she was all right.

"Isn't it strange that Hugo has brown eyes, but the baby has the most beautiful blue ones," her mother-in-law had said on first meeting Thomas on 22nd September. "I read that brown is the dominant eye colour."

"All newborn babies have blue eyes," Isabella had assured her in-laws—and husband. "I read that too...in some books." She smiled, remembering the only other pair of blue eyes that were almost as blue as hers from the first time she had gazed into them, as he lay on top of her, giving her more pleasure than she'd thought possible. The time with Danny had been time very well spent. She felt like a woman again and knew what it was to be adored and doted on.

Now Hugo was doting on her and Thomas, but that was quite different. It was a guilty doting, whereas Danny's had been an all-encompassing experience she hadn't wanted to end every time she left the hotel room.

At Thomas's christening, Sharon, that awful, coarse, common woman with her blonde hair and talon-like nails, mentioned the blue eyes again with a flash of her perfect, white-capped teeth. "It's funny that, innit, Isabella? I thought they started out blue but then went to the proper colour. But his have stayed blue. Funny that."

Isabella said, "Yes, they do appear to have remained blue. That's the thing with babies, as my dear aunt used to say, you get the baby that comes out. And this is the baby that came from me, and he is marvellous. I never thought I'd enjoy motherhood so much. At first, I thought I'd have to be back at work within a month or so, but I realised I couldn't leave him. Of course, you won't understand that feeling, will you, since you don't work and don't have children? It's such a shame."

Sharon had started to reply, until Fred jumped in and said, "It doesn't always follow. What about my Aaron? He's blond, and me and Camilla and Tamara, we're all dark. So you just get the baby what comes out, like Ky—Isabella said." He stroked Thomas's head then smiled to his sister. "I'm happy for you, sis. We both are. You've got a family now."

Chapter 38

FRED STOOD IN Camilla's kitchen in the middle of a long tirade about Aaron's future. Despite arguing for a while, Fred reflected he was no closer to winning. "I can't believe you've let it go this far. Bloody hairdressing college. No son of mine is doing anything to do with fucking hairdressing if I've got anything to do with it. What's wrong with Lux Sunglasses, or does he think he's above that now?"

Camilla said quietly, "You know as well as I do that he wouldn't think he's above anything. He'd sweep the streets, wipe tables, anything if he had to. He's a lot of things, but he's not a snob. And as for Lux Sunglasses, it's hardly like it's been in the family for generations, is it?"

"OK, so he's not a snob. At least something of me rubbed off on him." He paused to look at the kitchen he'd paid for the upkeep of for so long. "I've been meaning to talk to you about something, but what with one thing and another, I've not had time. I'm not happy about it, and I'm worried how it's affecting Aaron."

"What on earth are you talking about, Fred? I thought we'd resolved the financial issues."

"Not that. It's linked to the Lux Sunglasses stuff I suppose. It's all from that. He's not interested in that because he's had his head filled with all this bollocks about fucking hairdressing. And that's what I'm not happy with. This gay neighbour of yours, moving in with my son."

225

"First of all, he's *our* son. Second, he's not moved in with Aaron. He's moved in with us all."

"You're splitting hairs, love." Fred reached to pat Camilla's shoulder.

"Don't you *love* me. I'm not your love and haven't been for some time."

"Sorry. Whatever, it doesn't change the fact I'm not happy about what's going on with Aaron. What's going on under your roof. It can't go on."

"This gay neighbour has a name. He's called Charlie. So you can talk about him like a proper person, not just *this gay neighbour* you're talking about. Charlie's been a friend of ours for years. I used to go on dog walks together with him and his partner. And he's been very helpful lately."

"Yeah, since he moved in, I bet. From guilt about not paying you anything to live here. Coincidence? I don't think so." Fred huffed loudly. So this Charlie was crafty as well as being gay.

"Before that, actually. And he has been helpful since moving in, actually."

"Oh has he, *actually*? He's *actually* been helpful has he, *actually*." Camilla stared at her ex-husband. "No need to mock me. Charlie's helped an awful lot with what Aaron wanted to do, encouraged him to find out more about the things he's into. Got him to talk to local salons and go to the college to get a prospectus, find out what the course involves, how long it is, what the end will give him, what qualifications. He's very practical, is dear Charlie."

Why can't anyone else see it? "I bet he is practical, dear Charlie. And really the only one who's being a Charlie 'ere is you lot, being taken in by 'im and 'is crafty ways."

"If you're not going to have a mature conversation in my house, I'm going to have to insist you leave." She stood and gestured to the door. "If you don't mind."

"Oh, come on, Io…Camilla. I'll promise to be a good boy."

Hand on hip, she tapped her foot on the tiled floor, the noise echoing around the large room. "He's an awful lot of experience and knowledge from when he was a banker and his crafts and creative businesses."

"He's a banker, is he? Maybe I know him. I've probably bumped into him in the city bars. What's he look like?"

"I doubt it. He's about twenty years your junior, and there may have only been a few years when you were both working in the city. Look, I'm getting off the point. See? This is what you do to me. You've got me all flustered and I've lost my train of thought." She sat back at the table, and Fred smiled, pleased they could finally have this out properly.

"You were telling me how practical this Charlie is, and—"

"Yes, he's helped so much since moving in. I doubt I'd have been able to keep this lovely house if it weren't for him. He's teaching me some ways to save money. Home economics, it's called. He taught me to cook, and he helped me get the job."

"You've got a job?" Who had got rid of Camilla and replaced her with this woman before him?

"Didn't I tell you?" She avoided eye contact. "It must have slipped my mind."

"I'd have remembered that. What's it doing? Working at a shop or something like that?"

"I'm in the library down the road. I love it."

"As wonderful as it sounds that this Saint Charlie's been doing some sort of bloody Mother Theresa impression in this house, I couldn't really give a monkey's. I want Aaron to work with me at Lux Sunglasses, not be some mincing hairdresser."

"That's it. Out. I'm not having you talk like this in my kitchen." She marched to the door and held it open.

"That I've paid for," he mumbled, his whole argument crashing down around his ears, all because of his temper, damn it!

"What was that?"

"Nothing."

"The bottom line—as you'd say in your business speak—is Aaron will be what he wants to be, whether you like it or not. And we have Charlie to thank for that because let's face it, darling, neither of us had a bloody clue where to go with it when he told us he wanted to leave uni. If it were up to us, he'd still be here sitting around the house all day, getting up at noon, doing God only knows what in his room in the afternoon."

"I've a pretty good idea what he'd be doing in his room." Fred laughed to himself, remembering what he'd been like at that age.

"You don't have any guarantees with life. And with children, you get the child that comes out and the adult they grow into. We have Aaron, and he's our child." She pursed her lips, gesturing to the open door. "Are you leaving, or are you going to force me to push you out? The weather is coming into the kitchen, and I have to get on, so if you don't mind…"

"I will, but I'd like to talk to this Mister Perfect Charlie. See what twaddle he's been telling my son."

"*Our* son," Camilla corrected again, staring him down.

Fred stood but made no move towards the door. "Yes, *our* son."

Aaron walked into the kitchen holding Charlie's hand. "What about me?" He looked from one parent to the other, smiling.

Camilla looked at the two men, her gaze lingering on their hands.

Fred started to say something, but all that came out was a series of blustering vowels. He took a deep breath then said, "Aren't you going to do anything about this…this thing?" He pointed to their hands. "It's gotta be illegal, hasn't it? *He's* nearly my age, and *our son* is only just an adult. I'm gonna ring the police." He pulled his phone from his pocket and started to dial.

Camilla shut the door and stood in front of it, her arms by her sides. "What are you going to tell them?" she asked Fred. "What crime's been committed?" She smiled weakly at her son.

Aaron smiled back and squeezed Charlie's hand tighter.

Fred's hand shook holding his mobile phone. "But…but…but it's not right. He's his teacher. Aaron's his pupil. You said he'd been teaching him stuff. We've gotta do something."

Camilla looked at her son and Charlie. "Do you have something to tell us?"

Fred banged the table with his fist. The candlestick holders fell over. "For fuck's sake! What's wrong with you people? It's not like he's passed his driving test or something. We've gotta stop this!"

Camilla went over and rested her hand on Fred's. "I think it's a bit late for that. I think it's been going on for a while, and whatever they've done has already been done. Come on, now, let's all sit down."

Fred's mind flashed to an image he immediately tried to banish from his thoughts. His son and this man, *together*.

Aaron and Charlie sat at the table.

"We didn't plan it," Charlie said. "It just sort of happened."

Aaron nodded. "We've spent all this time together, and we have a lot in common. We get on really well."

Fred slapped his thighs. "Oh, well, that's all right then. Let's all jump into bed together, shall we?" He looked at Camilla, hopeful she'd say something sensible.

She shook her head. "Ignore your father. Carry on."

Aaron bit his lip. "Don't think I'm being taken advantage of. I'm nineteen. I was the one who did all the running. It took a long time for him to realise what I wanted."

Fred said, "I think I'm gonna be sick. I need to go 'ome."

229

"You're not going anywhere," Camilla snapped. "If you leave now, you won't see your son again. He's telling us something very personal and important, and we're his parents. We have a duty to listen to him."

Fred stared at the two men, then looked away. "A hairdresser is one thing, but a fucking gay one—that's a whole different ball game." He looked at his son again. "Where did this come from? Was it because I left your mum when you were young? Is that why?"

"Dad, didn't you think it was a bit odd I never had a girlfriend? Not one, and I'm nineteen?"

"I thought you was a late bloomer. I didn't get started with girls till your age, then I couldn't get enough of 'em."

"Mum, you must have had an inkling."

"A mother always knows, darling. I've suspected since you were thirteen but didn't say anything because I knew you'd have to work it out for yourself, and you'd do that in your own time. I did wonder if Charlie moving in would give you a little nudge in the right direction."

Fred couldn't believe what he was hearing. "*Nudge in the right direction?* Our son's a fucking queer, and that's how you describe it?"

"If you don't stop using that sort of language, you'll be out. I have a broom, and I shall sweep you out of here, no problem. And if you expect to be welcome here again, or in your son's life, you'd better behave yourself. He's always been gay. I can't believe you didn't see it."

Fred shook his head. How was he meant to deal with this namby-pamby new-age love-in when the real issue was being ignored?

"Anyway," Camilla said, "it's all out now. Granted, I didn't quite expect it to be this big of a nudge, but if you're happy, then…"

Aaron nodded.

Charlie took Aaron's hand again. "We are. I didn't think I'd meet anyone after Neil. I thought that was it, he was the one, and I would be alone forever. I always liked Aaron, but not in that way. And when he said he liked me, it went from there."

"Yeah, all right," Fred muttered. "No details please. If you suspected, why the fucking hell didn't you say something, Camilla? I'm the only person in here who's surprised by this? You two aren't surprised because you've been doing whatever it is you've been doing for a while." He turned to Camilla. "And you're not surprised cos you knew all along. So it's just me who's been in the dark, is it?"

"It does look that way, darling."

"Don't you *darling* me." He spat. All of them were making him look like some kind of twat.

Aaron shouted, "Will you shut up and listen? I'm trying to come out over here. If you don't mind." He laughed, then Charlie started to laugh too, followed by Camilla.

Fred said, "Oh, don't mind me. It's a fucking comedy, is this. A regular fucking Carry On film. *Carry On Mincing.* That's what it'd be called."

"Dad, you can do better than that, surely. I think I've known for a while but just didn't have the guts to do anything about it, not in real life."

"What do you mean?"

"Use your imagination, Dad." He paused while Fred tried to process. "I have my own laptop in my room."

Fred's eyes widened, and he slapped his forehead as he worked it out. *Accidentally ended up on the wrong porn category, my arse.* Why had Fred believed Aaron at the time? *Really?*

"But it wasn't until I met Charlie that I saw someone I wanted to do something about it with. I'd known him for years and always loved being around him. Walking the dog together, I used to make sure I walked with him when it was a group of us. I made excuses to go round after leaving uni. At first, I thought it was just because he was so interesting, so helpful and made me laugh. I knew I liked being around him, but as I got used to that, I realised it was cos I was, like, attracted to him. And when he moved in, I realised how I really felt for him, everything I liked about him. And he wasn't in a relationship anymore, so I at least stood a chance." He smiled at Charlie and squeezed his hand. "I knew he'd never do anything when he was with Neil cos he's not the sort of man to cheat. But once he was single...it just sort of happened."

Fred had listened to all this from his son and couldn't stop himself saying what came out next. "Not the sort of man to cheat. Just the sort of man who shags a neighbour's son while staying under her roof, even though the boy is twenty years younger than him. Only that sort of person, that's all."

"I knew you'd be like this, Dad. I knew you'd be all weird about it. He's fourteen years older, and that's nothing these days. I've felt happier than ever before, this last few months. Charlie's made me realise how I've felt all this time isn't wrong, it isn't anything to be ashamed of, it's just me, and love. It's love we have. And what's wrong with that?"

Fred turned to Camilla. "What you got to say about this?"

She shrugged. "It's the twenty-first century. Test tube babies, gay marriage, gay people adopting children, a black president in America, a BAFTA show about a group of people living in Essex, celebrity programmes full of people no one's heard of from other reality TV shows. The world's moved on." She paused to stroke Aaron's strawberry-blond hair. "He's not been that sulky, unmotivated, miserable teenager for ages. He has a sense of direction, and for the first time in years, he makes eye contact and smiles when I talk to him. If that's what Charlie's done to him,

I'm all for it. And if you're not, Fred, maybe you need to go away and think about why you've got a problem. As far as I'm concerned, we have a happy son and another son thrown in with the deal. You've not had to deal with the mood swings, the door slamming, the no talking for days, the miserable teenage years when he didn't know what to do. Well, now we know what was wrong."

Fred's eyes glinted. Aha, so she did agree with him! "So you do think it's wrong!"

"That's not what I meant, and you know it." Camilla hugged Aaron then Charlie. "When do you start this course? When can I expect my first free haircut in payment for all those dinners and clothes and school trips?" She turned to Charlie. "I suppose you'll be wanting to leave the spare room? It's a good job we got you a double bed, isn't it?" She smiled at them both.

"A while yet for the haircuts, Mum, but when I do, you're first in the queue."

Fred looked around the room, exasperated at how normally and quietly this had been absorbed into their family. "That's it, is it?" He pointed an accusing finger at Charlie. "You move rooms and share a bed with our son and everything goes on as normal while you—" and then at Aaron "—learn to be a fucking gay hairdresser?"

Aaron rolled his eyes. "I didn't read anything about the fucking bit. Maybe that's an extra module they didn't have in the prospectus." He pursed his lips, clearly on the verge of bursting out laughing. "I don't think the gay bit is a requirement for the course, but I might be wrong."

"Who's for a drink?" Camilla said. "I've still got a few slices of that chocolate sponge traybake I made."

Fred glowered. Camilla baking cakes? What fresh fuckery was this now? "You made it? On your own? You didn't buy it from a bakery?"

"Like I said, there's been a lot of change here."

"Fucking right, there has." He shrugged, realising he had to get his head around this. Maybe with time, it would all feel a bit more normal. "In for a penny, in for a pound. This evening can't get any weirder, unless anyone else has some revelations to share."

And so they drank and ate together, Charlie and Aaron holding hands while Aaron told his dad about the course and the salon where he'd be doing his placement a few days a week.

Although a small part of Fred wanted to shout and scream and storm out, he knew he'd be on his own, and if he wanted any chance of having a relationship with his new, improved son, he needed to push those feelings of distaste down and make an effort. He even talked to Charlie about their days in the city. No matter how awkward it felt, he had to make an effort with this man who meant something to his son, so he told Charlie about the biggest deals he'd done, and how he'd made his money to buy Lux Sunglasses. As it turned out, they had worked in the city together, not at the same company, but for a few years they'd overlapped and odds on had bumped into one another.

At the end of the evening, when Camilla said she'd see them in the morning and Fred made his excuses to leave, he noticed Aaron and Charlie sharing a quiet joke and laughing together, and even though he didn't want to think about what they'd get up to in their bed that night, he couldn't deny how much more upright, confident smiling his son had done recently.

Chapter 39

NEIL RETURNED TO his little house—it didn't feel like much of a home anymore—having worked away for four nights. He looked at Judy's empty bed in the corner of the living room. He would collect her from the dog-sitter tomorrow morning. No, not the morning; he had a report to write. He'd nip over to collect her at lunchtime. But no, he had an appointment for a personal trainer at the gym. OK, he'd definitely go to collect her tomorrow afternoon. Definitely.

He checked his calendar: he had three hour-long calls booked with three different clients in the afternoon, none of which could be moved and all of which could result in more work, so he'd be stupid to put them off. So five o'clock tomorrow afternoon, he would collect Judy. He'd spend the whole weekend with her, make an extra special fuss of her, since she'd been away from home, like him, all week. And she had now stopped crying for her other daddy since Charlie had moved out. She only sometimes jumped onto Charlie's side of the bed and howled, only the odd time, now.

He texted the dog-sitter a long apologetic message about his day tomorrow and how he'd collect Judy later than expected, and of course he was happy to pay.

He'd been doing quite a lot of paying for people to do things lately—things he'd normally not had to worry about since Charlie had done them without mentioning it. Between the Polish cleaner, the Spanish dog-sitter, the elderly lady who ironed his shirts and took his suits to the dry cleaners, he felt like he was keeping much of Chelsea in employment.

He loosened his tie and threw his jacket on the sofa on the way to the kitchen. It smelt of bleach, evidence of the cleaner coming earlier that day. He opened the fridge to a shelf of gold-packaged, *go on treat yourself*, premium-brand ready meals. The first week after Charlie had left, when he'd lived off takeaways, he realised his wallet and waist couldn't cope with that for long, but he didn't know or have time to learn how to make scrambled egg, never mind lasagne, casseroles, beef Wellington and other meals Charlie had prepared every evening.

He flicked through the phone book to the page for housekeeping services. He wondered if he could pay for someone to do *all* the house stuff, including cleaning—a bit of streamlining. That's what he'd advise himself if he were a client of his management consultancy business. Only he wasn't. He was a man in his kitchen, without his dog and without his boyfriend.

Since Charlie had left, Neil hadn't been too interested in sex, ironically since that was what had got him into trouble in the first place. Not that his and Charlie's sex life had been lacking. They'd never had any problems in that department. It was just that he'd got greedy and developed a taste for quick, instant gratification sex, then enjoyed it too much to stop doing it every time he was away.

"How was your day?" Neil leant against the work surface staring at the microwave where his meal turned slowly with a dim light and low hum of a fan.

The microwave hummed.

"Was it? That sounds very interesting. Tell me a bit more about that." He nodded a few times. "Really? Yes, I thought that too, but then I thought I'd leave it." More nodding. "Yes, I thought the dog lady would be all right. It's fine isn't it? Could you call her tomorrow? I've got a really busy morning." A pause. "No, I didn't think you could." He took a deep breath. "Because you are a fucking microwave, aren't you? Yes, yes. That's true."

The microwave pinged, and he took his food out, grabbed a fork and shovelled it into his mouth from the plastic tray, standing in the kitchen, leaning over the sink.

He nodded back at the microwave. "How's my week been, you say? Oh, well, let's see. It's been busy. Nicely busy, actually. I've hardly had chance to think about home, which is good. Training, meeting clients, travelling, sleeping when I got to the hotels. Not a minute to myself. Which is just how I like it as it goes." He wiped his mouth with a piece of kitchen towel, threw the plastic tray in the bin and the fork in the sink. "I know, I know, I should recycle it, but the way I feel now, I just can't be arsed." He stared at the oven, where Charlie had stood so many times taking out food for them and their guests to eat.

"I wish you were here to have an argument about the recycling, to tell me off for being a lazy arse." He wiped his eyes with the kitchen towel and turned to the microwave. "Yes, it is a shame. I agree. I've fucked it right up. I'm aware of that. But it's a bit late now. Can I get him back? He was very hurt. I hurt him so much, more than I've ever hurt him, I think. And although he knows I didn't mean to hurt him, I made the same mistake, time and time again. Which, being honest, doesn't really look good for my part, does it?" He tapped the microwave. "Well, it's been lovely chatting to you, but I really must go." He walked to the living room and put on some music to fill the emptiness. 'The Book Of Love' by Peter Gabriel flooded the room.

Neil stuck it on repeat and lay on the sofa, letting the music he and Charlie had danced to at his last birthday play away. He remembered Charlie reading some of his recipes aloud to ask his opinion. He remembered Charlie pleading and begging him to read one of his favourite pastel-coloured chick-lit books, which normally Neil wouldn't be seen dead reading, but when he'd read it, they'd had a conversation about how much they both liked it, and Neil had understood why Charlie read them to 'unwind his brain' after a long day of concentrating over figures or making new recipes. He remembered reading Charlie an important report he had written for one of his clients and how Charlie, although he hadn't understood much of it, had still given him useful pointers for the summary and opening page.

Neil wished with his whole being that he'd given Charlie a wedding ring and they were married. Even after his monumental, egregious, fuck-up, they would have been able to work through it because they'd have stayed together, rubbing alongside each other in their house. And if they'd have rubbed along with each other still, they wouldn't have been able to move apart as quickly as they had done.

The house that was technically his. The sofa they'd picked together. Their perfect home that felt like a perfect, empty cage.

He sat up, staring at the blank TV with tears streaming down his face. "What can I do to get him back?"

The TV obviously didn't respond.

"Have I said too much? Is there any going back on the argument at the start, or is that it? Is he too hurt?"

Neil remembered what the house had felt like a few months ago, days after he told Charlie what he'd done.

After the first argument, Charlie and Neil began to live separate lives under the same roof, and the house had been silent.

"Where's my shirts? I need one for work," Neil had shouted from the bedroom he'd stayed sleeping in.

Charlie was only making food for himself and had stopped doing Neil's laundry, but he hadn't told Neil that.

Neil banged on the spare bedroom door. "You awake?" He waited a moment, then opened the door.

Charlie lay in bed, his back to the door.

"Did you hear me? And what's for dinner tonight?"

Charlie didn't move and said quietly to the wall, "Iron's in the wardrobe in your bedroom. Washing machine is the white thing with the glass door in the kitchen. Washing powder under the sink."

"Is this what you're doing now?"

"Did you sleep with rent boys?"

Neil huffed, still holding the door. "Dinner?"

"Do what you want. You always do. I'm eating earlier. I'm not waiting for you to come back."

"Is this the game you want to play? OK, let's play this then."

Charlie turned in the bed to face the door, still lying down. "I'm not leaving. You're the one that fucked up. Fucked around. I've done nothing wrong."

"I've apologised. I don't know what to say."

"How about why you've cancelled the bank account and card for the account."

"I've taken legal advice, and that's what I was advised to do. Your contribution to it was negligible. It's basically my account. It's in my name anyway, so—"

"What about all the other stuff I do? Doesn't that count for anything?"

"*Did*. You're not doing it anymore. Not financially, no. You gonna iron me a shirt or not?"

"Not."

Neil slammed the door and left Charlie in bed. He hadn't mentioned Charlie's note about wanting to discuss how they could go forward with this, whether it was possible to, could they come up with a plan to get from where they were now to where they used to be? A sort of relationship recovery plan.

***

That evening, Neil had returned in a crumpled, already worn shirt with a takeaway for one in a paper bag. He greeted Judy at the door.

Charlie hadn't yet eaten. He sat at the kitchen table. "Enough for two?"

Neil banged the bag on the table. "You said I was to do my own thing, now you want to eat together. Which is it you want?"

"Ideally, I'd like you to not have fucked a load of rent boys, but since we can't go back in time, I would make do with some food and an adult conversation."

"I've only got for one." Neil tugged the containers from the bags and divided them between two plates. He handed Charlie the bigger portion.

"It feels like you've dumped a load of dog shit into a cake recipe instead of chocolate chips. That's what you've done to us. You've broken us. We're broken because of you."

Neil sighed. "I can't have this conversation again. I've said I'm sorry. I really am sorry."

Charlie picked up his letter from the table. "Read it, did you?"

Neil nodded.

"And?" He willed his boyfriend, whom he'd loved so much, with all his heart for so long, to say he thought they could work on their recovery plan.

"I've said I'm sorry. I won't do it again. You know that, don't you? You can trust me."

"That's the saddest thing about all this. I thought I could. Now I can't trust you. It's years of trust between us gone just like that." Charlie clicked his fingers. "What do you suggest?"

Please, please, please, say something about what you'll do.

Neil took the letter from Charlie and handed him another one from his bag. "From the solicitor."

"What's it about?"

"You're not on the mortgage. Never have been. Legally, it's my house. It's a notice to vacate." Neil stared, unblinkingly, at Charlie.

"If this is what you want to talk about, I'll go now. No big show. I'll pack and go tonight. If this is what you want."

Neil glanced at Charlie's letter and put it on the table.

Charlie packed a small bag of his clothes and some personal things, then stood watching Neil finish the takeaway from earlier. If he left now, they would never find their way back to each other; there would be no recovery plan. If Neil only wanted to talk about the house and didn't show any hope of them getting back together, this was it. The end. Charlie had come to the place where he could talk about what had happened without wanting to scream and cry and hit Neil. And if he could do that, why couldn't Neil?

"Do you want to read the letter? It's a proper one, from the solicitors."

Charlie waved the letter away, then pointed to his letter. "What about that one?"

"You said it was broken, that *we* were broken. How am I meant to come up with a plan to fix it? If a mirror's broken, you can't fix it, can you?"

"What if we're a cracked plate or bowl?" Charlie offered quietly.

"You said this was it. There was nothing we could do."

"Yes, I did say that, and you always agree with me, don't you?"

"I don't know what you want me to say. Just tell me what you want me to say, and I'll say it."

"If you need me to do that, after all this time, then it really is best if I go." He picked his bag up, closed the door and walked to Camilla's house, quietly sobbing with every step.

***

Neil had stared at the door as it closed behind Charlie. He'd felt pleased with himself for a clean break. The solicitor had warned him it may get nasty when he gave Charlie the letter, and he'd been relieved it hadn't, yet he'd never before felt so miserable. If only Charlie had told him what he wanted him to say, he'd have happily repeated it, but even now, he couldn't for the life of him work out what it might be.

Wiping his cheeks dry on his sleeves, he stared at the TV. "I suppose that's a no," he said, then turned it on, staring at the moving pictures, flicking through the channels, not paying any attention to anything except the quietness, the coldness, the emptiness filling the house, pressing down on his chest so hard so he almost couldn't breathe.

Chapter 40

FRED ARRIVED LATE and flustered to the café on the King's Road, where Camilla had suggested they meet.

"I'm not eating food in that house with those two, doing God only knows what upstairs, so you'll have to come to me," Fred had insisted.

"I don't have anything to say about *those two*, as you put it— one of whom is your son, and the other is your son's partner. It is what it is, and that's an end to it. So if you insist on seeing me, we'll meet near mine or we can talk on the phone."

So Fred had reluctantly agreed to a little independent café on the King's Road where Camilla often took herself for a bit of space and time alone.

He joined her at the small wooden table by the window. "What's good here?" He quickly scanned the menu for familiar territory.

"It's all good. It's been listed in *Vogue* magazine and *Conde Nast Traveller* as somewhere for non-Londoners to visit to get proper Italian coffee. So, take your pick."

"What are you having?" He looked at her glass filled with frothy milk and coffee, wondering when things had moved on from instant coffee and PG Tips.

"Caffè con panna. A shot of espresso with lashings of frothy milk. It's simply delightful."

Camilla's turn of phrase reminded him of Hugo, who had sex with men, didn't he? Just like their son. Fred shuddered. Yes, he'd definitely done the right thing meeting Camilla here.

"Anything the matter?" Camilla asked.

"Yes, no. Well, sort of, I suppose." He blustered. "Do I tell them, or will they come over?"

A young woman in her early twenties with dark hair tied back into a bun arrived at the table with a notepad. "You ready, yes?" She had an Eastern European accent.

Fred looked at his ex-wife. "You eating?"

"I could eat, if you think we'll be here long enough. Yes, I'm sure I could eat." She ordered a couple of cakes.

"Same, please," Fred said. "And a normal coffee. The most normal one you have."

Camilla touched the waitress's arm and whispered, "An Americano." She took a sip of her drink and sat back, glancing at the passing crowds pushing pushchairs and carrying paper string-handled shopping bags. She raised her eyebrows. "Yes, you wanted to talk to me?"

"I can't believe you're still letting that man live in our house. After...after...well, after you know."

"You can say it. It's not a crime any longer."

"I think it might be, actually. I been doing some research, and there's a pretty big age gap between them, isn't there? Aaron's eighteen—"

"Nineteen."

"And that man—"

"He's called Charlie." Camilla sipped her coffee slowly, continuing to meet Fred's eyes.

"That man, he's nearly forty, isn't he? It's pretty disgusting. That's gotta be some sort of minor being taken advantage of, isn't it? I read all this stuff about a teacher and a pupil, and he went to prison in the end." He left that hanging in the air between them, as the waitress arrived with their cakes and his large *Americano* coffee, whatever that was.

"Thank you, we'll let you know." Camilla smiled at the waitress, who reciprocated, then left. "Charlie is thirty-three, and Aaron, as we've just established, is nineteen. He'll be twenty very soon. That's thirteen years. Charlie's not, nor has he ever been, Aaron's teacher. He was a family friend, who Aaron always knew was gay. It's not like he's sprung it on him, taking advantage of our son. In fact, from what I can gather, it was rather more the other way around." She smiled at herself and took a forkful of cake. "Evidently, Aaron was quite the seducer."

"There must be something we can do." Fred didn't want to hear about his son being a seducer, especially not with it being a man he'd seduced.

"To do what? I'm terribly sorry, Fred, but I simply don't understand where you're aiming towards with this line of argument. We've had this conversation. I've made it very clear. Either you find some way to put aside your feelings or I doubt you'll be able to have any kind of relationship with your son. It isn't illegal. It's not immoral. What if the same thing had happened to Tamara?"

"I'd have punched his bloody lights out. Quick as you could say 'teenage daughter'."

Camilla sighed. "Oh dear. I'm not getting very far with you today, am I? Now, let me see." She took a deep breath, adjusted her hair in her reflection in the window and started again. "Imagine you liked the man Tamara was with. Imagine he made her really happy, the happiest you'd seen her for months, if not years. That Tamara had a smile you'd not seen for as long as you could remember—all because of this man. Would you still punch his lights out, as you say you would?"

Where was she going with this stupid bloody argument? After a while, Fred said, "No. Suppose I wouldn't as it goes. If he's making 'er that 'appy, and he's that good for her, then no.

Why would I?" He ran through the arguments he'd rehearsed in his head on the way there: age, illegality, immorality. "But you can't tell me it don't turn your stomach a bit. Thinking of them together, in the bedroom. Him doing God knows what to our son." He put the wedge of cake he was holding back onto the plate.

The sigh from Camilla was longer and deeper this time. "Close your eyes."

What was she playing at? "Eh?"

"Please humour me."

He did as asked.

"Now, imagine Tamara in her bedroom with this marvellous man you get on with so well. Got that?"

He nodded. "What they doing?"

"Oh, she's sitting at the dressing table combing her hair, and he's standing by the window. Got it?"

More nodding.

"Now he walks to her and kisses her neck. She turns to kiss him back, and they continue kissing and are lying on the bed. He takes off his T-shirt and…" She stopped. "How does that feel?"

Fred opened his eyes. "Fair point. Got it."

"I should imagine if either of our children thought about either of their parents having any form of sex, you with your wife, or me with—heaven hopes it may happen—some strapping young man, mid-thirties, with deck shoes, a red, short-sleeved shirt and dark-blue chinos…" Her eyes lingered on a man of that description standing by the till. "Then they'd be reaching for the bucket too. It's not what people do. Normal people do not think of their loved ones having sex with anyone, regardless of their gender.

Fred pushed his half-drunk coffee away. He leant on the table and rested his head in his hands. "What did I do wrong?"

"Why only you? We're both his parents."

"Yeah, but he's a man, and I'm his dad. It sort of comes from that, don't it?"

Camilla took Fred's hand. "You've not done anything wrong. I've not done anything wrong. It's just the same as why his eyes are that colour, or his hair."

Fred looked up. "I did always wonder where he got that hair from. It's no one on my side."

"Yes. It's just him. It's part of him, and it's not wrong or bad or anything. It's him. He'd obviously been struggling with this whole thing for some time. No girlfriends, and he's hardly smiled for the last couple of years, except when he was with Neil and Charlie, it seemed. When I thought back, that was the only time he lit up. Didn't think anything of it at the time, but now… Well, it makes sense, I suppose."

"He's 'appy, is 'e?"

"Now he is, yes. You should see how he's got into this hairdressing thing. You'd think he'd invented the feather cut himself. And there's all sorts of talk about dyeing his own hair. He's asked Charlie to help him. I said as long as it doesn't stain my bathroom, they can do what they like." Camilla giggled.

"What?"

"Just thinking of them in the bathroom bent over the bath, Aaron's head covered in some god-awful colour." She shrugged. "That's teenagers I suppose."

Fred took a bite of his cake and washed it down with some coffee. "It's cos I left you, isn't it? That's why he's turned out like this. I wasn't about enough, and he didn't have a father figure to teach him properly. All the things a dad's meant to do for his son. I didn't cos I weren't there. And now look what's 'appened."

"Aaron would be Aaron if you'd stayed or not. And besides, you know good and well why you didn't stay. I wouldn't put up with your nonsense any longer, and neither would the children. It was for all our best interests."

"I can't help thinking, if I'd have stayed, he'd have—"

Camilla threw a sugar sachet at him. "Quite frankly, you were hardly the model father! If you'd stuck around, he'd have learned how to sleep with his secretary and colleagues and tried to hide it from his wife. What sort of a learning experience would that have been? He'd have grown up a complete cheating little shit."

"That was low, Cam." He put the sugar sachet in the middle of the table, pondering his next move.

"Low, but true."

"So what now? If you're sure there's nothing we can do, what now?"

"I am quite, quite sure there's nothing we can do because there's nothing we need to fix. Aaron isn't broken. There's nothing wrong with him, so what on earth would we need to do? I've known Charlie for years, and I know exactly what he's like. If I were to conjure up a boyfriend for Aaron, I don't think I could have come up with anyone better than dear, kind Charlie."

"I can't handle them together, though. I'm not ready to see no son of mine kissing some bloke. Probably never will be."

Camilla signalled to the waitress for the bill. "One thing at a time. Would you like me to have a little word with them both? To bear that in mind when you're around? What about holding hands?"

"Maybe, maybe not."

"Ahh, so that's progress of sorts!" She paid the bill, which prompted Fred to ask how she was managing without his money, and she reiterated what she'd told him about Charlie helping her economise and how she enjoyed the job at the library. They talked for a while, companionably sharing their news, ending with Camilla promising to ask Aaron and Charlie to refrain from kissing when Fred was there.

"I'm sure they'll be OK with that little compromise, as long as they know you're making an effort. You'll just have to get used to the hand-holding, and rest assured, there's plenty of that. It's the longest, deepest honeymoon period. It's so sweet to see them together, making each other laugh, making each other drinks exactly how they like them. So as far as holding hands go, you'll have to *man up* I'm afraid, but fair enough about the kisses. I must admit, if I saw Tamara chewing the face off some male youth, I'd feel a bit uncomfortable. After all, they are my babies. Always will be."

"*Our* babies," Fred corrected with a smile.

Chapter 41

Paul was meeting Lady Reece Jones at a restaurant in Hertford, the small county town of Hertfordshire, less than fifteen minutes from Reece Jones Park. After a series of phone messages from Paul, chasing the balance of payment due to settle her account for Danny's services, she'd finally agreed to meet him—"But not at the house. Lord Reece Jones would find it too, too confusing. It's best to keep him completely out of it. I know a marvellous little place, tucked off the market square, very discreet."

Paul had found the place, no trouble at all, but arrived late, having been defeated by the town's parking system.

Lady Reece Jones stood to greet him, kissing both cheeks before gesturing to the waiter and ordering another gin and tonic. "What did you want?"

"Sparkling water. It's a bit of a drive back." And he wanted to keep a clear head for this meeting.

After polite introductions since they'd only ever dealt with each other virtually, Paul explained he was now looking after Danny's clients on both sides of the business—implying men and women without saying it aloud, given where they were—and with the assignment completed, the rest of the payment was due.

"Yes, my dear." Lady Reece Jones smiled. "I should elucidate as to why I've been so evasive. I do apologise for that, my dear, but perhaps I can explain."

"Please do." Paul internally rolled his eyes. This was going to be a long lunch.

"It is so sweet of you to meet me here. I do hope you understand I couldn't have you turning up at my estate. Lord Reece Jones doesn't know anything about this little arrangement. He's very sweet but very naïve. He doesn't really pick up on the signals." She continued at length, talking about how her daughter-in-law, Isabella, hadn't been able to produce the required son and heir and that she simply had to go so Hugo could meet the right girl and do his duty. "I was rather hoping she would remain out of their marital home. That was, you see, the whole point of this little escapade."

"He threw her out, didn't he?"

"Oh yes, but as soon as she announced she was pregnant, back she came. So it seems there wasn't such a problem in the first place. All it required was a little nudge in the right direction. And this is what I'd like to discuss with you. It seems an awful lot of money for such a small nudge. I was really hoping to get rid of her, to expose her for the cheating whore she is. While I now have the grandson, I still have to put up with her sour face. I hadn't planned on the grandson coming along at the same time as the affair coming out. So I wondered, could we have a conversation about the balance?"

Paul had known she'd try it on. Danny had briefed him well beforehand, and he had come here with one objective: to get the full £8,000 out of the *Duchess of bloody Hertfordshire*. With that goal only in mind, he took a sip of his sparkling water and began.

"I'm afraid we have no control over the ultimate outcome. Danny was asked to have an affair with your daughter-in-law, with the express purpose of her being discovered. I think you'll find the assignment was completed successfully. She was found out, and she was thrown out. End of."

Lady Reece Jones picked up her menu. "What do you think you'll have? It's all very good here. All locally grown, shot, raised, everything within a five-mile radius of this restaurant. It's marvellous. It's even called their five-mile menu—it says it at the top of the page." She stared at the menu, brows furrowed.

There would be no quick get in and get out with this one. Paul needed to lay on the charm, nice and thick, and he had plenty of time, so he figured he may as well lean into the lunch, enjoy it, make the most of the challenge. He waited while Lady Reece Jones gave her order, asking about each menu option and requesting they alter her choice in four ways. Paul bit his lip and overtly checked the time.

Once the waiter had left with their orders, Paul leant forward and gently held her arm. "Look, you know as well as I do, we won't get the police involved because what you asked Danny to do is illegal."

"Surely not!" She pulled away and put her hand in front of her mouth.

"If not illegal, then certainly a bit dodgy."

"I can assure you, I've never done anything *dodgy* in my life, and I'm not about to start now." Lady Reece Jones shuddered.

"Point is, it's hardly the sort of thing I can take down the Citizens' Advice Bureau, is it? But what I can do, which I think you'd find much less pleasant, is tell your neighbours and friends what you did. I'm sure a little notice at the back of your local paper would go down a treat." He spread his arms in the air, indicating the title of the article. "Lady Reece Jones sets honey trap for daughter-in-law with male escort. I wonder what your Women's Institute friends would say about that. And the others on the board of that school where you're a governor."

"How do you know about that?" she hissed.

He tapped the side of his nose. "This is my job. This is what I do for a living." The food arrived. "Shall we start? It does look delicious."

After more small talk and some dancing around what Paul could do if she didn't pay, Lady Reece Jones finally agreed he *had* fulfilled his side of the deal and pulled from her large Louis Vuitton handbag a silver leather cheque book and silver pen.

"I would prefer cash if you have it."

"I'm afraid I don't carry that much cash on me," she said, pen poised to write the amount.

"Bollocks. People like you nip out for milk and come back with a new fur coat or hat or something. I bet you've got thousands in that bag of yours."

She finished writing the cheque and waved it in front of Paul, then, when he refused to take it, she made a big show of fishing around in her voluminous leather bag, eventually pulling out a white leather purse bursting with fifty-pound notes. Strategically moving their drinks so no one could see, she slowly counted out the notes and handed them to Paul, who shoved them into an envelope with a flourish.

"That'll go straight into the new car fund with all the other money from you lot." He regretted that crass statement as soon as he'd said it, but he had what he'd come for so ignored the twinge of guilt. With a smile, he said, "It's such a great pleasure doing business with you…I didn't catch your first name?"

"I didn't throw it. Lady Reece Jones to you, if you don't mind." She put her cutlery down and wiped her mouth. "You have completely wiped me out. I've nothing left—" She stopped and stared at Paul. "*Us lot*? What on earth do you mean?"

Might as well have a bit of fun. "Your family made up over half of Danny's income for that quarter. It just kept rolling in. Between you and your son, you kept Danny a very, very busy man. He hardly had any stamina left for me when he got home." Paul smiled and winked lasciviously.

"Hugo? What does my son have to do with this?"

"Your Hugo—he kept coming back for more. Some months, he couldn't get enough of it. He paid in advance, then had to send extra to top up when he wanted another session with Danny."

"What nonsense! You silly little man. You really are the grubbiest, most disgusting individual I've had the displeasure of meeting. What business would Hugo have to see Danny?"

Throwing his napkin on the table, Paul leant back, casually crossed his legs and put his hands behind his head. "I thought you knew, my dear Lady Reece Jones."

"Knew what? What are you talking about? You despicable creature." She snapped her fingers and made the universal sign for the bill. She was already on her feet by the time the waiter arrived and threw some notes on the tray with the bill. "I bid you good day."

As she stepped past the table on a beeline for the door, Paul stood and whispered into her ear, "I thought you knew your son Hugo is pretty bendy, he's gay or bi."

She turned, her white gloved hand to her mouth. Paul steadied her as she sat again. The waiter lingered, and she waved him away, then leant across the table. "My son and Danny? But I met Danny. Don't you think I'd know if he were a...a...homosexual. And Hugo is *a married man*."

"Aren't they all, dearie?" Paul camped it up a bit.

"You're telling me my son Hugo is a homosexual? He's one of those men who plays with other men in public lavatories? Don't be so ridiculous. The idea's preposterous. I won't hear of it. It can't be."

Paul reached for his phone. "I have pictures if you don't believe me."

She pushed his phone away.

"Have you met your son, Lady Reece Jones? He is, as we say in the business, as gay as bunting. He's as camp as Christmas.

It's just shining out of him. I can't believe he married a woman in the first place! Was she blind?"

She grabbed Paul's arm and hissed aggressively into his ear. "Listen to me, you filthy, repugnant, little man. If you breathe a word of this to anyone, I will get you back. I don't know how or when, but I will get you back. *I have connections.*"

"If you say so, *dear.*" Paul stood, dropped a tip on the table and moved to leave.

Lady Reece Jones grabbed his arm, looking up into his face, confusion in her eyes. "They have a child. He can't be gay if he's given her a child. I don't understand."

"Isabella told Danny that she and your beloved, perfect son hadn't had sex in years." He picked her hand from his arm and waved his fingertips. "Toodles. It's been a scream! We must do it again sometime." He patted the pocket containing the envelope of cash, and then he was gone.

***

Lady Reece Jones looked around the restaurant to see if any of her other ladies who lunched had seen that particular scene. Thankfully, there was no one about she recognised. She wasn't used to being out-foxed by degenerates like that despicable man. That would be the last time she dealt with his type again, she was sure. But what to do about her degenerate and clearly ill son? She had been so pleased about the baby; it had solved all her problems in one fell swoop—except for that blasted daughter-in-law. Unfortunately, *she* was still around.

She couldn't allow it to get out that her grandson wasn't from Hugo. It would disgrace him and the whole Reece Jones family. Was she the only person who hadn't realised Hugo was...one of *those people*? Or was it quite obvious to the untrained eye? She suddenly felt very old and out of touch with the modern pace of life. *They* could get married now—not in a church, but it was still called a wedding. She hadn't paid much attention to the news at the time. After all, there were none of those people in her social circle. She had no reason to think they'd ever be part of her life. Only now, she had one as her son.

Her own, dear son, whom she'd raised herself—with a little help from a nanny and housekeeper, of course. What had she done for him to turn out so wrong? And what on earth was she to tell Lord Reece Jones? He'd probably want Hugo strung up and shot. Taken into a field and put out of his misery like a lame horse. Now, maybe that wasn't such a bad idea after all.

With a backwards glance, she gathered her belongings and swept out of the restaurant into the smaller limo she liked to take into town for less formal occasions.

"No rush to get home, driver. Take the scenic route. I've some thinking I'd like to do in silence." She pushed the button, raising the glass partition. There *had* to be a way to tidy up this beastly mess with a positive outcome for herself and her family.

Chapter 42

EVERYONE SQUASHED AROUND Camilla's kitchen table, big smiles on their faces. She'd briefed them in advance—no arguments or awkwardness—and told Fred, "We're all together to have some fun as a family. It's in the best interests of the children, so why can't us adults get along too?" To Aaron and Charlie, she'd said, "Don't be too much with your father there, please. Hands is OK, but no snogging."

"As if!" Aaron had replied with a wink at Charlie.

Camilla had left Fred to tell his wife about Aaron and Charlie being an item. The plan was that when they were all together, it wouldn't be an issue, they would just *be*, like a modern version of the Waltons.

Noticing Tamara in imminent sulking position ahead of the big family meal, Camilla reminded her of the chat she'd had with her father about him giving Tamara more interesting things to do at Lux Sunglasses. "I've successfully dragged your father into the twenty-first century. One foot at a time, granted, but he seems to be joining us."

Camilla, too, was finally 'with the times'. Gone were the pie-crust collars, Alice bands and pleated skirts, today replaced by a turquoise floaty dress from Monsoon that Charlie had taken her to buy after a long campaign of persuasion. At first, she'd said it felt a bit too 'Earth-motherish' for her, but once she'd tried it on with some sensible but fun sparkly heels, she'd noticed a spring in her step and had bought it.

Camilla carried the homemade lasagne from the Aga to the table. Its cheesy goodness and tomato garlic sauce aroma filled the room as it bubbled away in the earthenware dish. "Who's going to serve?" She looked around those gathered.

Fred volunteered. "Is this Harrods delivering again?"

"No, it is not, and well you know it. It's my...well, it's Charlie's recipe, but he taught me how to make it. So this is the first time I've flown solo. Or not quite. He was there in the background for various panics and questions."

Charlie smiled. "Never before has a béchamel sauce caused so much drama."

Nervous laughter rippled around the table as Fred served everyone a helping of lasagne. Sharon's laugh stood out as the loudest. She was on her third large glass of wine and already flashing her silver fillings to everyone.

"What's to go with it, Mum?" Tamara asked.

"Ah, yes, nearly forgot." Camilla placed a large glass bowl and some salad forks on the table. "A rocket, fig and pine nut salad with garlic truffle dressing. That's right, isn't it?" She looked at Charlie, who nodded.

Fred said, "This is you too, is it?"

Camilla nodded. "Tuck in. Don't stand on ceremony, everyone."

Fred chuckled. "Rocket, fig and garlic truffle. That's a bit gay, isn't it?"

The room fell silent as everyone stopped serving or eating and turned to him.

"Hah! That's a good'un!" Sharon said and took a large glug of wine. Fred tried to take her glass from her, but she dodged him and leant across the table to pour herself more.

"A bit fancy. That's what I meant. Wrong word. 'Course, wrong word. It just seems a bit much, with all the beche-whatsit sauce and tomato and beef in the lasagne, to have this as well. Dresses.

I mean dressy. Not that there's anything wrong with dresses. Yours looks lovely tonight, Camilla, doesn't it, love?" He turned to Sharon.

"Oh, yes. It really is pretty. Very nice. Where did you get that? I must see if I can get one for myself. It is such a nice colour." Sharon glugged her wine and waggled her glass in the air. "'Course, this is much nicer. Going down a treat, it is. Cheers, everyone!" She threw back her head and laughed loudly, treating them all to another flash of her fillings.

No one replied to Sharon's toast. Silence filled the room.

Charlie jumped in, straight-faced, and said very quietly, "It was Jamie Oliver, actually."

"What's that, love?" Sharon checked her nails in the light.

"The salad. It was a Jamie Oliver, so not that gay, really. I didn't change it at all. Straight out of the book, it is."

Fred didn't look at Charlie as he said, "He knows what he's doing, that Jamie Oliver. Don't wanna mess with perfection. Anyone fancy a bit more of this lasagne? I'm starving." He pushed the dish up to the other end of the table.

Sharon looked at her plate half-full of food. "Not for me, love. I shouldn't really have all this pasta, not with my figure." She tapped her minuscule stomach, her silver bracelets rattling. "I'm surprised you didn't add your own little twist to it, Charlie. You're *so* creative." In case no one understood what she was on about, she added, "The gays. It's like a creative gene or somethink. They're always into it. My friend, Paul—he's *well into* his dogs and dog shows. Grooming them, competing in the competitions. Everythink. It's, like, his 'ole life. Mine too as it goes. I don't know what I'd do with myself without my little furry doggy babies. I must introduce you to my friend Paul and his boyfriend. Paul does the dogs, and his boyfriend, he's a…a…"

"Executive assistant with one of them big consultancy firms." Fred removed the glass full of wine from his wife's hand. "That's right, isn't it, love?"

"What am I like, eh?" She laughed at herself then put a tiny forkful of salad into her mouth.

"It's like an episode of *Modern Family*," Tamara muttered.

Camilla smiled widely. "Yes. We are a sort of modern family, aren't we? All sat here, breaking bread together, so to speak. Isn't it so marvellously modern of us all?"

"It's an American TV show, Mum," Aaron explained. "Second marriages, gay dads, adopted parents—what a family is nowadays. Get it?"

"Yes, darling. Thank you. No need to embarrass Mummy. Have you told your father about starting at the salon and all your new friends at college? I'm sure he'd love to hear about it, wouldn't you, Fred?" She smiled firmly at Fred, then took a mouth of food in relief.

"Oh, yes. I'm all ears, aren't we, love?" Fred knocked his wife's elbow. Sharon nodded quickly.

Aaron told them about starting in the hairdressing salon on the King's Road.

Camilla breezed with, "It's where I used to get my hair done when we first moved here. I once had a perm on top of another perm, and let me tell you, that was a disaster. Of course, it's changed quite a bit since then!" She motioned to Aaron to continue his story.

He told them about his days at college where he learned the chemistry and science behind hairdressing, why you shouldn't perm coloured hair, what to do if a client is allergic to something you've put on their head, and how permanent and non-permanent colours work on the structure of the hairs. As he finished, he looked at his plate of hardly touched food and apologised.

"No need to apologise," Charlie said, squeezing his hand. "Be proud. Tell everyone. Shout it from the rooftops. You've found the something you want to do, and you're loving it. Think back to how miserable you were at uni compared to how you feel now. That's something to be proud of, to share with your family, isn't it?"

Aaron nodded and picked up his fork.

After a moment's silence, Camilla said, "Fred, you've got something you'd like to say to Tamara, haven't you?"

That was all the prompt he needed to start talking, at length, about issues they were having with Lux Sunglasses. Their range wasn't selling to younger customers, and he didn't know what to do about that.

"I've just done a unit on that on my business course, Dad. It's about segmentation for different customers…"

The two of them disappeared into a conversation while everyone else continued eating and chatting about far less stretching topics.

Camilla mopped her brow with a tea towel, thinking how it all seemed to be going OK. She was absolutely and completely fagged out—not that she could use that phrase these days, of course. She started to clear the plates as Fred and Tamara continued to talk. The others had broken into smaller groups of discussion.

Charlie helped clean up, despite Camilla's insistence that he sit. He argued he wasn't a guest, since he lived there, and grabbed Aaron to help too.

Camilla caught Fred's eye from the other side of the kitchen, still deep in conversation with their daughter. He smiled, and she smiled back, then leant to put something in the dishwasher, enjoying the feeling of achievement for pulling off a family meal with everyone there, no arguments and no food disasters.

***

Sharon sat back in the chair, allowing the wine to circulate through her system. It had all felt a bit odd at first, having dinner with Fred's ex. OK, so she knew she was there, in his life. She always got the update after he'd seen her. But sitting at *Camilla's* table, in *Camilla's* house, drinking *Camilla's* wine felt a bit closer and more involved than Sharon would have chosen. And all these gays everywhere—little Aaron, her friend Paul and, of course, Hugo. In a lull in conversation, she blurted out, "Everyone's gay now, aren't they? It's cute."

"I don't think everyone is, love," Fred said. "But it's a thing, more than it used to be. I agree with that. More people...'out', is it called?"

"My friend Paul, he's one. He's my dog friend. We met on the dog-grooming circuit."

"All right, love, we don't need your life story." Behind his hand, as if she couldn't hear him, he said, "She's a bit pissed, don't mind her."

"'Ere, never you mind I'm pissed. It runs in the family, don't it?"

"Come on, love. I think you've had enough." He tried to take the glass of wine off her.

Tamara sat upright with a mischievous smile. "Let her speak, Dad. I'm enjoying this."

Sharon held a large glass of wine in one hand, swinging it from side to side, bits sloshing out as she gestured to emphasise her point. "There's Charlie, the neighbour, and little Aaron, and my friend Paul. And then there's Aaron's uncle. That's running in the family, innit?"

Camilla leant on the table, brow furrowed. "Who on earth do you mean?"

Sharon clicked her fingers, trying to remember the name. "Him, posh one. Lives with 'er in the big house in Chigwell. Snooty parents, always look down their nose at you. Harry... Harold...Hugo! That's it! Hugo."

Fred smiled and grabbed his wife's hand to prevent her spilling any more wine. "There's a lot of it about."

Charlie said, "We are sitting here, you know. We're not toys or little dogs to put on your lap."

Sharon burst forth with, "Oh, I love them little ones. The teacup Chihuahuas. I'd love a coupla them, wouldn't I, love?" She turned to Fred.

Camilla pulled herself to her full height. "What are you insinuating? That Hugo, your brother-in-law, my children's uncle, is a homosexual? But he's married to Isabella. Dear, dear Isabella. She was featured in the society pages of *Tatler*, July eighty-four, as the most darling bridesmaid in her darling dress with the enormous darling bow around the back. I simply won't hear of it."

"Gay," Aaron said. "It's gay now, Mum, no one says 'homosexual' apart from doctors."

Sharon slurred, "Tha's e'sactly what I'm sayin'."

"But, but...I don't..." Camilla blustered. "How can he be? They've got little baby Thomas. How can it be? I can get you the edition of *Tatler* if you'd like. I kept it. Isabella looked so darling in it. Even if the marriage was shit, the wedding was a wonderful day."

Fred opened his mouth to say something, then thought better and closed it in silence.

Charlie said, "I think it's time we served dessert and changed the topic of conversation. Is it in the fridge? The pav, Camilla." He tapped her shoulder. "Fridge...pav?"

She waved him away and nodded. As Charlie searched for the pavlova in the fridge, Camilla continued her earlier train of thought. "How do you know this?" She was staring at Sharon now. "What evidence do you have? You can't just go around saying someone's a gay, willy-nilly." There were some giggles from around the table. "Sorry, unfortunate turn of phrase. Come on, you beastly woman. Where did this come from?"

Fred said, "No need for that, Cam."

"Don't you *Cam* me. I demand to know. Come on, out with it." She stared at Sharon.

So Sharon told them about her friend Paul who had an escort business, and about Hugo booking an escort and even added the pictures she'd seen for extra authenticity. "Danny, 'is name was," Sharon finished.

At the mention of Danny's name, Charlie left the room, and Aaron followed him.

"What's that all about? Lovers' tiff?"

"I doubt it," Camilla said. "They're very good together. If you wouldn't mind continuing with your sordid little story..."

The pavlova stayed on the work surface, uncut, its cream filling sagging in the heat from the Aga while Sharon glugged and gossiped the night away.

***

Fred drove home while Sharon swayed in the passenger seat, head lolling.

"You shouldn't have done that, love," he said. "We were told that in confidence. You swore on Dusty's life."

"Oh, well. Better out than in, eh?" Sharon giggled, trying to focus on her finger in front of her face.

"Hugo's not got an heir then. It can't be his, can it?"

Sharon shrugged. "Unlikely, from what Paul said." She stared out the window, trying to focus on a passing car, and failing. "You never know. They could've, you know..."

"It's a funny image, isn't it? Our brother-in-law being fucked by a big, strapping Italian."

"Yeah, it's hilarious."

"I feel a bit sick imagining it as it goes."

"Ah, well. No 'arm done." She giggled, asked how long until they were home, then fell asleep with her head leaning on the window, a bit of spit dribbling from her mouth.

Chapter 43
November 2014

ISABELLA ARRIVED HOME from work late again. She'd had an awful lot of these late nights since returning from her brief spell of maternity leave. She was so grateful for Irvana, the nanny—yes, that was her name. Isabella checked her diary to be sure.

Nowadays, her mind seemed constantly full of things she struggled to remember. She couldn't admit she wasn't quite the same as pre-baby. She daren't let anyone in the boardroom get even a sniff of that. But when she came home, her legs and brain sore from another day surrounded by men, having to hide any texts from Irvana or any baby-related calls, she slipped off her shoes and allowed herself to relax. She'd done it. She'd managed to get it all. The glamorous affair with the gorgeous European man, doing her duty as a mother—as far as her mother-in-law was concerned—and returning to the beautiful home she'd worked so hard to get. Not *work* in the traditional sense, but work with Hugo's parents, work to be the perfect wife in the face of Hugo being such a useless drip of a man. She'd been surprised how attentive and useful he'd been since baby Thomas had arrived—so surprised she'd thought about suggesting they try for another one, but to do that, they'd have to have sex at least once a year, and that really was too much *work*.

She walked to the nursery and checked Thomas was asleep.

Irvana was gently rocking in a chair next to the cot, darning or knitting or repairing something. Isabella never was quite sure what Irvana did with needles and material.

Isabella whispered, "I'm sorry I'm late. I just, well, it went on. You know how it is."

Irvana probably didn't know, but she nodded sympathetically anyway. "He was good. He is always good."

"Where's Hugo?"

She shrugged. "I been with baby all evening. I am looking after him. Hugo, he can look after himself, I think."

"Do go to bed, Irvana. I'm here now." Isabella left the room and walked around the house, calling Hugo's name. He wasn't in the living room or the TV room or the dining room or the kitchen or the bathroom. She checked if his car was in the drive, and it was. He wasn't in her bedroom, but why would he be? They'd had separate bedrooms for a long time. She walked into his bedroom and screamed.

Hugo lay on the bed, a typed note next to him and a gunshot wound to his head. A small gun lay by his side, surrounded by the dark-red sticky blood that was still flowing from his head.

Irvana ran to the door. "What is matter? What—" She screamed and covered her mouth with her hand.

The next few hours were a blurred procession of different professionals who came to the house, took statements, collected items in plastic bags, took pictures, eventually removed Hugo's body, until it was two o'clock in the morning, and Isabella knew she had to go to bed, but her mind was racing, the blood rushing around her body.

She collapsed on the floor in her bedroom and cried, deep, sobbing sadness, where she couldn't take a breath between sobs. The tears and snot ran down her face as she gave herself over to the feeling of total and complete loss she knew had happened but still couldn't quite believe was real.

Epilogue
Six Months Later

LORD REECE JONES looked at a photo of his grandson. He'd gone to Hugo's funeral without a single tear. He couldn't understand why his son would do something like that. "After what I saw in the war, I'm bloody well all right, and bloody Hugo. He does that, and what's he seen? What trauma and problems did he want to bloody well get away from? It's such a bloody, bloody waste. This little one will grow up and not know his father. We'll just have to bloody well make sure we spoil him rotten, won't we, old fruit?"

Lady Reece Jones nodded in silent agreement.

***

Lady Reece Jones took the framed photo and stared at baby's deep-blue eyes. "It's such a waste, but at least one good thing came from it before we lost him. We have little baby Thomas. We have some of Hugo that lives on. And we have an heir to the estate."

Baby Thomas may know his real father. He may know where he got those beautiful blue eyes from. But she doubted it. She wouldn't tell anyone, or it would all come crashing down around them. And she was sure her dirty whore of a daughter-in-law wouldn't tell anyone either, now she had the house and was playing the grieving widow role so well. With Hugo disposed of and his ugly, shameful secret gone with him, it was better for all of them.

It turned out she did have to see that despicable Paul man again, but he'd had his uses. A contact he could ask to get rid of her son. One final lunch with Paul, a few weeks after the first, back in that restaurant in Hertford, and this time, she'd arrived ready with the envelope of cash. She'd wanted it agreed and done with no further contact between herself and that disgusting individual. She hadn't been able to get her head around her darling son being one of *those* people, and she couldn't look at him after knowing that. She couldn't risk his being careless and the secret getting out and besmirching their family name, Reece Jones Instruments, Reece Jones Park—everything. So he'd had to go. She would never have need of dreadful Paul and his services and contact again, now that nasty business was all dead and buried.

***

Neil was alone in his flat, having sold the cottage he and Charlie had shared. It had been too full of memories of them together, so he'd moved to a docklands apartment near Canary Wharf— all glass, floor-to-ceiling, underground parking, portered reception. Totally and utterly soulless. Charlie would have hated it. Neil installed a voice-operated lights-and-blinds system so when he talked to the appliances during the long empty weekends in the apartment, at least something replied to him. His cosy cottage existence with Charlie seemed a lifetime away now, yet he was constantly reminded of what he'd broken whenever he stumbled across a property programme on TV featuring a cottage like theirs while he worked through the weekend, his papers on the coffee table and sofa, willing Monday to come rolling round once again, when he could go back to being *Neil the Consultant, Neil the Trainer*, not *Neil the Lonely, Neil the Cheater, Neil the Man Who Talks to His Appliances*.

***

Danny and Paul drove away from the London docklands Audi dealership in a brand-new, pearlescent-white cabriolet they'd bought outright.

At the traffic lights, Danny put the roof down and took Paul's hand. "The love bit is exhausting. Remind me not to say yes to any clients who want the whole relationship love bit. It's just too much to take. I want to get in, get done and get out again. Remind me, OK?"

"These presents are pretty fab, though, aren't they?" Paul said.

"They'll do, I suppose."

"So now you've expanded the business in both directions, how else can we expand?"

Danny shrugged, put the car into gear and sped off from the traffic lights. "That's what I've got you for, isn't it?"

"I fucking love you," Paul said with a smile at their twisted, dysfunctional relationship that, despite what everyone had told him when they'd first met, somehow seemed to work.

"I love fucking you."

***

Charlie and Aaron were walking their dog in a park with Camilla. Neil had eventually realised Judy would have a better life with Charlie than he could give her, cooped up in his apartment or left with dog-sitters for days while he was travelling around the country, staying in hotels.

Aaron babbled excitedly about his course and asked if Charlie and his mother wanted their hair cut now he'd done enough time at the salon to practise his technique. "You coming to see me at the Hairdresser of the Year show next year? The salon has sponsored me, as I did so well in the regional comps with my male styles." Aaron blinked at them both expectedly.

Camilla looked at Charlie and pushed her sharp bob behind one ear. "'Course we'll be there. Won't we, Charlie?"

He grinned. "Try and stop me."

"However, darling," Camilla added, "I don't think I'm quite ready to let you loose on this. Not just yet anyway. What about male hair? I'm sure that's so much simpler."

Charlie said, "Thanks for that. I've already told him no."

"Love is...letting your boyfriend cut your hair even though it might end up looking like you've had an argument with a lawnmower."

Charlie and Aaron shared a look at Camilla's first use in front of them of the *boyfriend* word.

"You heard from your sister?" she asked. "I hardly see her, now she's jetting off here, there and everywhere. Shame she couldn't come today."

"Dog walking? You've no chance, Mum. She's like the marketing and business development guru or something for Lux Sunglasses. She's gone totally *The Apprentice* on Dad, and he's, like, loving it, apparently." Aaron ran off after Judy.

Camilla raised an eyebrow at Charlie. Since he'd found the letter from Aaron's biological father, they'd tried to find Henry through Facebook and then old addresses but come to a dead end and agreed it was better to allow Aaron and Fred's relationship to continue improving, as it had been since Aaron had come out and found a new direction in his life.

Aaron ran past them both, grinning, his strawberry-blond fringe blowing across his face as he shouted at the top of his voice, "Aaaaaagggghhhhhh!" with Judy chasing after him.

Charlie and Camilla nodded slowly at each other, then turned to watch their beloved man tear into the distance again, a black-and-white blur at his heels.

***

Isabella walked slowly around the large, empty house she'd shared with her poor, dear Hugo, who'd not been able to take it any longer and had ended it all. She couldn't help feeling guilty in some part for that, for she'd told him Thomas wasn't his child but had given him no real choice but to let her come home after finding out about her affair. Now a widow and a mother, she couldn't ask Danny to help with Thomas, as that would get out so quickly around the village. And sometimes, during the evenings, when she returned from work having felt guilty all day for leaving her son with the nanny, she also felt guilty for coming home and not being able to work long hours, to give Lux Sunglasses her all like she used to, because now she had Thomas to look after.

It was at times like this when she did something she never thought she'd do. She missed Hugo. Although she'd thought him wet and a mummy's boy, at least there had been some sort of barrier between her and Lady Reece Jones' impervious will.

Living in this house, looking after the son and heir to the Reece Jones empire, had always been the plan, yet Isabella felt like a lodger in her own life and longed for the illicit afternoons in hotel rooms with Danny or even for the companionship Hugo had given her. For whenever her parents-in-law came to visit, they were straight to Thomas, their grandchild, and barely paid any attention to Isabella. She was, after all, only needed to raise the heir. Such was her lot. She had what she'd wished for all those years: a life without Hugo, and she had to make the best of it.

***

Every day at Lux Sunglasses, Fred was more and more impressed with the ideas, enthusiasm and work Tamara brought. As impressed as he was with how Aaron, once he found his vocation in hairdressing, had applied himself and was doing very well. And also, now Fred had got used to the situation, how good

Charlie was for his son. Even though he still felt a bit strange seeing his son kiss a man, he wished he and Camilla or even Sharon had the same relationship he saw between Aaron and Charlie— the way they helped and supported each other and were so happy in each other's company without the need for new cars or Jacuzzis or flash jewellery.

Sharon's appetite for those things had grown since she was no longer friends with Paul, having betrayed the secret he'd shared with her. Paul said there was no way he could ever trust her again. It had jeopardised his and Danny's business, so he didn't feel he could continue with their friendship. They sometimes bumped into each other on the dog-show circuit, and Sharon tried to be friendly, but Paul blanked her, only paying attention to her dogs these days. But obviously, that was the trouble with rent boys. It wasn't personal, it was just business as usual.

The End

About the Author

Liam Livings is an award-shortlisted gay romance novelist, creative writing tutor, and ghostwriter. His fiction focuses on friendship, British humour, and romance with plenty of sparkle. He's a member of the Romantic Novelists' Association and the Chartered Institute of Marketing and holds a Master's in Creative Writing from Kingston University.

He shares his house with his boyfriend and cats. When not writing, he bakes to indulge his dangerously sweet tooth, admires unaffordable classic cars, and drinks all the pink wine with friends. His favourite sport—of which he's a gold medal winner—is reading a romantic novel in a long hot bath.

Social Media

Website: http://www.liamlivings.com/
Facebook: http://www.facebook.com/liam.livings
Twitter: https://twitter.com/LiamLivings
Blog: http://www.liamlivings.com/blog

For Liam's other stories check out his website
www.liamlivings.com

Beaten Track Publishing

For more titles from Beaten Track Publishing,
please visit our website:

https://www.beatentrackpublishing.com

Thanks for reading!